# THE AGATE HUNTER

# The Agate Hunter

## John Moehl

RESOURCE *Publications* · Eugene, Oregon

THE AGATE HUNTER

Copyright © 2019 John Moehl. All rights reserved. Except for brief quotations in critical publications or reviews, no part of this book may be reproduced in any manner without prior written permission from the publisher. Write: Permissions, Wipf and Stock Publishers, 199 W. 8th Ave., Suite 3, Eugene, OR 97401.

Resource Publications
An Imprint of Wipf and Stock Publishers
199 W. 8th Ave., Suite 3
Eugene, OR 97401

www.wipfandstock.com

PAPERBACK ISBN: 978-1-5326-5719-1
HARDCOVER ISBN: 978-1-5326-5720-7
EBOOK ISBN: 978-1-5326-5721-4

Manufactured in the U.S.A.                                JULY 11, 2019

ALSO BY JOHN MOEHL:

Phobos & Deimos: Two Moons, Two Worlds

Closer to God

Ann—A Story of Intolerance

My efforts to convert words on paper to meaningful thoughts and insightful phrases are all dedicated to my dear Elisabeth, with whom I have shared my life—our life—a life that has in many ways provided the setting and highlighted the priorities for what I try to convey in the stories I tell. Her footprints are everywhere.

I would like to thank Marie for patiently reading these tales and Jacqui for taking my disheveled sentences and hammering them into something more presentable for the reader.

# Contents

*Author's Note* | ix
*Gems* | xi
*The Agate Hunter's Maxim* | xii
*Prologue* | xiii

| | | |
|---|---|---|
| Book One | The Beginning | 1 |
| Book Two | Near the Little Bighorn | 9 |
| Book Three | The Snows of Summer | 22 |
| Book Four | Breaking from Arapaho Tradition | 39 |
| Book Five | In the Shadow of Mpezeni | 64 |
| Book Six | Frozen Roots, Wilted Stems | 107 |
| Book Seven | Full Circle | 143 |
| Book Eight | Shiny Scraps | 176 |

# Author's Note

WE are often our sharpest critic. When young, we do not have enough time on the job nor the right lens to see how we are doing. Then, when we are old, we have an established track record. We have a history. We can look back and assess—but, it is too late to change—it is what it is.

From our vantage point as senior citizens, we may begin seeing our lives as incomplete—even as wasted when compared with others. How could we have been more exceptional, left more of a legacy? We wonder what we would or could do differently? Sometimes looking back makes us sad. Sometimes it does not.

This is story of life's pathways; sometimes seen as capricious, sometimes as threatening. This story is a work of fiction. The story, its actors, and their actions are fiction. While some of the sites are fictitious, in other cases, incidents may take place in real, well-known geographic locations. However, the story recounted at these locales is fiction. Similarly, at times historical persons or events are incorporated into the story to complement its telling. This does not imply any relationship between the story and these true historical figures or events. In the same vein, the story or its characters may be depicted at or on commercial or public entities that have existed or do exist (hotels, restaurants, bars, etc.). These interactions as well as any descriptions of the facilities or their services are completely fictitious derivatives of the story and in no way reflect on the real locales nor their staff or owners.

It may be worth adding a special note that the author is unaware of any existing or past company or entity named Delpro. Any connection to a functioning or former firm, business, or group is purely coincidental—all actions and events attributed to Delpro, or any other enterprise, in the following story are completely fictitious. Equally, all actions or events attributed to any public or private agencies come solely from the imagination and are not based on any facts.

# Gems

*Alert eyes, looking for glistening stones burnished by the sea's surge,*
*seeking luster in an opaque macrocosm that seems to shun radiance.*

*The winter wind whips the sea to foam, covering the brilliance,*
*making it harder for the seeker to find the object of his hopes.*

*Calmer seas allow the shimmering gems time and space to reappear.*
*Gifts—gems forged from Nature's mysteries to adorn the necklace of time.*

*Yet, time is a great press that crushes months and years into days and hours,*
*rudely pushing the seeker to new plains—new beachheads.*

*The urges of Chronos may dangle the seeker over the chasm of the unknown,*
*pursing growth, demanding celebrity, wanting wisdom.*

*The seeker is uncontrollably entrapped in the snarl of daily life,*
*painfully learning how to cope, how to love, how to lose.*

*The swirling tumult of being reshapes the young into the old,*
*but the seeker continues to look for the shiny scraps that make today unique.*

# The Agate Hunter's Maxim

Vigilance. Keep sharp eyes focused on the path before you, peering deeply, carefully studying to the left and to the right. Keep an ear peeled, and a slice of your vision focused on what is happening behind your back. That mighty sneaker wave—some say every seventh—may unexpectedly crash down on you, ruining your day.

# Prologue

It was an unusually warm day for October. Enjoying the warmth, he sat on a park bench on an outcropping above the pounding surf; the setting sun cast long shadows from his erect frame. He was still in pretty good shape, but old. He knew he was old.

He had seen so many sunsets, it was almost a metaphor. He had seen the sun slowly arch to the horizon then seemingly fall the last few feet into a boiling sea—thinking always he should be seeing the steam clouds from where he watched.

He once again waited for the steam cloud. It was his eyes that were cloudy with cataracts and age, but his mind was clear; sharp as the day he had left home to become a man—finding ultimately the need to return to stay a man.

It had been complicated. He guessed things always were.

Then the cell phone rang in the breast pocket of his Filson. He answered, knowing in doing so, he would completely change his life, his legacy.

*Book One*

# The Beginning

He had been born in a small hamlet on the Pacific Coast. The tiny town of less than a hundred inhabitants was squeezed between the Coast Range and the thunderous Pacific Ocean—in the shadow of Cape Verde. It had been named by the Spanish explorer Bruno de Heceta y Dudagoitia in the late 1700s, when he viewed the forested promontory from the pitching deck of the *Santiago* on his way north to Alaska.

The village was typical of the small communities that dotted the shoreline. There were basic local services for the citizenry—primary school, bus station, gas station, bar, restaurant, grocery store—in the village, but most jobs were outside in the larger port towns. One thirty miles to the north and the other twenty-five miles to the south, these ports encircled major rivers that drained the humid Coast Range into the awaiting sea. In the harbor townships, still small by any standard, there were jobs in the two major industries: fisheries and forestry. Fishers hooked, ensnarled, netted, and dug a variety of fare from the ocean's larder, while the lumbermen felled trees—some of the Stika Spruce over 500 years old—cutting them into boards for the country's booming housing market or shredding the trees into pulp for the fast-growing paper business.

*※*

He, his name was Edward (Eddie) Hall, had grown up on the rocky beaches and sandy shores of the Pacific—bouncing up and down the escarpments, in and out of the cold, crashing waves, like another piece of weathered and battered driftwood that littered the inlets and sloughs. He knew the sea's song, orchestrated as breakers smashed into walls of stone. He knew the sea's creatures, finding marvels beneath kelp, boulder, and pebble. He knew the awe and the calm inspired by the sea.

As soon as he was old enough to navigate the gullies and crags of the shoreline, he spent every free moment scouring the seaside for mementoes of its greatness with his ever-present companion, a golden retriever named Skip. He and Skip had a wondrous collection: glass floats broken free of far-off fishing nets; blennies and umbrella crabs pickled in formaldehyde in old mayonnaise jars; pieces of wood sculpted by the sea's lathe to look like reindeer; buttons from some bygone seafarer; and, bottles and cans with unknown writing from unknown lands. But mostly, they had agates. Wherever they went in their beachcombing, Eddie kept his eyes peeled for agates—studiously hunting these prizes that, like the sea's creatures, ultimately ended up in his mother's old jam jars.

Uncle Wilfred had a machine that polished the sought-after stones to a high sheen. But, lacking such an apparatus, Eddie kept his collection immersed in tap water, enjoying the sparkle and luster through the walls of the jars aligned on shelves in his bedroom—row upon row of, what he thought, could have been gems.

He was very good at hunting agates. It was relatively simple to spy the translucent stones on a wet beach, awash by the waves. But, above the tide line, the quarry hid under a cloud, like scum on a pond. Regardless of this deception, assuming the appearance of an ordinary stone, the agates could not hide from his keen eye. He was very good at finding his prey and always returned home with his pockets brimming.

---

He went to grade school in the village, so his favored routine was only slightly altered by the need to attend classes—an obligation for which he had no affection, and to which he freely expressed his opposition. However, when he turned thirteen, there were major changes; unpleasant conditions which, again, he could not avoid. Skip died after a long life and many good times chasing sea gulls. Equally devastating, he now had to go to Woodrow Junior High, which was in the neighboring town, eight miles to the north. This required daily bus travel that made it impossible for him to follow his old routine on the beach.

As a thirteen-year-old with salt in his veins, Eddie felt very mature—ready to take on his life and call his own shots. He knew what he knew, and he knew a lot. Unfortunately, society had colluded against him—the sheriff even brought him home when he was truant. Against all his better impulses, he was forced to accept that school was to be the centerpiece of his life for the foreseeable future.

※

Eddie's parents had their hands full. He was their first child and difficulties in his birth made it likely he would be their only child. And, often it seemed like one was too much.

They were even unsure what to call their son. They kept testing the options; the staid "Edward", the almost too familiar "Eddie", the alternative "Eddy", or just plain "Ed". Eddie himself thought of himself as "Eddie", not by choice, but as was so often the case in his decision-making, by a process of elimination. Edward was far too formal—kings were named Edward. Ed was simply too short—it fell off the tongue. So, he thought of himself as Eddie (for undisclosed reasons preferring the "ie" to the "y") but signed his name Edward. That worked.

Eddie's father, Earl, worked in a sawmill in the port city to the south; his mother, Irene, waited tables in the village restaurant. They worked hard, very hard—but he never doubted they were his family.

Earl was a saw filer—one of the most important and best paid jobs in the mill. He was considered more as an artist than a worker; his task to keep the saw teeth as sharp as a surgeon's scalpel—and in many ways, just as important. Mills bought logs and sawed them into boards—the efficiency of the saw was one of the major factors contributing to how much wood was wasted and how much was sold. A machine honed the saw, one tooth at a time. But the saw filer ran the machine. He got no credit if all went well, and considerable blame when it did not.

Earl, it was said, had sawdust in his arteries. His father had worked in a sawmill in the south of the state, mostly as a millwright but doing a variety of tasks. Earl's father's father had also spent his life in a sawmill—only for him, the mill was in Arkansas, the family moving west after the first great war. Earl himself had started doing clean-up when he was fourteen and worked his way through the ranks, being fortunate enough to find himself under the wing of a master saw filer.

Mill work was demanding. Earl was up well before sunrise, even in summer. The mill was about five miles east of the port, so he had a sixty-mile round trip every day in his rather beat-up eight-year-old turquoise 1960 GMC pickup. Work was seven to three-thirty; in winter, he got home after dark, the coastal road twisting and turning—often frustratingly slow if he got caught behind a log truck or a tourist caravan.

Irene was always home when Eddie came back from school, the bus dropping him off at the foot of their long driveway. Her earnings from waitressing were an important supplement to their family income, but she worked with conditions. She would take the breakfast or lunch shifts, but not dinner—she insisted on being home for dinner—home for her boys.

Irene was a local girl—hardy, with a big dose of practical knowledge combined with impeccable logic. She had grown up twenty miles inland from the village, her father operating a small dairy and tree farm. She was accustomed to tough jobs and rough living. She had met Earl at the county fair. At that time, he was a new employee at the mill, living right next to the plant. They seemed to be kindred spirits from the moment they met. Their marriage looked to be inevitable—the only provision from Irene being that they live in the village—she would not go far from her roots.

After losing several pregnancies, they had had Eddie when Irene was nearly thirty-five. They adored their son. As he grew and turned into a bit of a beachcombing vagabond, it was difficult for them to be separated from their scion. They organized as many activities as possible to keep everyone together—some functional, others more recreational. They would hunt doves, deer, or blue grouse, fish for cutthroat or steelhead—sometimes going down to the freshwater lakes to catch bass. They would take their squaw nets into the surf for smelt and clamber over the rocky outcrops for mussels. They would follow logging roads far into the heart of the forest to cut firewood. At low tides, they would dig razor clams on the beaches and gapers in the bays. They would harvest blackberries and salmonberries in season. Outings were painted with a brush of mystery and adventure.

However, given their son's nonstop, often seemingly reckless acts, in the back of their minds, Earl and Irene were always worried—more honestly scared—that Eddie would be the victim of some terrible tragedy. One day, when he was ten, when he did not come home on time from a jaunt on the beach with Skip, they were more than a little worried. If nothing else, Eddie was very punctual. After a few hours, Earl and Irene debated whether or not to call the sheriff. They did not want to give a bad reputation to a young boy—but they wanted their young boy home. The debate continued and after a delay of almost four hours, Eddie came to the back door—he and Skip soaked to the skin. They had been on the seaward side of a large basalt ridge that was separated from the main rocky outcropping by a canal—a canal they had been able to cross before high tide. Sadly, the tide peaked while they were still there. They were cut off until the tide turned. The ridge, their refuge, had been beaten by waves, but they managed to hold on and were happy to be home. That evening, Earl and Irene felt they should put a notch in the bedpost for one close encounter satisfactorily traversed. They knew it was just a matter of time until the next situation arose. They prayed it would finish in an equally positive way—in fact, they prayed all their son's challenges would be met and overcome without leaving too many scars.

※

Eddie did not have many close friends. There were classmates with whom he had schooled since first grade, but the Hall home was about five miles south of the village with few neighbors—none with children. Nevertheless, he felt no void. To complement the often-busy lives laid-out by his parents, he found the realm of Neptune to be his closest ally—spending hours and hours immersed both spiritually and mentally in the seashore's wonders.

To his frequent disappointment, inescapably, he had much less time to be on the beach in junior high and high school. Still and all, he managed to spend a lot of hours along the shore, missing Skip's company, but still making new discoveries. His collection of treasures grew. More and more pickle and jam jars full of agates lined the shelves of his room.

When graduation came and went, he felt like someone on a dock, getting ready to step on the moored boat, only to see at the last minute the boat was gone. He was left hanging in space.

He had, at his parents' insistence, applied to the state university. It was only eighty miles away—close enough not to be too intimidating. Everyone said the next step was college, so he guessed he might as well take it. But he was not sure the boat was there.

He had always been an above-average unenthusiastic student—his relatively good grades making it comparatively easy to get into college. Yet, he was unconvinced. Why keep going to school?

He tried to persuade his parents that, like many of his peers from the village, the best tactic would be to just get a job. They, however, neither having gone beyond secondary school, were adamant that he should at least try college to see how it was.

He argued it was too expensive and that it would be a real hardship for the family to pay all the fees. His parents partially agreed, but his dad had a solution for this too: Eddie would work in the mill during summer vacations to help pay for his studies—Earl had already cleared it with the office.

There appeared to be few options. Eddie packed his bags and his parents drove him to campus for freshman orientation. They agreed to come and get him for a respite at home by Halloween.

There was no major in agate hunting, so Eddie indicated his major as undeclared. He took boilerplate classes to fulfill requirements, as he had no specific area of interest that could be spelled-out in a college curriculum. Eddie meandered through classes like English Composition and Western Civilization; his keen eye, whetted by years on the beach seeking treasure, helped him take good notes and do well on exams. He continued to be an above-average unenthusiastic student.

His social life expanded with his academic life. His natural friendliness and winning smile made it easy to bond with the guys in the dorm. These guys, and his charisma, helped with finding a girl—or girls to be more correct. Eddie had had a girlfriend in high school, but it had been an on-and-off platonic affair that could not compete with the call of the seashore.

Now, the campus libertine spirit fostered a series of short and medium-term relationships that did a great deal to expand Eddie's heretofore nonexistent understanding of the female of his species. He also found he had an innate talent in the campus' chief intramural sport: drinking beer. After a kegger, it was not uncommon for him to find himself in an unknown rose garden or the dorm room of an almost unknown coed.

Nevertheless, good grades and an active social calendar were apparently not enough for him. He felt unfulfilled. He was where he was because of his parents' insistence—not because he saw any real value in being there. This disquiet gnawed at him—and he was not even sure why he was distressed.

At the end of his freshman year, he went home and spent every day for the first fortnight walking along the beach, revisiting his favorite places, listening to the waves and the gulls—getting grounded. He then started working in the mill, pulling planer chain, going back and forth to work every day with his dad.

In the fall, he returned to campus, more tired from the nine-hour, six-day-a-week shifts than eager to see his college friends. He remained unenthusiastic while the school terms came and went, still doing well in all areas—but halfhearted, at best.

His sophomore year was nearly a carbon copy of its predecessor: taking dreary core courses while partying hard without really enjoying it. At the end of the year, before going back to the drudgery of the planer chain, he accepted an invitation from some dorm-mates to spend two weeks hiking the Pacific Crest Trail.

The early summer alpine forest was splendid. There were patches of snow, high meadows in bloom, and a flurry of wildlife welcoming the warmer temperatures. Standing on the knife's edge, seeing the verdant river valley on one side, and the bronze high plains on the other, was the most dazzling panorama Eddie had ever seen. It was the land. He realized, his epiphany—it was the land. Even on the beach, he was attracted to the land, he realized, not really the water. The rocky crevices, the basalt outcroppings, and the agate bejeweled coves—it was the land. He had been born in one of the most covetable landscapes on Earth. He should acknowledge his good luck, protect the oneness, and help this land stay pristine and unique.

---

When Eddie got home for the summer, he resumed his spot on the planer chain, but on some afternoons, before going home, he persuaded his dad to make a thirty-minute stop at the city library where he rushed in to check out some books. On subsequent stops, he would quickly return an arm-full and grab replacements.

Eddie had never been a big reader. He easily managed to read all that was required in his homework. But he did not see himself as the kind of guy who would revel in lying in a lawn chair and enjoying a good book. Nevertheless, he now had a mission. He needed to know things he did not know. The library was the logical—and practically the only—source of knowledge over the summer break.

Eddie broke new ground in another area: letter writing. He had always been a reluctant writer, having to be chided by his parents to write his grandmother a thank-you card for his birthday present or send his uncle and aunt a note after receiving a much-appreciated Christmas present. He used the phone. But now he chose pen and paper to contact his roommate Michael, who lived in Billings—over a thousand miles away.

The results of his handiwork were unveiled to his family after they had returned home from the village's Fourth of July barbecue. With no fanfare and no advance notice, Eddie announced to his mother and father that he now knew what he wanted to do. He wanted to be a surveyor.

As he had learned in his readings, over two hundred years ago, Peter Jefferson had been a surveyor in western Virginia. His son had followed in his footsteps and then gone on to be President of the United States. So, if it was good enough for Thomas Jefferson, it was good enough for Eddie Hall.

Earl and Irene were relatively placid in view of this news. They realized their dear son was capable of far wilder antics and, after all, there was nothing wrong with being a surveyor—nothing at all.

Earl and Irene assumed this was just a matter of finally adjusting his major in college so that he would graduate with whatever was necessary to become a surveyor. Eddie informed them that, while this could be an option, it was not the path he had chosen. He understood that current trends were for people who wanted to become surveyors to do so by spending four years in college, learning all the theoretical bases—this was not for him. Fortunately, it was still possible to be an apprentice—becoming a licensed surveyor after four years of practical experience and after passing the licensing exams—this was the road for him. To wrap it all up, his roommate Michael had found him a slot on a survey team preparing for a major road renovation project on the road from Billings to Yellowstone Park. Wasn't it wonderful?

Not really. Could have been worse. But Earl and Irene were not ecstatic. Thinking of their boy that far away—their boy! The same boy who fell out of the apple tree, drove his bike off a boat dock, and took his mattress outside to soften the fall when he jumped off the roof with a flour-sack parachute. This boy, alone in the wilds of Montana? It did not seem to be prudent, let alone easy, for parents who had never really been separated from their offspring by more than a few dozen miles.

Nonetheless, by any reckoning, Eddie was now a man—albeit a young, naive, impressionable, inexperienced man. His parents had never really been able to compel him to do something as a child, now was not the time to start. Thus, when others were regaining their college dorms after a long, hot summer, Eddie was off on a bus to Billings.

*Book Two*

# Near the Little Bighorn

It was a long trip—the better part of two nights and three days. Upon arrival, it was not only a question of recovering from the long journey but adjusting to the elevation; Billings sat at over three thousand feet in altitude. This was no small leap for someone who had spent his life near sea-level.

Michael and Eddie only briefly crossed paths before Michael left on his way to start classes for fall quarter. They had barely forty-eight hours together, but this was enough for Michael to introduce his western visitor to his family—making sure they were on good terms before he retraced Eddie's steps back to the Pacific Coast.

Michael's father, Martin, was an engineer with the Montana Department of Transportation, working out of their Billings Maintenance Area Office. The Department was preparing to enlarge State Highway 308, fifteen miles joining the village of Belfry with the town of Red Lodge, known as the Gateway to Yellowstone Park.

The first step in the process was to survey the roadway. A contract had already been given to a Billings' surveying company, Jim Klein and Associates. As luck would have it, Jim Klein had several ongoing projects and was short one assistant surveyor. Martin had been able to propose Eddie as the new hire.

Martin and his wife, June, welcomed their son's ex-roommate—seeing him potentially as some sort of *de facto* stand-in while Michael was away at school. They even offered Eddie Michael's room until he could get settled closer to the job site.

Accepting the unexpected hospitality, Eddie felt strange sharing Michael's room with him for two nights until he left for his trek west. Still, it was a good chance to have some home cooking and to get to know the family—including two daughters, Samantha, a senior in high school, and Cheryl who was a freshman at the same school.

Michael's family, Eddie, thought, looked like something out of the pages of *Look Magazine*. They were tanned, athletic, and attired in leisure-chic clothing. They chatted excitedly about water skiing in Cooney Reservoir and Big Horn Lake as well as snow skiing on Red Lodge Mountain. They recalled the positives of volunteering for the Red Cross. They complimented each other about being below par golfers and above par tennis players at the Yellowstone Country Club, where they shared the greens with pronghorn. They were simply a great family.

Eddie was indebted to them for opening a door for him to what he hoped would be a new segment of his life where he could be as enthusiastic and feel as rewarded as when he put on his rubber boots and plodded off to the beach to the hymn of the breakers.

※

Eddie was quickly folded into Jim Klein's team. They were running against a deadline and needed to get the 308 job moving quickly. Late summer and fall in southern Montana were unpredictable seasons—it was difficult at best to know how long it would take them to cover the fifteen-mile-long job site. They hoped the field work could be completed in six weeks—but it was really anyone's guess.

Eddie, as a tenderfoot, was assigned to the chief surveyor on the 308 job. With advice from his new colleagues, he decided, as he had no roots in the Treasure State, to rent a room in Red Lodge.

With an advance from an understanding boss, he first bought an orange 1952 Willys Jeep CJ-3A. He then took his maiden voyage in his new conveyance to Red Lodge where he found a room at the south end of town, on Edrick Avenue, at Stan Coolidge's Cottages. He then drove the sixty-two miles back to Billings to get his stuff and say at least a temporary goodbye to Michael's family.

Red Lodge offered all Eddie needed. By comparison to the small coastal communities to which he was accustomed, it was a big town—albeit, a town that only had about a third of the population it had had at its zenith in the late 1800s and early 1900s when its economy was primed by mining that attracted a cornucopia of immigrants from all over Europe. In the Depression, the mines closed. Bootleg whiskey reportedly replacing coal and gold. Then, in 1936, the Beartooth Highway to Yellowstone National Park came to town and tourism became the epicenter of the economy.

Truth be told, Eddie could almost have been living anywhere and been equally oblivious to his accommodation. Much to his great pleasure, he was basically out and in the field from sunrise to sunset. He was with the crew, traversing the 308—learning how to skillfully use transits, stadia and range rods, chains, and dumpy levels. He would get back to his room dead tired but satisfied.

He thanked his mother for teaching him how to make a variety of stews and casseroles. He would shop for groceries Saturday evening and cook on Sunday. Usually, a meal like a big pot of Tilly's Irish Stew—one of Irene's favorites—would become his evening repast for the coming week. He would have some fruit and cereal in the wee hours of the morning before climbing into his Jeep—top off, the cold dawn air pummeling his face, a brown bag with a few sandwiches, thrown together the night before, at his side.

He thanked Neptune for having honed his agate hunting skills as his father had sharpened the blades and saws of the mill. These same keen eyes that could easily pick out an agate hiding in a pile of smelt sand could also pick out every dip and hillock populating their survey trail. He quickly saw and noted the topographical setting in great detail—often providing colleagues with valuable observations as to where to set up the tripod or the stadia.

He even, to his own great surprise, thanked his teachers for giving him a good understanding of the basics and the confidence to use these in the real world. His math abilities were put to practical tests for the first time as well as his abilities to communicate, both verbally and in writing. He passed all these tests. At last, the pieces were taking their place as part of the whole.

Eddie was happy.

The survey crew made good progress in covering the 308 and Eddie made good progress in covering the art of surveying. He was an eager learner and hard worker—a mix that did not go unnoticed by Jim Klein.

Through a lot of good luck and what Irene had called "elbow grease," the field part of the 308 job was completed in five weeks. Jim Klein was delighted. Eddie, however, was a bit nonplussed. *What next?* he thought.

Jim Klein asked Eddie to stop by his office. Uncertain of how the prevailing winds would push him, he decided to make arrangements to stop and see Michael's family while in Billings.

Trying to be a clever chess player, he went to Billings the day before the meeting with Jim Klein, spending that night in Michael's room. Martin gave him a hardy welcome, but June seemed almost ecstatic—whether it was his stand-in role as Michael, or because she just liked him, he could not tell.

Samantha and Cheryl too seemed pleased to see him, but totally preoccupied with high school life.

Over a much-appreciated, scrumptious dinner of pot roast topped-off with apple pie à la mode, Eddie provided his hosts with a brief recounting of his enjoyable past few weeks as an apprentice surveyor—a neophyte measurer. He concluded his tale with news of tomorrow's meeting with his boss, stipulating he did not know whether this was the end or a new beginning.

The girls smiled blankly, their good manners only just covering their total indifference. June seemed most impressed by Eddie's appetite, albeit sympathetic to his current uncertainties. However, Martin was resolute, as Eddie had hoped. Martin was certain Jim Klein, a fellow member in good standing of both Rotary and Kiwanis, would unquestionably want to keep Eddie on his team; bright young men were hard to come by. Nonetheless, should Jim Klein be so shortsighted as to let Eddie go, Eddie should not be worried. Martin had a lot of contacts and he was sure he could find something for this able young man.

This was exactly what Eddie had hoped to hear—he was not without options. He liked what he was doing and really did not want to pack up and leave. He certainly did not want to have to go back home as though he had failed at making a life for himself. Now he felt he had a cushion—if needed. Martin just might, once again, point him in a new direction. At times like this, Eddie felt he was like one of those wind-up toys, those metal soldiers painted all red and black with a big key sticking out of their back. If you wound the key, the little militia man would march forward, head on high, posture erect. But when he hit the wall, he would stand there looking like he was kicking the toe rail until the key had fully run-down. However, if you pointed him in a new direction, he would march forward ram-rod straight—until he hit the next wall, or his key ran out. Eddie felt, if he ended up hitting a wall, Martin would quite possibly be able to redirect him before his key ran out.

✷

Fortunately for all concerned, Eddie never had to test Martin's employment-finding skills. When he met Jim Klein, he was met with a pat on the back and good news for the days ahead. His boss was most satisfied with Eddie's progress and dedication. He offered him a raise as well as a plan for the coming months—emphasizing that this work was really all about making hay when the sun shone—taking it one job at a time. This volatility aside, Jim Klein proposed Eddie stay in Red Lodge. He would put him on a retainer while his office team put together the report on the 308 Project. If new data were called for, or validation of the field work was required, Eddie would go back on full salary, his new salary, for these assignments, if and when the need arose. In the meantime, Jim Klein was putting together a new project.

Rosebud Creek, some called it a river, emptied into the Stillwater River. The year before, there had been exceptionally heavy rains—the fast moving, high volume runoff damaging some of the rural roads. The erosion had affected a stretch from Fishtail, on County Road 419, for three and a half miles to State Road 78, and then for fourteen miles along 78, from Quaking Aspen Ranch to the junction of Adsit Ranch Road, with the exception of that portion of 78 that went through the town of Absarokee. The State had had a bill to, among other things, provide funds to improve water management along Rosebud Creek and the Stillwater River, including surveying the seventeen and a half miles of roadway. However, as always, this had become a political foil, become the object of heated partisan debates. Yet, no one wanted to let this area go through another winter without at least showing voters their good will to address what was seen as a worsening problem. Thus, at the very end of the fiscal year, they had finally approved the funds. The money was allocated. But there had not yet been the necessary discussions between Stillwater County, the State of Montana, and the City of Absarokee to agree upon the how's, when's, and by whom.

Jim Klein felt the preliminary talks would conclude by Thanksgiving and the political leaders at all levels would want to see something happening on the ground by Christmas, so they could show their constituencies how well they were doing their jobs. Jim Klein wanted Eddie on this team.

Eddy was happy.

He went by Michael's home to say goodbye to the family, only to be persuaded by June to spend one more night. That evening the pot roast was replaced by a ham-loaf with au gratin potatoes and fruit salad. And, that evening, rather than recalling the perhaps (through the eyes of others) dreary details of surveying, he regaled his hosts with his aspirations—now convinced he was that he was moving down a path that would lead him to the life he wanted to lead.

Back in Red Lodge, Eddie had only rare calls from Jim Klein—either asking him to follow-up on some detail of the 308 work (this generally requiring only a few hours of effort) or updating him on the progress of what was now labeled the 78 Project. Viewed from the other side of the ledger, he had a lot of free time.

At first, he got to know Red Lodge better—but there was not really all that much to get to know. He visited some bars and restaurants, but he still had to maintain a frugal lifestyle until he knew if he was going to have any work before spring.

What did surprise him a tad, however, as he meandered through the town at different times and went to different places, was that everyone seemed to be of European extraction. Well and good, he knew, you could not tell someone's roots by looking at the face—especially not in the increasing cold where people were bundled up from head to toe. Yet, being in the heart of the old Crow Nation, one might expect to find more folks saying they were of Native American (or indigenous) blood and fewer professing their origins (not that long ago) from Scandinavia or the British Isles. Apparently, the town's history as a mining area had drawn in the émigrés and driven out the rightful owners.

But that was a long time ago, if not that far away. The Little Bighorn Battlefield was over a hundred miles from Red Lodge—the site of Custer's now century-old Last Stand sitting squarely on the Crow Reservation.

Red Lodge had an Old-West-cowboys-and-Indians veneer. But this was all cosmetic, for the tourists. While the mining business had collapsed—the last mine closing over three decades earlier when there was an explosion that killed scores of people—entrepreneurs were still exploiters. The land baron mentality and hierarchy that had built mineral wealth for a chosen few at a great cost to the many continued with those same town elders, or their successors, calling the shots and pulling the strings to ensure that every possible tourist dollar found its way into their pockets.

Eddie had seen a similar version of the same scenario on the coast where the sawmill owners maneuvered and connived to control the stands of timber and the choicest markets—thereby dominating the major means of livelihood for hundreds of families. Tourism was now building on the coast too, and these same controlling interests were busy laying plans and purchasing assets to be able to maintain control as the economy shifted from the forests as the trees were cut and sold. This, in part, was a factor in Earl not opposing too vehemently his son's efforts to blaze his own trail. He foresaw all too clearly the shrinking forests and the ultimate decline of lumbering.

Eddie turned his attention to the world beyond Red Lodge, beyond Billings. He cast a wider net. He targeted a four-county tapestry as though he were surveying a small cove at home for the best agate sites. Big Horn,

Yellowstone, Stillwater, and Carbon countries were all close enough to Red Lodge to be able to bump around in his old Jeep—all possessing wonders he had not seen—semi-precious stones to be discovered just under a surface of slow-moving detritus, like the junk that accumulated in a tide pool after a winter storm. He just had to sweep aside the debris to find the treasures beneath only waiting to be discovered.

Of all the wonders from which to choose, Eddie was most attracted to the Crow Reservation—its nearest border less than fifty miles away. This affinity, he imagined, could be traced back to grade school and his childhood friendship with Willy Bray. Willy was one of a handful of Natives who lived in Eddie's village.

The tale of native peoples in the village was long and twisted. A year before the beginning of the Civil War, according to Eddie's fifth grade local history primer, several tribes from the southern coast had been held on a reservation in their village. Families were forcibly herded to this internment center, many dying on what they called their "Trail of Tears"—referring to the forced removal of the Cherokee People some thirty years earlier, when they were relocated from the Appalachian Mountains to the Ozarks. After almost twenty years of confinement, the government released these coastal peoples—after their tribal lands had been occupied by settlers, and when they had nowhere to go. Some, like Willy's family, just stayed put.

Willy's family lived up the river, not too far from Eddie. His father worked in the woods; his mother was a beekeeper. He and Eddie had gone through all the grades together. Willy had been an above average student, athletic, and well behaved. But to everyone in the hamlet, he was, at best, simply "that Indian kid"—perhaps, at worst, "one of them."

But to Eddie, Willy was just another kid. More importantly, he was another kid who knew a whole lot about the seashore. He and Eddie would scale the basalt precipices to sheltered coves where Willy would show Eddie a variety of heretofore unknown foods highly prized by his people and still harvested by his mother. Willy knew where to fish. He knew where to crab. He knew where to dig razors. Willy was really good to have around.

※

As Eddie explored the countryside, he was most fascinated by the Pryor Mountains. This chain of peaks, the tallest reaching almost 9,000 feet, occupied the southwest corner of the reservation, continuing southward to the state line.

These peaks received more rainfall than much of the surrounding prairie, offering a lush environment that had attracted the Crow centuries ago. According to Crow history, they came to the mountains to share in the riches, interacting in complete harmony with the "little people" who were the original dwellers. This endemic group lived in limestone caves, hunting with bow and arrow, and harvesting the natural bounty which they later shared with the Crow.

In the Pryor's, Eddie found a surrogate for the seashore. He hiked through Vermillion Valley, camped in Bear Canyon, followed Layout Creek, and visited Big Ice and Crater Ice Caves. In the absence of agates peeking out from the tide line, there were artifacts to find, hidden under the dust of time, requiring an equally keen eye to be resurrected.

Eddie scoured sites of tipi rings; more than a hundred rings present at one site alone near Bad Pass Trail. These vestiges of bygone societies and individuals reminded him of the shell mounds along the coast. Willy had explained to him how the village would go to rocky beaches, harvesting mussels, cockles, clams, and snails—bringing all these to a common pit for steaming and feasting. The mollusk shells would then be thrown on a heap—a kind of community dump. As the coastal areas were appropriated by settlers, these white shell heaps were overlain by erosion when the newcomers reshaped the land—the relics of the tribe's gatherings becoming geologic strata above their fossilized ancestors, some going back to the Paleozoic.

From the valleys that had housed thousands who had lived in harmony with their Creator, Eddie would scale the Pryor's peaks—on a clear day, looking across great expanses of savannah. Much like from Cape Verde, where he had gazed across the seemingly endless sea as the sun vaulted to its extremity for yet another day. From some vantage points, there was no sign of life to be seen, only boundless space. It was as though he was the first, or the last person on Earth. It was, he thought, perhaps dangerous to be at the pinnacle of your range, opening the door to feelings that you were king of the world.

King or not, Eddie was happy.

As cold weather set in, Eddie was forced to retreat from the higher elevations, shifting his exploring to the foothills and then to the lowlands (if 4,000-foot elevation could be considered as lowland). He would often go no further than the small town of Pryor; walking about the Chief Plenty Coups Park before going to the Double Spear Ranch where he would rent a cabin for the night.

As the temperatures dropped and the days shortened, he expanded his range in search of more accessible attractions. He would roam as far as the Interstate, visiting the Little Bighorn Battlefield National Monument not far from Crow Agency. This community had previously been the headquarters for the Bureau of Indian Affairs overseeing the sequestered tribe and was now the administrative center of the Crow Nation. He would venture as far as Garryowen, almost 150 miles away when one traveled through the reservation as he did. This was a tiny berg—even by Eddie's standards—that had the Custer Battlefield Museum and a few other interesting features. These were all the more interesting considering Garryowen was a nook of less than ten people, a backwater finding itself attached to the major artery that was Interstate 90.

---

True to Jim Klein's forecast, the 78 Project was ready to go before many had purchased their Thanksgiving turkeys. Most of the work would be postponed until spring. Nonetheless, there was considerable preparation, as well as a number of tasks that needed to be done on site and early. Living in Red Lodge, Eddie was the point man for these initial efforts.

Red Lodge was high and cold—certainly by comparison to his old coastal haunts. Yet, the real winter weather tended to come in February and March—even then, Red Lodge's average was less than twenty inches of snow a year.

November and December were snowless but cold, at times bone-rattling cold—the thermometer getting to forty on a hot day. Whizzing about in his Jeep was colder still. But with a good down coat and woolen gloves, Eddie was able to meet all Jim Klein's deadlines.

The 78 Project, supplemented by a good number of small jobs, subdividing farms, delimiting rights-of-way, and the like, kept the Jim Klein team busy through the next Thanksgiving. Eddie was gaining skills and confidence as he concurrently developed intimate knowledge of the Pryors—accumulating a collection of artifacts thanks to his sharp agate-hunting eyes—a collection that he would regularly hand over to the folks at Crow Agency as he felt they were the rightful owners. He was only the apt retriever who discovered things others had misplaced.

As he was more assured, both with himself and the job he was doing, he began going out on the town from time to time, frequenting any of the numerous drinkeries, but preferring the pub at the Pollard Hotel. The ambiance, going back to the hotel's origins in the 1890s, combined with the live music made for a calming atmosphere after hours spent in the sun and wind.

The Pollard was a favorite of tourists and Eddie would occasionally develop affinities with female visitors that could last for a few days, even a week—these, not infrequently, including romantic interludes. As his topographer and map-maker proficiencies improved, so did his social adroitness. Much as he evolved from a jack-of-all-trades into a good junior surveyor, he metamorphosed from an introverted beach comber and wayfarer into a more congenial, if not thoroughly extroverted, companion.

He found he very much enjoyed female company and was soon having to limit his social outings if he still wanted to be able to spend the prerequisite ten to twelve hours a day in the field.

However, when Jim Klein invited all his employees to Billings for a Christmas party, he took Eddie aside for quick chat. As always, work was being scheduled six to twelve months in advance. For the coming year or more, it appeared the bulk of effort would be needed to the northeast of Billings, not to the southwest as had been the case. The state was planning on working on a number of highways, including the 47, 39, and 447—all far from Red Lodge. Jim Klein suggested Eddie consider a move. A good base for the upcoming jobs would be Hysham, county seat of Treasure County.

※

So, it was, Eddie left Edrick Avenue, the Pollard Hotel, and Red Lodge, moving to Hysham—a community sandwiched between Interstate 94 and the Yellowstone River, with less than one-sixth the population of Red Lodge and at about half the altitude. He found a room in the Village Apartments, just a few blocks from the post office, hardware store, and high school that formed the community's epicenter. This cattle-raising and wheat-growing shire town was eight miles northeast of Billings via the Interstate and about sixty miles due north from Crow Agency.

The job sites were further apart, requiring Eddie to spend more time bouncing about in his Jeep. But, pragmatically, he realized he had little else to do on a work day. There were no more tourist spots nor transient visitors looking for excitement. This was a tight farming community. He did occasionally venture into the Brunswick Bar for a beer and a rare chat with a local—but there was no real social life.

On weekends, weather permitting, he continued his jaunts into Crow land—less frequently in the Pryors, now concentrating more on the closer northern part of the reservation as well as expanding his scope to include the neighboring Northern Cheyenne Indian Reservation.

Benefiting from living next door to the Interstate, additionally, he began making more frequent trips to Billings. He still stopped regularly to see Michael's family, but now generally stayed on his own dime in the historical Dude Rancher Lodge, unless an unplanned romantic adventure took him elsewhere.

With more time in the big city, Eddie's dating began to increase, opening a covey of new fun and surprises. With no small degree of hesitation, he even decided to ask Samantha to go with him to a jazz concert at the Fox Theater in Billings. She was now attending Rocky Mountain College, but still living at home. He had considerable misgivings about going out with her, but was aware that she, like he, enjoyed jazz and he knew few other jazz aficionados.

It went well.

Unexpectedly, with the help of Samantha, Eddie greatly enlarged his cultural horizons. Growing up, the closest thing to a cultural event was the Fourth of July Parade at a port city or the Catholic Church's Nativity. Concerts, symphonies, theater, opera, dance, and seminars were things of the big city—at most, only read about in the statewide newspaper which Earl perused religiously, but which had never become habit-forming for his son. Eddie was a void as it concerned "events". His consumption and appreciation of music, especially jazz, was limited to the local AM radio station. His recognition and admiration for the arts was limited to an earnest, nearly fervid delight in seeing Nature's wonders painted on Her own canvas. Aside from conscription in grade school, he had never attended a play or a concert. He had never voluntarily listened to a speaker. He had, in fact, never wittingly, sat quietly in a room full of people while others spoke, sang, or acted.

Samantha changed all this. She kept Eddie informed of various events scheduled by Billings' organizers—the two attending some sort or other performance at least every other month.

However, their relationship was isolated to these events. He did not invite her to explore the mountains or savannah with him. She did not invite him to scholastic or family affairs. There was no romantic commitment—but they were good friends.

To say Eddie's romantic life was sparse is to be overly generous. There were the random exceptions when he would find himself with someone who was looking for a short, superficial relationship—be it for an hour or a week. Rarely, he could literally bump into a willing someone at the grocery store or the gas station, or, more often (though none were often) meet someone while taking care of paperwork at the county courthouse.

Eddie would laugh to himself. He remembered in the sawmill when he was a kid, one of the men had been sobbing on a coffee break and said that if he did not get laid soon, he would go blind. Eddie guessed he was just active enough to avoid blindness.

---

On the work front, Jim Klein was very effective. The company ended up getting contracts for the 47, 39, and 447 Projects, as well as some add-ins.

Thanksgiving had become a default milestone and Eddie was coming up on his second holiday living in Hysham when Jim Klein rather unexpectedly organized his Christmas party two weeks earlier than usual.

When all were gathered in the Billings office conference room, each with a glass of some variety of cheer, Jim Klein called for quiet, raised his glass to salute all his colleagues-*cum*-employees, and announced he had sold the company to Millerman National Land Company. Jim Klein expanded. The terms of the purchase were that all ongoing work be completed by the present management and that all staff be integrated into Millerman activities. Jim Klein translated. All would remain as it was until sometime between Easter and Memorial Day when he estimated all current jobs would be completed. At that time, all employees would be transferred to the Millerman payroll. However, this did not mean that Millerman would keep the transferred staff in Billings or even in Montana—people would be assigned based on Millerman's needs and project load.

Jim Klein's announcement was met with neither sobs nor applause. No one really knew what it meant—including Jim Klein. The subtext clearly indicated he had been made an offer he could not refuse. But the implementation of the new structure and its impact on the current staff remained to be seen. What was clear was that, at the very least, it would be disruptive.

Among all Jim Klein's employees, the planned changes had the least impact on Eddie. In some ways, the announcement of these changes was a big help to him. He was entering the field of surveying through the portal of practical experience and not through an academic program. Nevertheless, he was still required to take two general exams: Fundamentals of Surveying as well as Principles of Practice and Surveying. Once he had passed these tests, he would be able to sit for a state licensing exam. He now knew he had to complete these exams before Jim Klein handed the reigns over to Millerman.

To no one's surprise, things seemed to happen much as Jim Klein had predicted (he was rarely wrong). A week after Mother's Day, all the projects were wrapped up, the results reported, and the payments made. On an unseasonably warm May Wednesday, the Jim Klein crew formed a semicircle around the Billings main entrance as the bronze plaque that had born the Klein name for three decades was replaced with one that now identified the portal as the Millerman National Land Company's Billings Office. As wine and cheese were served to commemorate the new management, Phil Schumer was presented to the group by Jim Klein as the newly appointed manager for Millerman's Northern Rocky Mountain Region with offices now open in Billings.

Phil Schumer made a brief statement filled with generic pleasantries before going to the heart of the matter: over the coming month, he would meet individually with each employee to review their role in Millerman—a list would be posted in the main hallway indicating the date and time for each's appointment.

Eddie's time came in early June. Pretty much as expected, Phil Schumer spent a few minutes applauding Eddie's hard work and dedication to doing a good job before pivoting to the core of the discussion; as a relatively new employee, an employee without a family, and an employee who had already moved twice in recent years, Eddie was a prime candidate for a transfer to another office. Schumer explained his attempts to blend long-time staff inured to the Jim Klein culture with experienced Millerman staff who knew how this much larger organization did business. To make these adjustments as painless as possible, they were doing all they could to keep former Jim Klein staff in the general vicinity of the Rockies—proposing a transfer for Eddie to Fort Collins.

Eddie was scheduled to take his second exam July 21st. So, he agreed to the move to Colorado as long as this could be postponed until after the test date. His condition was readily accepted. Eddie had a memorable Fourth of July celebration with Michael and his family; Michael was home for the summer before starting law school at the University of Chicago. After the fireworks, he and Samantha spent the night at the Northern Hotel to wish each other well. A little over two weeks later, he passed his exam and, before the end of the month, was heading south in his old Jeep.

*Book Three*

# The Snows of Summer

EDDIE had no idea of what was in store for him in Colorado or in Fort Collins. He knew Fort Collins was almost two-thirds the size of Billings. He was going to, for him, the big city. He had studied the map, noting that Colorado State University was located in the north of town, adjacent to downtown. Millerman's offices were situated in the northwest part of town, between Riverside Avenue and McHugh Street, about three miles due east of Colorado State University campus and less than a mile south of the Lamey Avenue bridge over the Cache la Poudre River.

His first task was to find accommodation—reasonable if not cheap accommodation. This meant going the opposite direction from the University where kids' parents were willing to pay inflated prices for their children's bedrooms. Before seeking any professional help, as from a real estate agent, he decided to drive around the southern suburbs, just skirting the city's boundaries.

His stars must have been shining brightly on that occasion. As Eddie reached the outskirts, near Horsetooth Reservoir, along West County Road 38, he saw a small "for rent" sign on an old fencepost in front of an even older farmhouse. Always being one to turn over the stone to see what was underneath, he went up to the house to enquire.

His knocks were met by an elderly gentleman who bade him come in, calling to his wife as Eddie took a seat in a well-used living room. When a simply, but somehow nobly dressed grey-haired lady of equal age entered the room, Eddie indicated he was just enquiring about the "for rent" sign— expecting that it was probably in regard to a room available in the rather large and well-kept house.

The couple insisted on serving Eddie a cup of coffee before discussing accommodation. He sipped his too-weak-for-his-taste coffee, answering their questions as to what he was about—apparently needing him to fill in some background before they felt comfortable talking about their offer.

Hearing their guest was a newcomer to the area with gainful employment, the lady of the house explained they had a bungalow in the back that had been the base for their son before he had joined the military. She pointed to his photo on the mantle and explained he had been killed in action in Vietnam.

More recently, the chalet had been occupied by their nephew who had come from the family's home area of Nebraska to attend the University. However, he had flunked out after two years and the cottage had been vacant for months.

This all sounded most interesting and Eddie asked if he could see the rooms. With an obvious mixture of melancholy and anticipation, the couple accompanied him out the kitchen's screen door and across a small yard with a clothesline supporting sheets and jeans, to a small brick structure with a carport on one side. The bungalow proved to be a wonderful surprise: there was a large living area with a combination living, dining, and kitchen area with expansive picture windows that looked away from the main house, over rolling pasture outlined by the foothills. Next to this great room, there was a large bedroom with bath. The builder had thought of everything and there was even a large storeroom. It was even fully furnished with all appliances including a washer and dryer in the storeroom. It seemed to be just what Eddie needed.

They sat on the plaid divan and concluded their arrangements. There was mutual agreement on both sides. Eddie would sleep in the bungalow tonight.

His new abode was approximately fifteen miles from the office—with little traffic it made for a quick commute. The first time he made the trip, his armpits were already sweated-through before he got to the office. He was unsure if it was due to the early August heat, already sultry in the early morning, or due to the nerves of walking into a strange office for the first time.

※

Things were all the same and all different. Steve Stewart was in charge of the office, working under Phil Schumer in the regional office. Steve and some of the senior staff had individual offices surrounding an open space filled with dozens of cubicles—one of which was assigned to Eddie. However, in assigning the workspace, Steve made it abundantly clear that he rarely expected to see Eddie seated in this area—his job was in the field.

After making the introductions and chaperoning him through a perfunctory tour of the facilities, Steve took Eddie into his office to explain his exact assignment. Millerman had landed a big contract with Weld County, the third-largest county in the state, to survey many of the county's roads—starting with roads 31, 35, 37, and 39. They had arranged with the County Assessor to have temporary space in the county's offices on 17th Street in Greeley. For the foreseeable future, this would be Eddie's base.

Eddie, a complete stranger to the whole state, quickly asked colleagues about Greeley and Weld County. The city, called "the garden city" and home to the University of Northern Colorado, was a little more than half the size of Fort Collins, located just west of the confluence of the Cache la Poudre River with her bigger sister, the South Platte. The county, going all the way to the Wyoming border, with over 4,000 square miles of area and less than 250,000 people, was a lot of open range, including the Pawnee National Grassland. It was barely thirty miles between the Millerman Fort Collins Office and the Weld County Assessor's Office, with most of the job sites in between. Eddie decided this did not require another move when he had just found his comfortable chalet near Horsetooth Reservoir—he would commute.

The first of the several sites was only a little more than twenty miles away from his new home, near Woods Lake (Eddie was to learn, not to be confused with the Woods Lake in the south of the state at the foot of Mount Wilson in the San Miguel Range). Through the upcoming road improvements, the county wanted to increase access to the lake in the hopes of attracting more anglers—the reservoir offering an array of warmer-water fishes over and beyond the much-loved native cutthroat trout.

※

Slowly, but perceptibly, Eddie felt himself putting down roots—tentative, fragile fibers, not tough taps, but underpinnings, nonetheless. The more he moved about, the easier the moving about became. He wondered if he was now destined to follow the winds, having no permanent base. He wondered if he would ever see Cape Verde again.

One day after work, he stopped for an early meal at the Blue Lotus, a Chinese restaurant that had excellent spring rolls and a Szechuan stir-fry that made his mouth water. After a spicy meal that left him with a pleasant afterglow, he cracked open his traditional fortune cookie over one last cup of green tea.

The fortune inside read, "your present will cast a net for your future". He did not know why, but he folded the little slip of paper and put it in his wallet.

<hr />

Eddie enjoyed his new surroundings. The western fringes of the great prairie lapped against the bulwark of the Rockies. The frosty peaks, that scratched the sky at over 14,000 feet in elevation, slowly slipped away into the grasslands, like a scoop of ice cream lazily melting on a summer afternoon. Fort Collins was just over 5,000 feet, not too far off the altitude of Red Lodge. The slide eastward continued, with Greeley at a few feet above the 4,600 mark and the border with Kansas descending to about 3,800 feet.

Although there was nothing to compare to the Crow lands for his hikes—in search of exactly what, he was not sure—there were the Pawnee National Grasslands about seventy miles to the east, and the Soapstone Prairie Natural Area about thirty miles north, on the Wyoming border. These areas offered great stretches of nothingness into which he could lose himself—surfacing refreshed, but with few tangible signs of his efforts. His agate-hunter eyes found little worthy of stuffing into his daypack. Nevertheless, this did not dissuade him, and he roamed the hills whenever he had free time, enjoying the nearly constant breeze in his face and, at the right season, the fertile scent of the prairie.

Work, however, as a now-seasoned surveyor, was becoming an all-too-familiar stew—Weld County Road 68 looking more and more like Treasure County's Taylor Road. He enjoyed the work; of that he was still sure. He enjoyed the challenge of transferring precisely what his eyes saw to paper. He enjoyed the idea that what he did would make things better. He enjoyed being outside. He enjoyed in many ways being the master of his own time. But he was worried. He did not want his job to be a re-run of what he had so often seen in the sawmill: work becoming the doldrums. So many of the men started off their shift grumpy, becoming only angrier as the hours passed, just waiting to leave the damn place to have a cold beer. He did not want to fall down this pit. And, so far, he did not even feel like he was teetering at the edge. He was still excited every morning—still enthusiastic. But he felt something was missing.

Unbeknownst to him, this missing piece was becoming clearer as he was leaving the County Assessor's office after reviewing with this fine gentleman the work of the previous fortnight. The Assessor, Paul Jenkins, had mentioned the Union Colony Civic Center and the vacuous expression on Eddie's face must have been clear confirmation that the connection to this—what Paul had assumed to be well-known institution—was obviously lost on Eddie.

Paul then informed his young uncultured guest that the center was named for the original Union Colony, the precursor to Greeley. The colony was an experimental agricultural utopian community founded in 1870 by Nathan C. Meeker. Meeker, a newspaperman, entrepreneur, and community founder, later became an Indian agent and was killed by the Utes in 1878. While his story was an important part of the city's history, Paul pointed out that the town herself had been named after Meeker's editor, Horace Greeley. Paul, nearly swelling with pride, concluded by animatedly underscoring to Eddie that today the center was one of the largest performing arts venues in the state, hosting a variety of shows, concerts, performances, and other magnificent entertainment.

At the time, his host's exuberance for the preforming arts was almost a subliminal event, like seeing someone on a passing bus who reminded you of your favorite aunt, but only realizing it days later. Eddie's mind was focused on the deadline for his current assignment—performing arts a distant thought that was filed somewhere in the less-used reaches of his brain.

※

Several weeks later, before heading home, Eddie was having a sundowner beer at the Old Chicago Taproom (something not possible prior to 1969 when Greeley gave up its dry status) when his eyes fell upon a handbill for an upcoming performance of *Chicago* pinned to a fly-speckled bulletin board. This, unconsciously, opened the door to the reclusive corner of Eddie's mind where he kept all variety of miscellaneous items. A performance. A performance at the Civic Center. A renowned and greatly esteemed civic center. Was this something of interest for an unsophisticated beachcomber?

With an almost physical jolt, this brought back memories of Billings and Samantha and all the events the two had shared—events he never would have explored without Samantha's guidance and encouragement. He thought of the song from *Chicago*: "All That Jazz." Jazz had been the initial bridge with Samantha. Why not?

So, he called her. She was still living at home, having transferred from Rocky Mountain College to the Montana State University's Billings campus to pursue a degree in sociology. He felt disquieted calling his friend's baby sister, although she was only four years his junior and a mature woman in her own right, but old memories die hard. He could still picture her at the dining room table with her parents and her siblings, a high school student full of vitality and hope. But there was also a very vivid memory of a night in the Northern Hotel. This latter was the more persuasive, pushing him to invite her to come south for a visit.

The decision made; this did not abate Eddie's apprehension. He had no idea what kind of social life Samantha led. She was an attractive and outgoing young woman—almost certainly popular and the target of many erudite, libidinous young men who almost predatorily roamed the Billings campus. And with whom she most likely had much more in common than she had with an under-educated, rough, unpolished, bucolic mapmaker—or so he saw himself.

This insecurity notwithstanding, Eddie was happy to hear her voice and even happier to note some level of reciprocity on her part. After a few minutes of everyday generalities, he learned she was enjoying her studies and hoping to get a place of her own in the future. But this future was still elusive. She was midway through her junior year and, feeling very unworldly, toying with the idea of trying to spend the summer and the first part of her senior year studying abroad. If all went well, she would return to Billings for a quarter before graduating. Beyond this, she had no clue.

She was, Eddie thought, already a step ahead of him. When he was a college student, he did not even have enough presence of mind to acknowledge that he did not have a clue. He was not, moreover, even sure the situation had changed much today.

As Samantha trailed-off into the mantra of the ennui of campus life when one lives at home, Eddie saw an opening but was reluctant to take it. He swallowed hard, crimped his eyes shut, and stepped off the edge, asking Samantha if she had ever visited Colorado—a seemingly, he hoped, innocent enough question.

As frank and self-effacing as always, both reassuring traits Eddie thought, Samantha, with a laugh, clarified that her unworldliness was not really just a question of not having traveled outside the United States. She had never been more than a hundred miles away from Yellowstone County. She was, by her own admission, a country girl who had never been far from the country.

With the road open, Eddie forged ahead, complimenting Colorado on its natural beauty and impressively varied countryside. She should really come and see for herself. Remember, he urged Samantha, the longest trip started with the first step and this was far from the longest trip. Colorado was really still in the extended neighborhood.

Her quick agreement so surprised Eddie, he nearly forgot to continue the conversation. Tongue-tied could not begin to explain how he felt. Stumbling about, nearly at a loss, he was greatly relieved when Samantha herself came to his aide, saying she would love to come and see him over next Easter's school break.

---

Eddie was filled with both anticipation and trepidation about Samantha's visit—still months away. While he began to mentally plan each day, each hour, he continued his routine—measuring, mapping, plotting, analyzing. Work-wise, things were on the verge of becoming tedious when there was a great kerfuffle at the Millerman Fort Collins Office. Kent Whittaker, a longtime employee on the Fort Collins team who had really helped Eddie grasp the ins and outs of office operations and politics, was being called before the State Board for Professional Engineers, Land Surveyors, and Geologists, accused of false accounting and negligence. The accusation, lodged by a group calling themselves the Friends of Gateway Park, alleged Kent had intentionally, and for direct and significant compensation, established false boundaries for the Fir Forest Products Company off Highway 287. Then the company harvested 3,200 acres of state land, claiming it was part of their private timber stands—this determination based on demarcations established by Kent—boundaries now purportedly completely fraudulent.

The embroilment received a great deal of unwanted press—press that Millerman did all they could to downplay. However, when the board found Kent guilty of inappropriate professional behavior, taking away his license, and the state lodged civil cases against the Fir Forest Products Company and Kent—pending possible criminal charges and seeking compensation and penalties for the illegally procured timber—Millerman had to do all they could to distance themselves from their now former employee. This included going to the bulwarks to prove emphatically and categorically that Kent was acting on his own, with no knowledge of his employers.

This was no easy task for the surveying firm. Kent had been on official assignment surveying, as Eddie so often did, easements for Poudre Canyon Road and the drainage of Owl Creek. He had seemingly satisfactorily completed this job, submitting all the prerequisite reports, maps, and data. However, it appeared that while on the Poudre Canyon project—this part of a contract with the State of Colorado—Kent had made personal arrangements with Fir Forest Products to prepare and present another project with updated forest boundaries to the Colorado State Land Board.

Ultimately, the Land Board, the Board of Professionals, and the State Attorney General's Office all reviewed Millerman's role in the wrongdoing—all deciding, after due deliberation, that the parent company had had no prior knowledge of, nor input into, Kent's nefarious actions. Millerman did not see the regrettable saga end without first receiving a formal and severe reprimand from the state for not keeping better tabs on its staff.

Throughout this entire drama, Eddie had been a spectator. Kent worked to the north and west of Fort Collins; Eddie covering the south and east. Their zones did not overlap. Eddie had no ties, not even the thinnest threads, to Fir Forest Products. He was completely out of the line of fire. This notwithstanding, the whole sordid affair did mean he would now have to do more, document more, clarify more, to ensure his work was fully chronicled for the scrutiny of all and, it seemed, the frustration of he alone.

When all was said and done, the resulting additional bureaucracy for a deeper and deeper paper trail added a minimum of four hours a week of new mandatory and stifling office tasks. In addition to this unappreciated drudgery, the Kent story underscored the possibilities for misuse of surveyor skills and responsibilities. There were evidently always options for crossing the line and maybe a lot of folks did so; Eddie was now unsure.

As Kent's actions attracted the focus of several investigations, it became clear he had been falsifying data for years, having an ample offshore account to show for all his illicit endeavors. Kent's empathy for his fellow employees, his natural outgoingness, his church-on-Sunday and Best-Dad awards aside, he had led almost a double life. He had been a model employee of Millerman and, at the same time, a clandestine self-employed mapmaker willing to formally present the most erroneous of figures as long as the compensation was large enough. His malfeasance shocked the company. It also broke up some of Eddie's growing monotony while surveying the new job on Road 74 near the now completed survey of Road 31. Before the frenzy over the Kent kerfuffle, the increasing colorlessness of rural Colorado roads was only diminished by the occasional special attraction—the Maxwell Washing Machine Museum near the junction of the jobs for the two backcountry thoroughfares one of Eddie's favorite local landmarks. Kent's misconduct now stole the spotlight from all other diversions.

※

It was well into early spring when the dust from the Kent matter finally settled. It was nearly time for Samantha's arrival.

Eddie had eagerly explored options for this much-anticipated visit. What would Samantha like? He reviewed everything. He thought about going with her to the well-trafficked byways of Denver, the famed and flamboyant walkways of Aspen, the isolated pathways of Spanish Peaks in the south, or Arapaho Reserve in the north. He was still mulling over the possibilities when he got a call from Samantha. She wanted to reconfirm her plans and let Eddie know she would only be able to spend the period Wednesday to Friday after Easter with him in Colorado. She was sorry. She had to spend the holiday with her family—Michael was coming home for the first time in a long while. Then the next weekend she had to spend her time studying since she had exams immediately after classes resumed. She hoped this was OK.

Eddie wanted to yell, "No! It's not OK." But he said nothing other than he was glad she could still come and share whatever time she could, given her busy schedule. He was at a loss of what special events could be arranged for two nights and basically two days. He set about laying more modest plans.

He discovered the Union Colony Civic Center was having a rendition of *Hello Dolly*. He was able to get tickets for Thursday. Sally, the Millerman receptionist, then told him about the Ace Gillett Lounge in The Armstrong Hotel. Named after the hotel's original, and now deceased, owner who, as a secret bootlegger with a love for jazz, had drawn loyal crowds in the previously dry town, to listen to the wonders of the local jazz trio for over three decades.

Not knowing when she would arrive on Wednesday or leave on Friday, and with Ace Gillett on Wednesday and *Hello Dolly* on Thursday, Eddie felt he had reshuffled things as best he could to meet the demands of a much-shorter-than-hoped-for visit that would go who knew where. He was still bummed-out about the brevity of Samantha's visit. But he remembered the old adage he had heard somewhere, "half bread is better than none." Who knew? Maybe they were such a mismatch, as he often feared, that their fifty-some hours together would already be such an overload the two would never speak to each other again?

Inwardly, Eddie was a "ruminator," mentally digesting and then re-digesting things. He was probably now going through far more iterations than many would consider as good for his spiritual well-being. Outwardly, however, in terms of doing, he was pragmatic. Once the inevitably of something was clear, he fully accepted the circumstances as those with which he must deal—moving resolutely, if perhaps unenthusiastically, ahead.

Eddie dove deeper into his work to avoid any self-inflicted wounds from phrenic histrionics provoked by overdoing his rehashing of Samantha's upcoming stay. His data collection and mapping moved carefully forward—east along County Road 74, toward County Road 33. He was retracing certain parts of the Overland Trail, the Nineteenth Century major east-west link that dipped south in Colorado. The trail and the road crossed the Eaton Ditch, named for, and built by Benjamin Harrison Eaton, the Ohio-born Governor of Colorado from 1885 to 1887 as well as a member of the Union Colony and large land owner who diverted the water from the Cache la Poudre River for farmers north of Greeley.

Eddie read the signboard on the canal bank, "BH Eaton Ditch—40°28'07.4N 104°56'00.5W". A dispassionate reminder of a very passionate subject—power and money. The canal, built in 1878, as local residents had told Eddie, had, to the ire of many, diverted water upstream from other users. This ultimately, but more slowly than many would have wished, led to legislation that protected the water rights of downstream farmers. Whether Kent or Benjamin, Eddie reflected, people tended to use their positions to their advantage. He wondered, was this simply a question of predators and prey—the natural cycle of nature?

---

Easter was in April, a capricious month in northern Colorado when the morning temperatures could be in the high thirties while the afternoons could warm to the high sixties. It had been a relatively mild winter, with about seven inches of snow in March and only a little snowfall continuing into the next month. Eddie had lost little work due to inclement conditions and was ready for a break—taking the full week after Easter off in honor of Samantha's visit.

Like treacle, the days oozed by, Samantha calling on Tuesday night saying she would be in Fort Collins by lunchtime. She had actually already left Billings, spending the night with a friend in Casper. They agreed to meet at the Wild Boar Cafe on College Avenue, not far from the CSU campus and an easy spot for Samantha to find. Eddie was still not sure of the sleeping arrangements and wanted to go slowly until he was able to gauge the temperature face-to-face.

When she pulled up into a parking space right in front of the cafe in her 1975 Dodge Dart, Eddie was standing near the coffee house's entrance, trying to look nonchalant, albeit he had been standing there ramrod straight for over half an hour. However, he savored much of his anxiety melting as, when she saw him, she jumped from her car, leaving the door ajar, and flew into his arms—which were as ill-prepared for a steamy embrace as was his brain. He kind of stumbled into her, looked into her eyes, kissed her on the forehead, inhaled the bouquet from her hair, exhaled far too deeply, then gave her a sultry kiss that embarrassingly slipped on and off her lips. He was, happily, greatly rewarded by feeling her full-bodied response to his attention. It seemed the ardor from Northern Hotel had kindled a flame that still smoldered in both of them.

When they were finally suitably seated in the cafe, they seemed to be at a loss for words, each staring into his or her own coffee cup, relishing the aroma—whether of the coffee or each other was uncertain. Then, after a calming silence that reminded Eddie of what he noticed in the congregation after taking communion, they settled into a comfortable cadence of small talk—catching each other up on what they had been doing since they had last met.

After four cups of coffee, two *pain au chocolat*, and lots and lots of stories—for each, some fascinating, some somniferous—it was time to make a move, if not the move. Eddie asked Samantha if she was too tired from the long two-day drive to go out for some jazz that night. As he had hoped, and secretly expected, she was ready for some good music accompanied by a good drink.

Eddie then tiptoed out onto the ice, asking what kind of room she would need. There was the Best Western University Inn just up the street, the Hilton Fort Collins, just about as close in the other direction, and even a Northern Hotel, he said with a smile, on the north side of town.

Whether it was his contagious smile, the reference to the Northern Hotel, or just her own preplanned ideas of how the visit would take place—whatever the reason—with a delicate mien, she said she had heard so much about him living in a charming place next to a waterbody with such a charming name that she really could not go anywhere other than this, by all accounts, most delightful place to spend the night.

The ice did not crack. Eddie was jubilant. Almost forgetting to pay the bill, rushing to the door, he said he would quickly get his Jeep and she could follow him to West County Road 38—the most warmhearted place in town.

They almost missed the jazz at Ace Gillett. Eddie had no more helped Samantha with her small duffel bag, then, as soon as the front door closed, she was in his arms. From his arms to the couch to the bed, their ardor heightened and then was warmed by an afterglow that made staying in bed considerably more appealing than driving back into town for some music and a drink. But, with a twinkle in their eyes, they agreed it was better to stretch things out, and an enjoyable musical evening would make the sequel all that more enjoyable too.

They did appreciate the music and the ambiance, happy to have come, at times the deep throbbing bass tones penetrating them like small seismic tremors, somehow seeming to form a metaphysical bond between them. They sat at a dark corner table, holding hands, absorbing the intense intertwined rhythms of bass, sax, and drums. Eddie sipped Henry McKenna on the rocks and Samantha had a glass of chilled Liebfraumilch.

They returned to Eddie's bed after midnight with renewed fervor and passion. They had what many would call a "lay-in," finally nearly crawling from the sheets at almost midday, ravenous but somehow satiated. After a savory brunch of fruit, omelet, toast, and scalloped potatoes, skillfully orchestrated and assembled by Samantha, they drove to Rotary Park and took a languorous walk along Horsetooth Reservoir, saying little, watching the waves skip across the water's surface, teased by the cool breeze.

After an invigorating time feeling as though they had grounded themselves with nature, becoming a natural part of things that were and would be, they returned to the comfort and security of Eddie's cottage. There they warmed themselves on each other's incandescence before taking a shower and marveling at the curves and folds of each other's bodies. They then got in Eddie's windy old Jeep, Samantha preferring this to her more conformable and certainly warmer Dart and headed to Jay's Bistro where they had reservations for an early dinner before going to the Civic Center for the performance of *Hello Dolly*. They thoroughly enjoyed the play, even if it was sprinkled with prickly shards of acrid poignancy as each realized in a matter of hours, they would again be separated by five hundred miles of forest and plain, mountain and valley, river and gorge. They felt as though they lived in two very separate worlds that would rarely cross paths, that would seldom intersect, that would only whimsically offer such ephemeral, if elegant times of joy and intimacy. In many ways, with all the constraints, it seemed almost masochistic to seek to forge such a personal and deep partnership.

However, as is well known, emotions can, and often do override rational decision making. They felt profound bonds had been sculpted in a miraculously short time—bonds that should be nourished and reinforced. Unique, once-in-a-lifetime bonds like those no one had ever experienced before—their bonds, their wonderful, priceless bonds.

As much as they may have tried to wish it away, Friday morning did arrive all too soon.

In the wake of a spartan breakfast of coffee and buttery croissants they had picked up after leaving the Civic Center, Eddie and Samantha embraced as though each were trying to suck the very essence from the other—Samantha then heading down the drive to West County Road 38 and thence northward to Billings.

Eddie immersed himself in his work. As planned, his project moved progressively eastward. When Road 74 transformed into Collins Street in the little community of Eaton, Eddie and his crew turned north along Road 35, following their contract, keeping to Weld County thruways.

In the quiet of his bungalow, he would revisit the all-too-short time he had shared with Samantha. Through these visits, he realized he still knew very little about her or what she wanted to do when she finished her studies. They had whetted their appetites. They had focused on the pressing urgency of now, today, without addressing tomorrow.

His concerns about dating his friend's sister and about dating a girl several years his junior were alleviated. Michael's name had never come up—he was a non-issue. Furthermore, age had not been a factor in any way. They had interacted like two adults, never wondering who was the older or more mature. Barriers, real and imagined, seemed to be falling away. But his overactive mind was still overrunning the factual events of only a few hours together—turning the pages of an imaginary book that foreshadowed his future. Was this their future?

He felt pulled in new directions. This was not his first romantic fling. He had seen relationships—long and short—end. At times, the ending was foreseeable from the beginning. At other times, the door seemed to slam shut totally unexpectedly. Yet, he had never been concerned. Things were what they were. Or, things had been what they had been.

This time seemed different. This time felt different.

Was his avid imagination driving the process? Was he, as he often did, fantasizing—embellishing a small piece of reality into a historic tale?

He would call her at least once a week—not wanting to overdo it for fear of the impression it might give her parents, as she was still under their roof. He hoped she had, at the very least, told them she had been traveling to see him and, upon her return, had told her family that they, the two of them, had some sort of connection, be it ever so causal. This, he hoped, would downplay her parents' possible—he felt probable—concerns about their daughter's unscripted actions.

The fact that he was unsure of exactly what and how she had told her parents was exemplary of what a small slice of the bigger picture they had actually dealt with—the imperative having been to live for the moment—the second—the millisecond. But it was now time to think in broader strokes. It was time to change the lens and look at things more clearly.

This was what he wanted. At least, he thought it was. He knew he did not want something he thought of as special to become commonplace and then to be lost. But what did she want?

They were not able to have this discussion over the phone; both because this was not a suitable means of conveyance for these messages and because it required more time than she could easily invest while living at home and studying. They needed to sit down, one-on-one, to see where they thought their lives were leading them.

As a mapmaker, he mapped out a strategy to fill in the blanks. They would get together for the Fourth of July. It should not be again at his place. Here it would be too easy to avoid the future and enjoy the present. They would meet halfway, on neutral ground where they could objectively see the lay of the land—where better to do this than from a mountain top?

Thus, he proposed to Samantha they meet to spend the Fourth together camping in the mountains, at Bow River Campground in Wyoming. Uncertain how much convincing she might need, he recalled in splendid detail how July was summer in the Rockies—a time of rejuvenation and beauty. Wild flowers would be in bloom, meadows would port malachite cloaks, the aspen would be approaching their leafy majesty. The Fourth of July was the gist of an abbreviated but sumptuous summer season.

The campground itself, at over 8,500 feet elevation, near the Medicine Bow River, was swathed in crisp, clear mountain air that would liven their spirits and enrich their souls—this latter descriptive, he feared, a bit overboard, even for his own tastes. They would, he added, not knowing if he had made his point, not be too far from the 10,000-foot Pennock Mountain if they wanted to get to an even higher vantage point. They could meet in the small town of Elk Mountain, sixty miles northwest of Laramie, where she could leave her car and they would continue in his Jeep to be better able to handle rough roads should this be necessary.

Samantha needed no convincing and was more than ready, willing, and able to campout with him—leafy trees and crisp air or not. She told him she already had a tight-fitting red, white, and blue T-shirt she was eager to model for him. While she assured him that her parents were alright with everything, he suggested it might be more prudent to tell them she was visiting a classmate in Laramie for the holiday.

※

Eddie had booked a room for the first night in the historic Elk Mountain Lodge. He was particularly happy when he found the hotel, dating back to

1905, had a room named after Louis Armstrong who, a few years earlier, had received great acclaim for his singing of *Hello Dolly*. This was serendipity.

Again, the days seemed to pass at such a slothful pace; Eddie felt summer would never arrive. But arrive it did, first in the lowlands, then in the high plateaus—at the same time, they finished their Weld County project. Steve Stewart was more than satisfied with the results and welcomed Eddie's request for a few weeks off after months of slogging through rain, sleet, and snow.

Eddie was so anxious that he left Fort Collins two days before his appointed rendezvous with Samantha, saying to himself he needed to check out the hotel. This worked out well as he was able to confirm the Armstrong Room as well as ensure Samantha could keep her car at the hotel when they went into the mountains. He also verified they would have a camping site at Bow River, while making a run down to Laramie to get some red roses to adorn the room when Samantha arrived.

When Samantha did arrive, she was effusive about all: the hotel, the room, the flowers, the camping out. They spent a rapturous night accompanied by the spirit of Louis Armstrong. Then after a filling English-style breakfast of eggs, sausages, blood pudding, tomatoes, mushrooms, bacon, and toast—all washed down with a great pot of delicately roasted coffee—they moved the Dart around to more secure parking at the side of the hotel and took off into the northern reaches of the Medicine Bow National Forest.

They followed Ranger Station Road, then, soon after crossing into the National Forest, took a short detour to Hanging Lake where they ate a picnic lunch the hotel had prepared. The food, the sites, the sounds, the nearly palpable aurora—everything was stimulating, leading them on, promising even sweeter fruits just over the next rise.

It was several hours before sunset when they finally arrived at the campground. There were only a few other people partaking of the proffered alpine hospitality; Eddie and Samantha found a secluded spot to pitch their tent and began preparing their evening meal.

They had simple meat-and-potatoes fare that required minimal time and effort to get on and off the table—the table in this case being a two-by-twelve board the Forest Service had kindly affixed between two stumps. Hand in hand, they took an evening promenade into the forest, marveling at the calmness and pretending they were taking air with the nobility of 18th century Savannah, complaining, with a laugh, about the unbearable heat and humidity. Soon it became quite noticeable that the temperatures were rapidly falling—Eddie and Samantha assumed this was all part of the normal cycle as the day drew to a close.

By prearrangement, Eddie had brought a double sleeping bag. Thus, as the cold began to seep through their jeans and windbreakers, they decided it would be much more comfortable to snuggle in their tent than to try to build a campfire to keep warm.

Later, through giggles, they noted with satisfaction that they had no close neighbors, as these folks might have been distraught by the noisy contortions they had chosen to keep themselves warm.

They finally succumbed to sleep, not hearing the Great Grey Owl that flew overhead, just inches above the tent's mast; the raptor was constrained to low altitudes in his hunt due to the stormy night sky.

Eddie awoke, expecting to see a summer sun welcoming the day, but finding an oppressive grey sky and four inches of snow on the ground, the tent, and the Jeep. Snow in July—who would have thought! But there it was, everywhere.

He gently brought Samantha back from another world where she had been softly mewing, with a smile of satisfaction. He held his palms over her eyes and asked her to sit up. He then flipped up the tent's flap as he removed his hands, chuckling as a look of astonishment seeped over Samantha's face. Snow!

※

There was no real problem. The Jeep could easily handle the conditions. Their tent was strong and their sleeping bag warm. But did they want to pass the Fourth of July covered in snow? They thought not. Almost as if they had telepathically agreed, they quickly packed up, retracing their steps to try and find again the spirit of Louis Armstrong.

They got back to the Elk Mountain Lodge and, finding their room available, with great grins, told the receptionist they would be staying a week. They joked about finding their independence in their hotel room, celebrating their freedom carnally—the pleasures of the flesh merging with those of the spirit to memorialize the founders who had also built this fine establishment with the soft cushy beds.

While they did spend a great deal of time woven into love's cocoon, they began to realize they were in fact getting serious and, as such, needed more dialog—what was to happen? Inadvertently, Eddie outlined it well when describing to Samantha how he had been, and still was an agate hunter. He had adopted a habit of casting his eyes to the pathway before him, often seeing all sorts of treasures, from beautiful stones to historic artifacts. Now, however, though his eyes were still focused forward, he saw nothing.

He no longer knew what path he was following. It had all been so clear before. Now it was so fuzzy, so murky. There were no gleaming pebbles or ancient remnants peeking out at him from beneath the shrubbery. There was only haze—haze, or fog, or vapors, or puffs of air—that carried the scent of her hair and the perfume of her soul. He felt his agate hunter skills were no longer enough. He felt he was lost for the first time in his life. He felt they were lost. He felt the path had led him to a maze—a tangled web wherein somewhere lay the map, and he a mapmaker—a map, a chart for moving ahead through his life—through their lives.

Eddie remembered his grandmother talking about the mythical Greek tale of Theseus and the Minotaur. The nasty Minotaur threatened people's lives as it ate unwed girls, protecting itself by living in a labyrinth. With the help of his love, Ariadne, Theseus navigated the maze and accomplished his goal of killing the Minotaur. Would he and Samantha kill their Minotaur?

*Book Four*

# Breaking from Arapaho Tradition

WHEN Eddie and Samantha bared their souls at the Elk Mountain Lodge, in the shadow of Louis Armstrong, Eddie learned that jazz, and maybe now he himself, were not Samantha's only passions. Her studies in sociology had taken a twist, almost a cultural anthropological bend. She was very interested in—one could say devoted to—helping marginalized people. Within the framework of her experiences in Montana, this meant Native Americans, a group mistreated, abused, and maligned for centuries. Their stay at the hotel, close to Medicine Bow, had put things into a different perspective for her. Much as Eddie had gone back to his agate hunter analogy, she too used her childhood as a construct to explain how she was prioritizing elements of her current life's plan.

When Eddie had first mentioned Medicine Bow, Wyoming, her initial thoughts had been to remember back to one of the first western TV shows she had seen: *The Virginian*. The 1902 novel, and the 1962 TV series of the same name, had roughly followed the same tales of ranchers heroically fighting for survival in the Wyoming Territory. Those following these popular stories had never seemed to consider that the land for which these ranchers were so valiantly fighting was not theirs—it belonged to, and had belonged to for centuries, the indigenous peoples.

It was often difficult to say precisely what belonged to whom—much easier to say to whom nothing belonged. The indigenous tribes were unquestionably the original owners. To the limited extent Samantha had been able to look into this question before coming to meet Eddie, and as it related to this part of the state, it seemed to her that the Shoshone, coming from the West, may have been one of the leading occupants in recent time. They were then partially displaced by the Cheyenne, Arapaho, and Lakota Sioux. But it was hard to know. The tribes themselves, to greater and lesser degrees, were nomadic. They were also in frequent conflicts between themselves and with the intruding white settlers. When the white people took control, they moved them about like pawns on a chessboard—often translocating them to strange places far, far away from their homelands.

It was a complex, all too often horrific mosaic. It was a maze of deep historical import that had often been reshaped by recent tellers—reversing roles, making the intruder the hero.

In her research, Samantha had decided in her own version of the agate hunt that it was necessary to turn over one leaf at a time—her current target, the Arapaho people. While all were equally subject to injustices and prejudice, the Arapaho, going back to her sociological foundations, had a very interesting social structure.

Samantha had explained to Eddie that, according to the reports she had read, in Arapaho culture, girls often married their brother's friend—the comparison with their arrangement not lost on Eddie. However, unlike their situation, these were arranged bonds—the girl's family selecting their future son-in-law, apparently frequently based on the girl's brother's recommendations, from amidst those young men who had traversed the rites of passage. These tests, among others, demonstrated to all that the young man in question had the necessary skills as a hunter to be able to take care of a wife and a soon-to-be family.

Samantha had quipped that she hoped Eddie was a good hunter. She then continued with her sketch of Arapaho conjugal customs.

Given the prerequisites for marriage, the groom was generally ten to fifteen years older than the bride. When the couple had made all the arrangements, the marriage was sealed by the groom's dowry—most often horses given to the bride's family. The girl's family would reciprocate by providing the newlyweds with property; setting up their own tepee for them, where they would spend their wedding night.

Samantha, with a glint in her eye, had added that the story would not be complete without mentioning that the Arapaho, like many of the indigenous peoples of the Great Plains and the tribes of the southeast, had been polygamous, unlike the Pueblos and the tribes of the northwest. If the man had the means, he would marry other women—not infrequently, marrying his first wife's sisters. Samantha had wanted to make sure that Eddie had no thoughts about Cheryl. She had also wanted to clear something else up. Arapaho men, like the men of most Native American tribes, had a greater chance of an early death since they were the ones involved in the relatively high-risk activities of hunting and war. A wife prematurely losing her husband was often picked-up by her deceased husband's brother. Samantha had expressed her delight that Eddie did not have a brother, underscoring that, like a second wife, Eddie should wipe from his mind any thoughts of an early departure from this world.

Samantha had completed her high-spirited tale of the Arapaho saying she did not know if her father wanted any horses, but they should not expect him to provide them with their tepee. They were going to break with Arapaho tradition.

When Samantha had been telling Eddie about the Arapaho, she had been fetchingly sitting in her tight red, white, and blue T-shirt on the black and gold chintz bedspread in the Louis Armstrong Room. Her demeanor and tone had been light, almost carefree. However, underneath her blithe storytelling was a very serious undercurrent; Samantha expected to marry Eddie. Moreover, Samantha intended to focus her professional life on trying to understand and help other people.

Eddie had finally been overcome by his hormones and could take it no more. He tackled Samantha, sliding her T-shirt up as the two tumbled on the oriental rug in a hot embrace. But even as his ardor rose, he understood she had truly opened her heart to him and told him what he needed to hear. He now needed to find a new lens through which to view his life, their lives. Everything had changed. Their worlds had collided and fused.

※

When Eddie and Samantha left the Elk Mountain Lodge, he going south, she going north, they each realized their own lives would no longer be the same. Each understood the other more clearly, more fully. Beyond knowing each other in the heat of passion, they now knew each other's hopes and aspirations, fears and trepidations. They had crossed a bridge and now needed time to digest the results—to see how they should react, what they should do.

Eddie went back to Horsetooth Reservoir and Weld County. Samantha went back to her parents' home and her school books. They still had their weekly telephone calls, reinforced by irregular, but more flowery letters and cards. Samantha assured Eddie that her parents were fine with their "friendship." Eddie assured Samantha that he was fine with their being fine.

They managed to organize nearly random places to meet for a weekend or even a stolen day, irresponsibly depriving their busy schedules of their personal inputs for thirty-six hours. They met in Crowheart, Wyoming, and spent a weekend dividing their time between their big sleeping bag and Yellowstone Park. They met in the Arbuckle Lodge in Gillette. They even went back to the Elk Mountain Lodge—twice.

Eddie had suggested they keep meeting at the Elk Mountain Lodge until they had slept in all twelve rooms. Samantha was fine with a dozen visits, but preferred Louis' spirit to oversee her intimate relations. Eddie agreed the manifestations of their loving desires were well suited to an accomplished musician who knew how to play all the right notes. However, he felt variety would be good. They should at least sample the Nellie Tayloe Ross Room as Nellie had not only been the fourteenth governor of Wyoming from 1925 to 1927, she had been the first woman governor in the country and later the first woman to head the national mint. This was, he admitted to Samantha, a high bar to top, but Samantha, as a talented and motivated, and beautiful, he added with a blush, young lady of the 20th century, would certainly go on to do things that made poor Nellie's modest accomplishments pale in comparison.

Although Eddie tended to make light of the sometimes torturous adjustments they each made to be a couple (when actually not being a couple), he did find the whole process frustrating. He was able to laugh it off with Samantha, but still, his overtime-working psyche felt there had to be a better way. He equated it to taking care of an aging aunt. He kept going to her bedside. He kept offering words of encouragement. He kept a smile on his face. Yet, all the time, he knew things would probably not work out all that well. Eddie longed for stability in their relationship. It was not that he needed the validation of some sort of ceremony, nor that he wanted to start a family right away. Those were not the issues. He just wanted stability. And, critically, he did not want stability to evolve into stagnation. He wanted to continue to learn, to explore, to discover. He wanted to put his agate-hunter eyes to the test every day. He wanted to grow every day. To be stable was not to atrophy, he was certain. But now there were too many moving pieces for him to be comfortable. He wanted to simplify his life. Nonetheless, he felt this was a selfish position. He accepted that more flexibility and uncertainty were required at the moment—hopefully with a promise for greater tranquility in the year to come.

At this stage of their relationship, under the prevailing conditions, he begrudgingly accepted they had to have a lifestyle resembling a traveling circus. So be it.

Given their penchant for stylish old hotels with stories to tell, they had chosen The New Occidental Hotel in Buffalo for a three-day get-together over the long Memorial Day weekend, now well over a year into their relationship. Samantha arrived first since she had only about half the distance to travel, considering the long haul her beau had to make to come all the way to northern Wyoming. Like Elk Mountain, the Occidental named their rooms—here after places and not people—and Samantha chose the room called the Bordello as being most appropriate for their stay. She hoped Eddie would like the gauche bright red appointments.

Laying out a gauzy, pink negligée that she thought was a nice contrast to the crimson bedspread, curtains, and upholstery, she knew she would have planned to arrive before Eddie even if they had chosen a spot where she had had the furthest to travel. She had news to share. News she was not sure that would be a welcome addition to Eddie's views on their relationship. She needed to prepare so she could gently tell him, while the summer abroad was indefinitely suspended, she was now planning to break her studies and take an appointment at Saint Joseph's Indian School in Chamberlain, South Dakota, right on the Missouri River.

She did not think it was a big deal. After all, Fort Collins was about the same distance from Billings as from Chamberlain. And it was an opportunity. She could go as a student teacher for two quarters, get credit toward her degree, and get excellent hands-on experience. Although many college students went into student teaching, there were not many opportunities at Saint Joseph's and not many that offered a two-quarter program. It was a good thing. She hoped Eddie saw it so.

Not only would this be good for her professionally, but it would also, in effect, constitute her moving out of her parents' home. She had long since passed the point when she felt she needed to be out from under their roof. The time spent in classes and with Eddie had minimized the time she had actually been at home—this making the arrangement livable, at least for a little while longer. But now, when she went to Chamberlain, she would really be moving out. Yes, she would have to come back to Billings and spend one final quarter on campus before graduation, but this was more like living on measured time.

There was, of course, a down side. As a student, she had managed to adapt her schedule to the needs of others, being quite malleable and hence able to slip away on a regular basis to spend time with Eddie. As student teacher, she would have a full-time job—her time would not be her own. It would be harder to balance her relationship with Eddie. But it was just for a few months. Fingers crossed.

Eddie arrived in high spirits, a bouquet of red roses in his hand that melded into the room's *fleur de lis* emblazoned wallpaper. After a long and hard hug topped off with a deep kiss—better than the first time, he silently congratulated himself. He told Samantha he hoped he was able to live up to the reputation implied by the room's name—he fully agreed with her choice for them to go to the Bordello together.

After they had sampled the bed, during that warm period, as Eddie reminded Samantha of the depiction of the afterglow in 1930's films, when the man and the woman would sit in their underwear, smoking Turkish cigarettes, and sipping Champagne, Samantha asked Eddie about work at Millerman and the dry spring in Fort Collins. Eddie's antennae immediately twitched. This was the small talk of small talk—not one of either of their fortes. Samantha did not have the gift of saying much about nothing—she had an agenda.

As he twirled a lock of her hair between his thumb and forefinger, he suggested it might be better to go straight to the point. Trapped, she acquiesced, telling him of her plans.

His reaction was more moderate than she had imagined. He was clearly not thrilled by what he saw as new churning of the hodgepodge that had become their life. But he had not shot off the bed in a snit. His thoughtful respect for her plans, her priorities, made her love him more.

※

It was not that Eddie had no objections—he had—and plenty. But he had grown to know Samantha well enough to know that when she had made up her mind, he would not be able to change it by a frontal attack. So, he really had no alternative than to go with the flow. And much to his satisfaction, things worked out better than he had feared they might.

Samantha got settled in Chamberlain without any major glitches. Martin had driven down with his daughter, taking two cars to make sure they could carry all she needed without stressing her already stressed Dart.

As was her ilk, she quickly got, as her mother would say, "down to brass tacks." There was a job at hand and she immediately focused all her considerable energies on accomplishing this task.

Miss Weaver—with an emphasis on the *Miss*—was her supervisor, really overseer. She was a rather bleak, aging spinster—made all the more leaden by her seeming complete disregard to her appearance. Apparently, being clothed from head to toe—including a somber scarf more suitable for mourning—was, in the good Miss Weaver's view, all that was necessary.

Yet, underneath the more than drab exterior, Miss Weaver was a very knowledgeable person and a skillful teacher. Though nearly wooden in her disposition, she managed to take an immediate liking to Samantha, generously sharing her thoughts and artistry.

Even more profound for Samantha was getting to know the students. This was practically her first chance to really get to know people of another culture, another ethnicity. After all, things in Billings were pretty homologous, one might even say humdrum.

These were great kids—emblematic in Samantha's eyes of decades of marginalization and victimization. She so wanted to help. But it was far from easy.

They may (or may not) have been great kids, but they were not all inherently great students—far from it. Just tackling the basics of early primary education proved challenging—frustrating. Many of the students came from homes that did not encourage learning—homes fractured by abuse of many kinds, both intramural and extramural. Her initial goal had been to move the whole class up the ladder of knowledge. Ultimately, she decided she would be successful if she could help at least three kids.

She zeroed in on two girls and a boy; each independently seemed to have some fire in their eyes, some deeper desire to learn. In so doing, she felt a great weight of guilt. Playing favorites. Was it so wrong? But, whether wrong or not, it seemed right. She was, at the very least, conflicted. Nonetheless, she continued working with her trio before and after classes and sometimes over the lunch hour. They became her charges. She rationalized her disproportionate efforts by the fact that she was a short-termer. She could already see the end in sight. She wanted to be able to accomplish something in her very limited stay, and these three seemed like the best possibility for having a lasting impact.

When not shepherding her threesome through the mysteries of learning, Samantha was intrigued by this school, started by French and German-born fathers in 1927, these founders assisted by four nuns from Glen Riddel, Pennsylvania, two years later. These early architects had begun with fifty-three Lakota Sioux pupils. Today, the school offered classes from grade one through twelve, accommodating more than a hundred students.

The Patron Priests had targeted youth from the Cheyenne River Indian Reservation, home to the Teton, Two Kettle, Sans Arc, and Blackfoot bands of the Lakota Sioux. The reservation, covering more than 4,000 square miles along the west shores of the Missouri, had been established thirteen years after the battle of Little Big Horn. Sitting Bull was one of the most renown residents of this vast space until his death at the end of 1890.

St. Joseph's was, in Samantha's view, trying to make a dent in combating years of mistreatment when native peoples were literally put in a box to be forgotten in the attic. The invaders had never wished to invest in combating the illnesses they had inflicted, while always more than willing to invest in the wars themselves. It was sad. St. Joseph's efforts seemed so small—still more than half the kids from the reservation did not obtain a High School diploma.

She was often tempted to see if she could change her arrangements and become a permanent member of the teaching staff—trading her plans of graduate school for a more immediate and pressing need. She might well have taken this decision to its endpoint had Eddie not repeatedly intervened, prompting her, cajoling her, convincing her to stay the course.

Eddie managed to get to Chamberlain every two to three weeks. It was a long haul, seven-and-a-half hours via Scottsbluff and eight hours via Rapid City. The first few trips, he had traveled straight through, driven by a desire to hold Samantha in his arms. While their fervid embrace did seem to make it all worth it, to turn around and drive another full day back to Fort Collins was more than a little exhausting. It began to affect his work once back on the job.

He decided to take it slower. He began taking some leave time, making the whole trip last at least three nights—the first in Rapid City, when he was then only about three hours from Chamberlain. However, rather than rushing to the goal, he opted to take a bypass—to go slowly. He would get on the road very early the next morning, swinging through Badlands National Park on Highway 240. He stopped at random spots where he could wonder across the nearly deserted prairie, taking great gulps of the savory winds of times gone by, and getting his agate eyes back to work, looking for any artifacts or even bits of debris from earlier passersby.

These stopovers in the Badlands served as a time to not only reawaken his keen searching eyes, but also to revisit his inner self. He spent much of his life outdoors, in the bracing wind—hot and cold, parched and soaked. But at work, he was fully at work, concentrating completely on the assignment at hand. Wandering almost aimlessly over the Badlands, he cast his attention inward.

He knew he deeply loved Samantha. He knew he very much liked where he was in life—he enjoyed his work, his living conditions, and his lifestyle. He was happy. But he sensed a pending tremor. He felt like he felt when he saw the great rain clouds swirling and foaming high above the plains—a storm was coming.

Samantha was changing. She was the same, but she was different. She still, perhaps more than ever, demonstrated her love for him. She was still that spirit he loved—that dynamic, energetic, outgoing, thoughtful, pensive, imaginative, and even patient person with whom he was so happy to share his life. But her carefreeness was being shed like a butterfly shedding its chrysalis. She was trying her wings, metamorphosing into a new life. However, in this transformation, a new woman was coming from the cocoon. There was a deep seriousness, nearly a sadness, practically a pathos overlain by a compassionate poignancy that seemed very unfamiliar to Eddie.

When in Chamberlain, Eddie stayed at the Old Bridgeview Inn, a modest, run-of-the-mill lodge that was made special not by its comfort or architecture (both very plain) but by its wonderful location at the river's edge. The hostelry was not only on the banks of the mighty river, it was strategically located for a young man who could only meet with his best friend when she was out of school. The Anchor Grill was only three blocks to the southwest and a good spot for a meal or to sit for an hour with a book and a cup of coffee that grew cold as he stared out the window. The American Creek Recreation Area was about seven blocks to the north, also on the river's shore and a fine place for a walk or a commune with Pan and the nymphs who, according to Samantha, were responsible for protecting the wild areas and their inhabitants. The Akta Lakota Museum was less than a thirty-minute walk north—right next door to St. Joseph's.

From a variety of sources, Eddie learned about his newest home away from home. The town had been named after Selah Chamberlain—one of the builders of the Erie Canals in the 1830s who turned to railroads in the next decade, becoming the director of Chicago, Milwaukee, and St. Paul Railroad. In an average year, the town would get twenty-six inches of snow. There was good walleye fishing on some parts of the river. The population of just over two thousand was eighty percent white.

The town was about thirty miles south of the Crow Creek and Lower Brule Reservations, an umbilical of sorts for these groups being the intervening community of Ft. Thompson. This borough of almost 1,500 inhabitants was ninety-five percent Native American, nearly two-thirds of the population living in poverty.

Eddie learned a lot of bits and pieces. What he did not really learn, at least to his satisfaction, was how Samantha was doing.

Yet, neither this concern, nor the hard fall and winter weather, could dampen the hunger of their visits. All in all, their bonds grew and strengthened over these months. Through it all, Eddie did not come to any epiphany. But, in walking for hours and hours along the banks of the Missouri and through the nothingness of the Badlands, he had gone through enough self-analytical gymnastics to feel he was more aware of how their world was evolving.

For her part, Samantha was diametrically opposed to Eddie—at least in terms of self-analysis. She was totally fixated on what lay before her—the tangible results of what she saw as grave and unreconciled injustice where her helping hands could make a difference.

She was still being tugged in two directions: wanting to stay, to dig in, to devote herself to the most-worthy cause of St. Joseph's and wishing to return to Billings and finish her degree with the hopes of continuing on to graduate school.

The conundrum was finally, if inexactly, settled by Eddie's argument that she would be a more effective tool of righting wrongs if she had more tools in her own bag. She could only do this by honing her skills through further education.

Spring came, and Samantha said a somber and almost crushing goodbye to St. Joseph's, including a tearful au-revoir to her trio—doubting she would indeed ever see them again. Nonetheless, feeling she had somehow, in some small way, contributed positively to their schooling, and hopefully to their lives.

Martin again helped his daughter relocate.

She promptly got her things in order in Billings and then met Eddie for a weekend at the Elk Mountain Lodge before starting her final quarter at Montana State University's Billings campus. That summer she would be graduating with her bachelor's in sociology.

Eddie concentrated on a new job in Larimer County—an assignment that would have initially been Kent's, but with his disgraced departure, work areas had shifted.

---

Midway through Samantha's classes, Eddie invited her again to the Elk Mountain Lodge. Their schedules had kept them apart for more than a few weeks and, anxious to see him, she was jubilant to have a chance to be together in a place that had such good memories.

When she arrived, the Satchmo room was filled with red roses, but Eddie was nowhere to be seen. After she had unpacked her overnight case, he was still nowhere in sight. Just as she began wondering what had happened to him, there was a knock at the door.

When she opened the rustic pine portal, she found Eddie, in coat and tie—a rare event in and of itself—on bended knee, offering a pink pillow which supported a golden ring. He was proposing. She nearly fell over.

After she had breathlessly said yes and they had celebrated in their own intimate way, as candid as always, she wanted to know why now. It was midterm, he was mid-assignment. Why now? It seemed practically out of place.

Taking no offense at her burrowing for the truth, he could only reply that he really did not know. He just woke up one day last week and decided that every day they were apart was a lost day in their lives. There were no doubts they were in their own eyes, and everyone-else's, a couple. It was time their union was more permanent, even if their futures were not.

As Eddie had said, their espousal was a surprise to no one—at least no one east of the Rockies. Samantha's friends and family, Eddie's co-workers, all knew of their now well-established relationship—none finding marriage unexpected, even if the timing was a bit strange, since Samantha still had not finished school.

The same could not be said of Eddie's parents. While he had in no way intended to shun them, since leaving, he had not returned to the shores of the Pacific. He called at least once a fortnight, sending cards and notes at different times throughout the year. However, as he himself knew, he could not claim they had been privy to his life on the other side of the Great Divide.

Eddie had decided he owed it to his parents to go home and talk to them face-to-face. Samantha agreed, while maintaining that, contrary to Eddie's plan, she should not accompany him. Her immediate priorities were in Billings—wrapping up the present and preparing for the future. She would meet his family in Billings for the wedding. Maybe, she noted, not the best form in terms of introducing parents to their new daughter-in-law. Nevertheless, her absence was a way to ensure there could be honest and open discussions in her in-laws' household, without having to talk around an unknown fiancée.

Somewhat reluctantly, Eddie accepted Samantha's conclusions and, as a gainfully employed surveyor, made his plans to go west to spend the Fourth with his family. The days passed, and the time arrived. Ticket in hand, he parked his Jeep in the long-term parking at Denver Airport, learning from the sign on the wall as he walked into the departure hall that this airport had the largest land surface area of any airport in the country. He wondered who had surveyed it. Maybe, just maybe, there had been a little extra in it to adjust the numbers and make the place bigger to fit the big shadow the operators wanted to cast. Probably not, of course. Most people were completely scrupulous. Most numbers were as accurate as one could make them. But, then again, you never knew.

This was Eddie's first time flying. He, in no way, felt worried. He had no concerns that this tube of aluminum would come pummeling down onto the snowy slopes of the Rockies. He knew it was perfectly safe and a damn sight quicker and more conformable than the bus. So, it was not fear that was gnawing at his innards as he showed his boarding pass to the attendant when the flight was called—it was just that he did not know what he was doing, what one did when one traveled in an airplane. And he did not like not knowing.

His apprehension proved unwarranted. He found traveling by plane nothing all that special. He had an aisle seat and was able to stretch out a wee bit. The middle and window seats were occupied by a young couple who had absolutely no time for him—only for each other. He hoped he and Samantha would be like that when they traveled.

The flight was just a little over three hours. He had a few beers, a light lunch, and a short nap. He arrived in Portland feeling ready to embrace his family. He rented a small car and took the road along the Columbia straight to Astoria and then south on Highway 101, right to his front door. He had forgotten how absolutely spectacular the coast was. He felt a shudder in his veins and a tingle in his scalp as he smelled the sea breeze and heard the seagulls cry.

His parents' unobtrusive cedar-sided house, the home of his youth, was there; at the base of Cape Verde, squeezed into that tiny strip of pine scrub between Highway 101 and the embattled rocky beach that was beaten incessantly by the crashing Pacific surf. He had not told his parents he was coming. This might have been cruel. It probably was selfish. But he wanted to surprise them—a decision he had not shared with Samantha and for which he felt guilty up to this very minute.

Still in all, it was his plan, now it had to be implemented.

He waited until late afternoon when he knew they would be home, then he drove down the driveway, sure they would come out to see what outsider had absently stumbled into their yard. Unlike people of today, his parents were old school and welcomed, even respected, strangers. They were always ready with a kind word and a helping hand.

As expected, they came out to see who was coming in this small car, much more suitable to the big city streets than rough coastal roads. When their son hopped out of the driver's side, they nearly fell in a heap. After strong cries of consternation and equally strong embraces, they all went inside to the combination living-dining area that overlooked the roaring waves.

Eddie was taken aback by his parents' appearance. His father was stooped and stiff—probably understandable after years of bending over, inspecting thousands and thousands of saw teeth, especially on those big forty-foot band saws that would not fit into this room. His mother was grayer and looked more fragile. But there was still the air of unbendable steel in her backbone.

They were concerned—very concerned. What could bring their errant son home unannounced? Only tales of woe. But he did not seem woeful. His smile seemed to hold promise for good tidings.

In close to a pro-forma way that made Eddie feel he was behaving more like he should in a Millerman monthly meeting than a family reunion, he apologized for not giving his family more forewarning and, moreover, for his lengthy absence. He had no real excuse. It just was that life was complicated.

At this point, Earl strained a bit to get out of his favorite chair and went to the kitchen to get three beers. Irene put her feet up on the ottoman.

They all sipped their beers as Eddie recounted in not too fine detail his work, his life, and his love since leaving home. Although the abbreviated version, it was long enough for Earl to go twice more to the fridge for refills.

When Eddie drained his third bottle and wrapped up his tale, ending with their pending wedding, there were smiles all around. Irene and Earl were delighted. Eddie had not gone on through the hallowed halls to become the first member of the family to get a university degree, but he had done damn well. They remarked he was healthy, seemed happy, and was much more mature than the young boy-man who got on a bus east, what seemed like so long, long ago.

They were happy for him that his career had worked out and that he had found a woman to love, and who loved him. Things had worked out well.

Eddie, relieved and enthusiastic, pushed from the past through the present to the future. What about the wedding? They had to come.

He explained he had wanted Samantha to come with him, so they could all meet here on the beach where the wind would rumple her hair as she saw, with wonder, the fantastic place where he had grown up. However, to her credit, Samantha did not want to take anything for granted. She wanted those who could soon be her in-laws to be able to discuss in complete freedom their thoughts and feelings about the marriage; there was plenty of time to get to know one another later.

Irene and Earl agreed with Samantha—recognizing, after such a long and complex absence, it was good for just the three of them to talk candidly. Nevertheless, they also knew that Eddie would do what he would do—feeling that if she were good enough for him, she certainly would be good enough for simple folk like them. They wholeheartedly gave Eddie, and Samantha in absentia, their blessing.

But there was one small possible snag. Irene and Earl were still poor, working folk. They could not just pick up and head to Montana on the drop of a dime. To be safe, they would need to have six weeks to be able to work out with their bosses how they would get the needed time off.

Eddie assured them this was no big deal; they would do whatever needed to be done to make sure both families were there to celebrate their marriage. Furthermore, to be perfectly clear, he would be paying for their trip, so they should not be concerned about this aspect.

Satisfied things were quickly working out, and in the best of ways, in the back of his mind, Eddie was making other calculations—studying the terrain—making adjustments.

It was the first of July. In six weeks, it would be mid-August, exam time for Samantha. His intentions, when he had been on his knees in Wyoming at Satchmo's door, had been to get this done quickly—very quickly. To try and grasp that stability he so sought so that the two could explore as one. This was not to be the case. They would now have to re-plan for a wedding after graduation. This was better in many ways, but just further off.

Eddie wrapped up the discussion—his parent's debriefing, as it were—by saying he had intentionally come home early so that there would be enough time to make the necessary arrangements for all concerned. It would be a fall wedding, so he would call them well in advance once the date had been set, so they could arrange for their time off.

The formalities completed, Eddie slipped back into a more laid-back mode, making sure his parents knew he planned to be home for another four nights, hoping to spend the Fourth of July with them.

This news was met with high spirits, as they had thought, their now very important son, would have to quickly head back to his awesome responsibilities on the other side of the world (or so the other side of the Rockies seemed when one sat on the Continent's edge).

Irene said she needed to set another place at the table—not to worry, there was plenty in the pot. Earl picked up his newspaper and turned on the TV, Eddie immediately recalling the routine when Earl, amazingly to Eddie, watched the news and read the paper at the same time. Some things never changed.

Eddie went to the car, got his duffel bag, threw it on the bed in his clean and as-he-had-left-it old room on the north side of the house, and then went out for a walk on the rocky beach. It was near high tide, the surf was heavy, there was fish-oil-scented foam scooting in front of the surge on the onshore breeze. A pair of pelicans, rare sites in this area, slid on the breeze, seemingly welcoming him as they tilted their wings and went into a lazy upward spiral. He took a lungful of the moist air, relishing its flavor. He was home.

After a twenty-minute walk south, driven to the path on the bluff by the lapping tide, he went home. Earl had laid a fire and Irene had set the table with their special Friendly Village plates. It was a homecoming appreciated by all.

After a dessert of blackberry cobbler, his parents asked Eddie if he had any special plans for his stay. He admitted he had nothing particular planned other than seeing them. He had to leave here on the fifth to spend the night in Portland and leave early the following day for Denver. Other than that, his only plan was to celebrate the Fourth with them.

Irene said they had in mind to go down to the river with a cold dinner in the picnic basket to watch the fireworks. She added, almost offhandedly, her brother Hal would be joining.

Eddie indicated this would be great, skipping over the Hal part as he tried to remember who Hal was—he could not remember an Uncle Hal.

Eddie called Samantha, collect, slept in late in his old bed, helped his mother with his old chores including splitting wood—his father now too old to do this himself, a neighbor kid coming in twice a week, chopping for a fee. At low tide he would go into the coves and see if his agate eyes could still do the trick—returning most times with at least one pocket of his jeans half full. At high tide, he would walk along the escarpment, the rumble of the surf surrounding him; delighting in the sea's salty breath, still awed by the rooster-tails trailing back from the great breakers, enjoying the flash as the shock of the wave's arrival reverberated up his legs. This too was home.

The time passed quickly, his mother taking time to prepare his favorites for dinner—clam chowder, steamed mussels, crab cakes.

He secretly and carefully inspected his parents. They were older—quite a bit older. This was to be expected, of course. Yet, he was uncertain, he did not know how to know, if this aging was what everyone went through, or if there was more than just age in play. His father seemed bent and his mother shrunken. They no longer moved with the fluidity he remembered from his childhood. There were fewer jokes, less laughter; there were more grunts accompanied by plenty of "remember whens." It was not a sad household; it was just changed.

As he would think of his youth while falling off to sleep near Horsetooth Reservoir, he would think of his years growing up in living color, like watching *The Brady Bunch*. Today, he saw his family in black and white like watching *Father Knows Best*. Still his family that he loved, but somehow discolored with age like an old photograph.

On the Fourth, his parents had an uncommon chance to sleep in. They had a late brunch. Then Earl and Eddie went for a walk on the beach while Irene filled the picnic hamper.

There was a sandy spit where their little river entered the Pacific, occupying the waterway's south side for the last 800 yards of her run to the sea. The north side of the river rose abruptly to a large knoll that housed the village.

At sunset, the Hall Family spread one of Earl's old army blankets on the soft sand, waiting for the village mayor to sound the siren used for tsunami warnings—but today to be used to announce the community's valiant attempt to put on a fireworks display.

They had just opened the small cooler—Earl taking care of this, while Irene was the overseer for the hamper—taking out three beers, when a long shadow was cast across the olive-green blanket.

Eddie looked up and saw a pretty ordinary man, a little younger than his mother. He was muscular with good posture, short hair, clean-shaven, wearing opaque sunglasses, khakis, and a golf shirt along with blue boat shoes with, Eddie's keen eyes noted, *Sperry Top-Sider* emblazoned on the heel. The unsmiling man stood nearly at attention, as though awaiting an invitation; which he got when Irene looked up, looked startled, stood up, beckoning the man to join them while introducing her son to his heretofore unknown Uncle Hal. Through all this, Earl sipped his beer and watched the swallows skim above the river's surface—only turning to shake Hal's hand in a limp sort of way once his brother-in-law was seated next to his wife.

The entire awkward interlude, as far as Eddie could tell, was thankfully immediately suppressed by the hoot of the village siren as the mayor announced the beginning of the firework extravaganza.

As the last of the somewhat disappointing fusillade fizzled and floated to Earth, the foursome sharing the old blanket was finishing their repast, all licking their fingers after sampling more than just a smidgen of Irene's fine meal. Not having said more than a dozen words, Hal vanished almost as stealthily as he had come. Earl and Irene seemed to act as if he had never been there, cleaning up the crumbs and folding the blanket.

On the short drive home, Eddie tried to ask about Hal, but only got a perfunctory reply that he had been in the neighborhood and had decided to just stop by.

The next day it was back to work for his parents and back on the road for himself, so they said their goodbyes over one final beer, then went off to bed with promises to keep in better touch.

✳

Eddie had stopped en route to Portland to buy a large quantity of the coast's prized smoked salmon that he generously shared with Samantha's family and co-workers at Millerman—making old friendships all the stronger and new ones with people he had never seen before. After a few days of enjoying the sea air, the mountain drafts seemed weightless and tasteless—the seaweedy tang of the Pacific lingering on his palate for several days.

He and Samantha had a spicy reunion that drove the last remnants of seaweed pungency from his mouth. She came down to Fort Collins soon after he returned to get the full scoop, as she put it.

As they lolled on his tousled bed, he gave her nearly a minute-by-minute recounting of his trip home. She was overjoyed by the actions and reactions of Eddie's parents. She was happy he had been able to ground himself on the basalt outcroppings of his beloved beach. She knew he was disappointed by the need to reshuffle their plans and wed later but pointed out that waiting until after her graduation did, of course, make sense. She suggested they aim for a Halloween wedding—they could all go in costumes of Prince Charming and Sleeping Beauty, she chuckled, as he grabbed her, entwining her in the sheets.

Later, over a simple dinner and a good glass of wine, as the setting sun cast a golden light through the plate-glass windows, they agreed a Halloween nuptial was, indeed, a realistic and intriguing target. With that settled, Samantha informed Eddie what he already knew—she had not been doing just nothing while he was frolicking in the Pacific Ocean.

Reminding him that when she was seriously considering staying on at St. Joseph's, he had underscored the importance of her education, of her honing her skills, of her going to graduate school. Well, he had been right. She had, in his absence, decided once and for all that she did want to go to graduate school, and had started applying.

This was sweet news to Eddie. He imagined her enrolled in Colorado State University's Graduate School here in Fort Collins—her studying while he was working in the hinterland, planting the Millerman flag. It was that stable and secure life for which he hoped—it was within reach, or so it seemed.

---

They went ahead and announced their plans for a Halloween event—albeit many were confused whether this was a costume party or a wedding. This did allow ample time for Eddie and his parents to make the necessary preparations. For their part, Samantha's family made arrangements with the minister at their Methodist Church for a wedding ceremony on All Hallows' Eve. Unlike Martin and June, the good vicar seemed to think a wedding on the eve of All Saints' Day would bring blessings to the newlyweds.

In the meantime, Samantha devoted her energies to applying to graduate schools, having received her diploma from the rector's hands in mid-August—a hot month for the prairie and for the couple. She was effectively living at Eddie's—filling application forms, walking by Horsetooth Reservoir, tidying up, or trying to assuage their spirited carnal desires. She smiled to herself when she thought of her mother's reaction to her choice of a bisque-colored gown as opposed to the pure white of fresh snow. Bisque was, she giggled, a more earthy color.

The wedding was a great success. Eddie's parents had, by their recounting, a marvelous trip to Billings, enjoying every bit of it—even the queuing at the airport. Samantha's parents had arranged for an elegantly simple gathering on the eve of the ceremony, seeming to hit it off quickly with Earl and Irene. The wedding itself was charming. Some of Eddie's colleagues did show up in Halloween costumes and someone put an enormous jack-o-lantern with a lascivious grin on the stoop of the reception hall next to the church.

After the rather leisurely reception, Eddie helped his parents with a rental car and a good map with notes, sending them on their way south for a much-anticipated trip to Yellowstone. Although the park was closed, there had been little snow and the roads were clear. One lodge was open, and Eddie had booked a room for Earl and Irene for five nights. They would then continue on to Fort Collins to see the couple one more time before going on to Denver, staying two nights there to see the sights before heading back to Portland. A wonderful trip for people who rarely were more than fifty miles from home.

For the bride and groom, there was not any real honeymoon, however. After attending to all the required matters, they left for three nights in their old haunt of Louis' room at the Elk Mountain Lodge. They got back to Fort Collins Saturday evening, a few days before Eddie's parents, with time for Eddie to rest before jumping into work on Monday.

Earl and Irene arrived as planned, effervescent about all they had seen and done. Eddie had booked them into the Edward's House B&B, he and Samantha meeting them there the evening of their arrival and going out to dinner at the Colorado Room. The next day, Eddie was at work and Samantha took her new in-laws for the grand tour—really more an effort at bonding than sightseeing.

In truth, little effort was needed. Irene fell immediately in love with her daughter-in-law. She was the daughter she had never had and, she hoped, the answer to her son's restlessness that had doubtlessly made him a sort of bittersweet waif since his early childhood. Irene found in Samantha the unique mixture of energy and empathy she felt necessary to help her son find the life he sought. Irene was the first to admit that she herself did not know what this long-sought life looked like—but so far, she had the impression her son had no more of an idea of what this would look like than she did. Now, with a little luck, she hoped Samantha, grounded and steady, would be better able to accompany Eddie to where he and the two of them could be happy—really and deeply happy. This promise alone was enough to build a bond with Samantha. But, over and beyond this prospect, she simply liked the girl very much.

Where Irene went, so went Earl—the couple, as they left Fort Collins, was very happy indeed with how everything had turned out.

---

The winter weather worsened, keeping Eddie more in the office and Samantha more homebound. She continued to dig deeper into graduate schools, spending considerable time prowling the University's Morgan Library.

They enjoyed this almost cloistered period, getting to know the little previously unnoticed shards and slivers of each other that so contributed to their individual persona—details often kept in the shade during the burning height of a new romance. They learned how each other held their fork, folded their underwear, put on their shoes, and even broke wind. It was a good time.

As the new leaves appeared on the trees, daffodils and tulips reluctantly leaving the warm earth, they began taking walks around Horsetooth, enjoying the reawakening. On one such jaunt, as they cuddled on a bench against the stinging wind whipping off the reservoir, Samantha said she had news. She had been accepted into graduate school.

Eddie hugged her harder, kissing her intensely as he whispered congratulations for a job well done.

Samantha, basking in both her accomplishment and her husband's appreciation of her hard work, hugged him back, even harder, whispering in the wind she hoped he would like California.

His surprise was palpable.

She took a deep breath, the numbing gusts, she somehow feared, not as cold as the reaction she would get from Eddie. She took his chilly face in her hands and told him softly but firmly that she had been admitted into Stanford. Stanford was the number four school nationally in anthropology and the area of social anthropology in which she wanted to focus was one of their strengths. It was really terrific news and a once-in-a-lifetime opportunity.

To his benefit, Eddie tried. He tried to hide his surprise, his shock. This was not, definitely not, Colorado State University. This was, yes California, but the California of San Francisco. He knew roughly where Stanford was to be found: on the San Francisco Peninsula, between San Mateo and San Jose. After all, he was a mapmaker. This was nowhere close to Horsetooth.

She waited, impatiently.

Eddie almost visibly shook himself, like Skip used to do when he got out after swimming in the river.

He found his voice again, telling his wife, his lovely and loving wife, that this was indeed wonderful—if totally unexpected. He would be back near his beloved Pacific Ocean.

※

By mid-July, their heads still spinning, Samantha and Eddie were settled in a small apartment in Menlo Park. Samantha was to start orientation in early August. Eddie had been fortunate enough, or persistent enough, to land a job serving at the Dutch Goose, a burger and brew joint not too far from their flat. Not what an experienced, certified surveyor expected, but what the hell. Something else would surely pop up later, and this was a way to put his time to productive use.

Their finances were not too bad despite topsy-turvy goings-on. Martin and June, more than just a little happy their daughter would be going to graduate school at Stanford, had agreed to pay for her studies. Their stipend even paid part of their living expenses. Eddie's savings, not insignificant due to a frugal lifestyle, had so far been protected. His unexciting work at the Goose would provide the balance of their immediate expenses—it could be worse.

Eddie had given notice to Millerman, with a June thirtieth departure date. They had gone to Denver and traded their Jeep and Dart in for a low-mileage 1980 Peugeot 505 wagon. They had let their exceptional landlords know they would be leaving after the Fourth. They spent the Fourth at a barbecue organized at Steve Stewart's where they said goodbye to friends and colleagues.

The next day, they loaded their Peugeot, said silent adieus (not au-revoirs) to Colorado—not expecting to come back for anything more than a short visit, but admitting that one never knows. They drove the well-used tract to Billings to spend a few days with Martin and June before embarking for the unknown, and somewhat intimidating, life of the greater San Francisco Bay Area.

Samantha was an apt student—her studies progressing smoothly as Eddie learned that there was a lot more to being a server than he had initially thought. It was a tough job. Maybe not like pulling chain in the mill, but it sure was not without a lot of challenges—not the least of which required dealing with a rainbow of people. This interpersonal requirement, however, was met with some sort of a twisted welcome.

Eddie was well aware that most of his working days had been spent either alone or with a small crew, tramping across the hinterland. He had had relatively little regular contact with what one might consider as society at large—he was getting this now, by the boatload. He was learning about how to deal with people. It was not easy. It was frustrating. It was all too often unpleasant. Nonetheless, he knew it was an unavoidable requirement if he were to continue along his life's path—he accepted it in this vein.

Within six months, Eddie had acquired a whole new set of people skills while Samantha had plowed through her studies and was starting her thesis on the impact of populations' coping strategies in dealing with vulnerable segments of their society. Otherwise put: how do different societies take care of their more needy members and what impact do these actions have on the overall society's developmental trajectory? A mouthful to get at the core of Samantha's passion—helping those who needed help.

After a wet and mild (by their standards) winter—after Easter—Samantha and Eddie were strolling around the Bair Island State Marine Park—one of their favorite haunts—when she pulled him onto a nearby bench, huddled next to him, and whispered into his ear her latest secret. After graduation in a little over a year, she already had a job lined up.

On the surface, this seemed like good news. But the setting was all too familiar. Samantha had a way of making things anything but simple. Eddie tried to dig a bit deeper.

The news he received was even more shocking than that time not too long ago, on the shores of Horsetooth Reservoir, when his relatively secure, if perhaps rather dull, life had crumpled into a mound of sand. This time, with an enchanting smile across her face (with wrinkles at the corners), Samantha informed him, pending his approval of course, she had tentatively agreed to work for a well-established NGO: AMORE Children's Aid, in the Albaycín District of Granada in Andalusia, Spain.

This could be a dream come true.

Samantha explained that AMORE Children's Aid was a highly esteemed international organization dedicated to helping orphaned and abandoned children. They were wonderful. For a long time, she had admired their work. They had a strong program on children's rights. Their Spanish operations dealt with a lot of unwanted migrants from Africa who were otherwise, at the very least mistreated, and all too often put in serious risk. If Eddie agreed, she (or they) would do volunteer work for one year. If, after this period, both parties decided to go ahead, she would be considered for a management level position at one of the operational hubs. It was a once-in-a-lifetime opportunity.

Eddie was amazed at the number of these once-in-lifetime opportunities; he did not know how many more he could take. But this was Samantha. The life he had crafted and hoped to build upon was in storage—he served beer and burgers to drunk college students. Why not? He had never been to Spain. Hell, the furthest east he had been was when he visited Samantha in Chamberlain—she seemed to be his St. Christopher.

---

As he had already witnessed, when Samantha got things rolling, things happened quickly. They both enrolled in some evening Spanish classes at Cañada College. Samantha took her last exams before Christmas, worked on her thesis over the holidays, successfully defending it just after Valentine's Day. By May Day—the Labor Day celebration for most of the rest of the world—they had sold their car and most of their possessions, got their visas and tickets, packed, and were awaiting a flight to JFK with connections to Madrid then on south to Granada. AMORE, of course, paid for the travel: she as their volunteer, and he as what they called a "non-matrix spouse".

For Samantha, this all seemed almost effortless. She dealt with the rigors of international travel with aplomb. They arrived in Granada and had a sound sleep in the small auberge where AMORE had reserved a room and where they had full pension and accommodation for a month while they got their affairs in order. Samantha hugged Eddie tenderly in the early morning hours as they awoke for the first time under a Spanish sun.

On day one she calmly picked up her duties and began working with kids from all backgrounds and speaking all languages, accomplishing this with ease, as though she had been doing it for years.

Eddie was jet lagged, confused, and overwhelmed. He had no clue what to do or where to start.

Fortunately, AMORE had been here before and they had arrangements with a local expeditor—kind of a hybrid welcome-wagoner and real estate agent—English-speaking, nonetheless. Estelle, Eddie's new best friend, shepherded him back and forth across the city as Samantha plunged deeper into her heart-wrenching work.

With Estelle's skippering, Eddie found a quaint, small, furnished apartment with a wee veranda. Once Samantha had given her blessing, Estelle then oversaw the setting-up of a bank account, the turning-on of utilities, and even the purchase of a not-too-bad-off Fiat.

Before cutting the umbilical cord to his custodian, Eddie garnered all he could about different enterprises that might possibly employ a skillful surveyor. He doubted his waiter skills were competitive but hoped his mapping skills were.

As Eddie worked down his list of businesses hopefully interested in hiring a topographer, he was surprised to see one name in English: Delpro Industries. He remembered, along the bus route he had taken in Menlo Park to the Dutch Goose, seeing this name atop one of the many steel and glass towers that adorned the peninsula. Here in southern Spain, this was certainly not the same company—just a quirk with two businesses on opposite sides of the Atlantic having the same name. This likelihood notwithstanding, Eddie put Delpro on the top of his list as he scheduled visits.

From the outside, the Granada Delpro, whatever its affiliations, looked nothing like its sparkling and stylish California still-to-be-determined sibling. The office was located on the top floor of a six-story building with a 1940's vintage stone façade, in an old and rather shabby part of the city. The empty and dimly lit reception area was adorned with dirty Moorish tiles on the floor and unkept mahogany siding on the walls—all speaking of better times gone by. There was an old steel and bronze lift with a metal accordion door and open, screened sides. It grunted and groaned with Eddie as its sole occupant and he wished he had taken the narrow stairs that spiraled around the elevator shaft.

The aged lift bucked to a halt, the grate screeching loudly as Eddie stepped out onto a rather wide and well-lit paneled corridor—the paneling looking much more ship-shape than its relatives on the ground floor. There were doors at each end of the corridor with frosted glass windows; Delpro was simply stenciled on one and "private" on the other.

Passing through the Delpro door, Eddie found himself in a contemporary office space that could easily have been Millerman's regional office in Billings. To his right was a marble-topped counter, serving as a parapet for a modish glass-topped desk at which sat an equally modish and youngish, well-groomed blonde woman who greeted him with an unmistakable Brooklyn accent.

Eddie was a bit maladroit—unaccustomed to sharing his thoughts with complete strangers. Nevertheless, the modish receptionist knowingly set him at ease, and he was able to somewhat succinctly indicate he had come to see about a job. He was a surveyor, (obviously) an American.

The blonde woman smiled, asked him to take a seat on the nearby leather divan, and picked up her phone.

About fifteen minutes later, as Eddie was thumbing through an old issue of ¡Hola!, a rather rotund late-middle-age gentleman with an impeccably tailored suit silently appeared at his shoulder.

The gentleman extended a firm and toughened hand, introducing himself as Horace Smith.

Eddie, trying not to smile as he thought the name Horace had been lost a century ago, stood, still holding Mr. Smith's hand, and thanked him for taking time to see him.

Mr. Smith guided Eddie down the hallway to an office with good-quality but functional furniture and a remarkable view of this piece of the city. Offering Eddie a seat in a captain's chair, he took his place behind an ample and well-organized desk, asking how he could be of service.

Eddie handed him an envelope from his breast pocket—it contained an ordinary sheet of A4 paper typed *recto-verso* with the story of his life, his résumé. As Mr. Smith perused the sheet, Eddie added he and his wife had just arrived from the States—she working for AMORE, he now, as Mr. Smith could plainly see, looking for gainful employment.

Mr. Smith let just a faint sliver of a smile slide across his closely shaven face, as he asked Eddie if he was really a good surveyor.

After Eddie had assured his host that he had gobs of experience (perhaps not the best term in retrospect), Mr. Smith let the smile actually take hold, saying, by pure chance, they were looking for a surveyor.

Eddie was stunned. He had not expected to land a job, at least, not this quickly.

Mr. Smith elaborated. Delpro did a lot of things—they were very, very big and very, very diversified. They were everywhere. Here their prime focus was agriculture. They had barley and wheat fields. They had olive, fig, and lemon orchards. They had greenhouses—lots of greenhouses. They raised vegetables: green beans, tomatoes, lettuce, asparagus, rocket, and peppers—much of this exported to northern Europe. They had a lot of land—irrigated land, waterfront land, rain-fed land, peri-urban land, rural land, highland, lowland, and wetland. But the Spanish land tenure system was archaic and highly variable. In truth, they were not really sure how much land they had.

So, and here was the lucky part according to Mr. Smith, the company had just decided to answer this question: exactly how much land do we own? The thing was, they were not sure how to go about answering this question.

Thus, Mr. Smith said, if Eddie was interested, they could put him on contract to develop a plan of action—using his experience and skills, describe how Delpro could get to know what it needed to get to know.

Later, in their cozy apartment, over a late dinner (people in Spain eating much later than those in the Western US), Eddie told all to Samantha—ending with how he had left the rather grungy ground-floor reception with a signed contract in his pocket. The start-up date was the first of next month and in the meantime Delpro would take care of all the formalities.

He told Samantha that he had asked Mr. Smith about the building in Menlo Park and it was in fact the global headquarters for Delpro Industries. It was kind of like destiny.

They agreed this was an amazing quirk of fate. The gods had truly smiled and now they were, for the first time, together and each working in an exciting and challenging area that could open whole new avenues for their careers. It was fantastic. They felt so lucky.

*Book Five*

# In the Shadow of Mpezeni

Eddie found his new job much more difficult than he had first imagined—much more. Everything Mr. Smith had said had been true. But he had just glanced over the subject. It was, after closer examination, very complex, indeed—a real Gordian knot to unravel. Delpro was as big and varied as promised, but he had had no idea how complicated the local land use system was—and he really understood very little written Spanish—certainly not enough to interpret the tomes of convoluted legal documents.

However, Mr. Smith was undaunted, immediately approving the temporary hiring of a bilingual legal aid to work with Eddie to sort out all the necessary background texts.

Maria Helena was at his side in what seemed like an incredibly quick two days. She was a charismatic young woman in her mid-thirties with impeccable language skills and, perhaps even more importantly, what seemed to be a good, practical head on her shoulders. Together they went to the legion of national, regional, and local agencies that dealt with land and water use. With Maria Helena's charm, they seemed to have easy access to archives and were soon filling pages and pages with notes on the prevailing codes, regulations, and laws.

The work had started smoothly and was building momentum. However, it was a Herculean task. Delpro was truly as amoeboid as depicted—its pseudopods far-reaching, gliding into a large variety of places—some totally unexpected. Eddie and Marie Helena had to cast a wider net and dig deeper if they were going to accomplish their task. On the surface, it was a simple enough assignment to identify whether or not all the necessary steps in land ownership and water use had been followed—all the i's dotted and the t's crossed, all the signatures obtained, all the fees paid.

But, as they explored, they found a growing matrix, really more of a maze. Eddie winked at his inner self in an imaginary mirror as he thought back to that first visit to the Elk Mountain Lodge when, recalling his grandmother's tale of the Minotaur. He remembered how he had thought at that time he was trapped in a tremendous labyrinth. He now had to admit that Spanish bureaucracy was even more of a twisted web than his life had been what now seemed like a lifetime ago.

Delpro was not only invested in a wide range of agricultural enterprises, but they were involved in an equally large number of import and export markets as well as with immigration issues in relation to, according to the formal documentation, arranging visas for specialized technical staff.

As a multinational, Delpro's various purchases, leases, contracts, letters of agreement, memoranda, and accords were often conditional on acceptance of, and adherence to a whole covey of diverse requirements from immigration control, to food safety, work safety, environmental impact, and civil rights. These diverse, and often cloudy, requirements made the assignment all the more entangled—the approvals for ownership or use frequently contingent on the annexed requirements. And these requirements had to be verified before the ownership or use could be validated. It really was labyrinthine.

It was like a three-dimensional chess game. But Eddie had good spatial perception—perhaps, he thought, due to his agate-hunter eyes. However, in this case, he was not envisioning spatial arrangements of roads or canals, but of twisted bureaucratic and legal channels. Nonetheless, the picture began to take shape like those old eight-by-ten, black-and-white photos that began to magically appear in the trays of developer in the Photography Club's darkroom in high school. Slowly, as if materializing from the stratosphere, very slowly, he began to have a picture of how the processes worked—the actors, the steps, the products.

He discussed this with Mr. Smith. The job was ballooning as they began to fully grasp the extent of the subject matter. What had first been seen as a relatively simple plan to inventory assets had turned, given the intricacy of Delpro's holdings as well as convoluted legal and tenure systems, into a puzzle challenging the most agile mind. They needed to reset the target.

Mr. Smith agreed. They would have to undertake some case studies for different categories of operations and then merge these into a template for a plan that could be applied more broadly (underscoring he himself would pick the pilot sites). The work was growing and growing.

Mr. Smith would bolster the team. He would ensure that Maria Helena would have an assistant and that a car and driver would be assigned to the project.

True to his word, in just a few days, David, an intrepid-looking, native-born Granadian with two-years of university-level English appeared as a jack-of-all-trades for the team. He was accompanied by Alberto, a driver who was in turn accompanied by his metallic blue SEAT sedan. It was a modest vehicle for a modest team. Yet, Eddie was surprised, even impressed, by the level of support he was receiving. It was clear that Delpro, through Mr. Smith, was paying attention to his efforts.

Discovering Alberto spoke a basic amount of conversational English, far better than his sad attempts at Spanish, Eddie decided he would begin visiting some of the agricultural sites to better understand the true situation on the ground.

What Eddie found left him perplexed.

※

As Eddie came to grips with his latest surprise, Samantha was coming to grips with the enormity of the AMORE task. Quite simply, the Iberian Peninsula was the hoped-for destination of thousands of illegal immigrants from across Africa. Most came from Northern Africa and the Sahel, but others traveled from the equatorial regions. Some even came from as far away as the southern plains.

The Strait of Gibraltar, less than nine miles wide, separating Africa and Europe, was like a magnet for economic refugees fleeing war, famine, pestilence, and poverty. All seemed to be seeking the European panacea. Refugees endured all measure of sufferance and indignity. Many felt they had nothing to lose. Lamentably, no small number of these people realized they had something to lose when they lost the little they had—be it tangible or spiritual—to traffickers who demanded exorbitant offerings to put emigrants' lives in dire risk.

The immigrant children who almost magically appeared in Samantha's care were youngsters covering the full spectrum of humanity, some barely more than toddlers and others mature and aloof teenagers. Some had arrived, having lost their parents en route. Some had been found by authorities, sleeping on streets, sick and malnourished. Others had been picked up by police for panhandling or pickpocketing to try and garner a few pesetas to feed themselves and their families. A few of the unfortunate older kids had even already infiltrated themselves into local crime groups—chiefly involving drugs and prostitution. All the children were at risk of having human predators befall them for the sex slave trade. It was so often heart-wrenching.

Samantha was seeing so much she never knew existed; so much of human kind of which she had previously been blissfully unaware. It was so far from what she had known in Billings.

On the bright side, if there was one, Samantha was not challenged by her level of Spanish language proficiency. Her very basic ability was fine. After all, most of her charges spoke Wolof, Hausa, Fula, Mossi, Mande, or Bambara. Those from the more distant lands spoke Kiswahili, Kikongo, or Yoruba. Samantha's Spanish was, in fact, better than most of her gaggle of kids. Still, she found herself generally communicating in English or high school French.

Her task was to first ensure the health and safety of a child, then to determine if there was any family nearby. Families that could be reunited were. Children with no place to go were integrated into social programs that took care of the welfare and education for varying periods of time and under varying conditions. Samantha was their conduit—either back home or to a new life.

She learned quickly that, for her own survival, she needed to distance herself. Initially she had wanted to do it all. It was like, as a little girl, when she had gone to the pound with her father to get a puppy. She had wanted to take all the dogs home. Reality was often unpleasant, but it was reality.

She now understood how the doctors had been when her grandmother had been in the hospital with the stroke that ultimately killed her. As a small grandchild, she could not understand how these men could be so cold and just stand there. *They had to do something;* she had thought. How could they simply stand around while her grandmother died? Now she understood that if you really wanted to help, you had to keep your emotions in check.

This was also the key for a happy home. Both she and Eddie were tired and somewhat frustrated by still trudging along the learning curve of life in Granada. They kept their equanimity, and maybe their sanity, by not talking about work, or current affairs, or even local traffic. They would go out to see the *carnicero* (butcher), *panadero* (baker), *verdulero* (greengrocer), *pescadero* (fish monger), and *vendedor de frutas* (fruit seller), no supermarket (*supermarcado*) for them. They would go out to look for choice items to grace their kitchen. Then, they would both dive into preparing a sumptuous evening meal using fresh ingredients which had previously been totally foreign to them. They would sit on the tiny veranda and listen to jazz. They would walk along the promenades. They would play cribbage. They would make love.

As Samantha learned to develop calluses over those soft parts of her heart, both for her own protection and for the good of those in her custody, Eddie began exploring farms, leaving much of the now deep diving into Spanish bureaucracy and justice to Maria Helena and David. After all, he was a field man. Walking the fields, fence lines, and lanes would tell him more than pages and pages of legalistic jargon.

However, before separating from Maria Helena and David, they developed a schematic of Delpro's holdings in Granada Province. They realized the city of Granada was less than one percent of the provincial territory although it was home to nearly half of the province's roughly one million inhabitants. They located company operations precisely on a detailed topographic map. For each site, they outlined relevant categories of regulations and legislation, summarized Delpro's internal description of activities, and identified a local contact. Then, while the "office crew", as Eddie called them, filled in the blanks regarding the administrative and financial management, Eddie, with his surveyor's eye, went to inspect a subset of randomly selected facilities.

Under Alberto's guidance, they elaborated a calendar where they followed a different point of the compass each day. They would make an appointment with the contact person and then visit the farm. While Alberto took pictures of the installation, Eddie sketched all on a big pad of A1 paper he had found at a neighborhood *librería* (bookstore). Eddie wished he had had a car-load of instruments with him, but his perceptive eye was able to capture most of the major features as well as validate the infrastructure and crops to be found.

At first, Eddie was unsure. He had little idea of what he would find on the ground. The layers and layers of twisted bureaucracy and legal passages were daunting, serving to magnify the complexity. The tangled webs caused him to wonder if he would really be able to provide the means for his employers to answer in full their questions as to the status of their holdings. More times than not, these answers seemed to be fuzzy and elusive. But they were needed if the team was to be able to produce the desired plan.

The questions aside, once he had good ol' dirt on his boots and the breeze to his back, he was able to see things much more clearly.

A rhythm developed. Surprisingly quickly, Eddie felt he was on top of the work. As he and Alberto visited farms, the truth of Mr. Smith's effusive statement became apparent: Delpro was very big. There were row crops, orchards, pig pens, chicken coops, and lots and lots of greenhouses. There were service buildings, housing, water storage, and irrigation structures. There was an abundance of everything.

Yet, regardless of the size of the operations, the sites seemed almost masked. There was never a signboard identifying a Delpro investment. There was rarely any public indication of the farms at all except for some sort of mundane guidepost giving a local name and address for mail delivery.

Eddie assigned each site his own identifying number that he used on the pages and pages of his large format pad. There he would draw the complete enterprise to scale including roads and public utilities. Within three months, he had filled four pads and visited ten operations.

He decided they needed to pull back and digest the material they had collected before adding more to the great pile of A1 sheets that were now in piles throughout their apartment. The work to date likely provided more than enough detail for Mr. Smith to select a few pilot farms where they would need to burrow even deeper.

The whole team, therefore, compiled a dossier on each operation: Eddie's sketches, Alberto's photographs, along with Maria Helena and David's legal and financial data. Eddie then went meticulously through each dossier. The results were unanticipated.

※

Eddie would make his farm visits from Monday through Thursday, reserving Friday for team work and recapping events. On Saturdays he and Samantha would go to a local restaurant to drink in the culture and the good wine, while numbing some of the neurons that had been abused during the week. Then, on Sunday, after a lovemaking lie-in, they would take public transport to one of the hundreds of notable sites that could be found within a few miles of their bed.

※

While Eddie was digging through papers, Samantha was digging through her emotions as though she was necessarily, but regrettably, scratching off scabs. The sores were there. There was so much sadness, injustice, and neglect. There was so much that was just wrong. She remembered years back, in response to a fellow student's complaint about what was felt to be an unjust grade, one of her most accomplished professors, with a thick Mississippi Delta accent, had replied almost placidly, "Life ain't fair."

A truism she was painfully seeing, painfully living, each day.

The effortlessness of accomplishing her routine on good days would be replaced by dense shadows of indecision.

Everywhere so much unfairness.

When the weight of the problems seemed overwhelming, she felt like she was teetering on the brink of a dark and inhospitable river that was sucked into the Earth's innards, that was trying to suck her into the abyss. The River Styx? She was balancing on the edge.

She pulled back. *Inhale, exhale,* she told herself. If not her, then who? There was a job to do. Best get to it.

These self-doubts of her resolve, these questions of the enormity of the task and the near futility of her efforts, these misgivings visited her on a regular basis. Her uncertainty swelled during days fraught with too little sleep and too many suffering eyes looking to her for solace.

She had seen so often the bright eyes, ecstatic at reaching salvation, reaching the land of *"les blancs".* The hope and the promise of having succeeded, having overcome the worst of obstacles and having reached the destination. She had seen all this dashed as if torn apart by a tornado of indifference and misunderstanding; a storm of racism and fear.

When she felt the ground crumbling under her feet as the river rushed by, she would find Eddie. She and her lover would sit in the darkness of their apartment, only filtered light from the street creeping through the curtains. She would breathe in his fragrance and welcome his love. In the morning she would awake refreshed.

Then with time, the shock lessened. And, in some ways, to her this ebbing of awe at the pain of the human condition became more worrisome than the initial emotional stress derived from her charges' suffering. It was not normal. It should not become normal. It should not be tolerable. It must be addressed.

As Samantha dredged up her soul, Eddie drilled into the data the team had harvested from Delpro farms. The issues that had perturbed him at first glance only magnified as they bore into their paperwork. It was almost as though the results from Maria Helena's and David's efforts were from a totally different world than the field information assembled by Alberto and himself. In most cases the official approval, regulatory license, and monitoring reporting seemed to significantly underestimate the scale of operations recorded by Eddie. In some instances, the crops and even the operations on file were completely different from what was seen in the field. Regularly, the physical size of operations declared in the formal documentation was much smaller than that seen first-hand—smallholder farms turning out to be large commercial enterprises. This, at the very least, represented numerous inconsistencies. What appeared to be systematic could, he thought, perhaps be attributed to the nearly opaque and impenetrable bureaucratic structures that conceivably could just as easily produce erroneous results as viable data. But there could be other explanations.

Ultimately, Eddie decided they were all working for Delpro and their employer deserved the benefit of the doubt. The riddles that seemed to be embedded in their work would certainly be unraveled as they undertook the pilot studies. Thus, Eddie prepared a synthesis for each operation they had examined and, with a cover letter only vaguely referring to any inconsistencies, he presented Mr. Smith with their interim results.

As usual, Mr. Smith was appreciative, earnestly receiving Eddie's report with a warm smile and a promise to, based on the team's excellent efforts, have a list of pilot farms within forty-eight hours.

Eddie scheduled a team meeting with the boss to review Mr. Smith's list of pilots, thinking there may be need for some discussion with their leader as the list was finalized. To his surprise, when Mr. Smith met the group, he simply handed them a small sheet of paper with five names—stating with no ambiguity that these were to be the object of the remainder of the team's work.

To the even greater surprise of Eddie and the team, none of the pilot farms were chosen from the list of farms already examined. In fact, only one farm, which they had never visited, was in Granada Province; the other four farms were equally divided among the neighboring provinces of Málaga and Almeria.

Mr. Smith was gone. Eddie looked for an explanation. They certainly had done very thorough preliminary examinations. Maybe they had done such a good job so far that Delpro felt they already had enough material on those firms reviewed in the first phase and they wanted to encompass an entirely new group of farms in the second phase. After-all, Delpro's aim was to have a bigger picture of all their operations. Couldn't it be a logical next step to shift the focus elsewhere?

"Damn," Eddie said to himself. Analyzing all this through a magnifying glass would lead exactly nowhere. Samantha and he needed the money and Delpro had proven to be a generous employer. He had a job to do and he should simply get to it.

This was, coincidentally, the same conclusion Samantha had reached regarding her self-searching dilemma—she wanted to help, and she was helping. Full stop. Get on with it.

Thus, it was, each dove into their tasks despite misgivings; Samantha questioning her impact on what seemed an endless problem, Eddie unsure of the aims and veracity of his work. Questions apart, they understood this was a trial period—this was temporary. The extent to which they could reconcile their questioning could well influence their willingness to continue along these pathways. But for the moment, it was best to carry on.

While each engaged his or her concerns, these were quite different. Samantha was dealing with an intrinsic query: peeling off the emotional packaging, was she suited to a person-centered assignment where failure was often more likely than success? Eddie, on the other hand, was confronted with an extrinsic situation: understanding his thorough and transparent job ethic, was he able to undertake an assignment based on incomplete and potentially flawed data?

They discussed their individual uncertainties, knowing full well, though inherently intertwined, they were predicaments each would have to answer to their personal satisfaction if they were to be able to move forward as a duo with mutually supportive lifestyles.

Eventually, pragmatism overcame what may have been overactive emotions and imaginations. They were young. They were free from the at times almost puritanical viewpoints of western America. They were living just down the street from a renowned nearly 3,000-year-old palace that had been the home to both Yusuf I as well as Ferdinand and Isabella. They were living the dream. Or so it seemed.

While Samantha tried to convince herself all was for the best, Eddie was perhaps more successful in diverting his attention from the risks of wading into a possible quagmire by allowing himself to be fully consumed by the new pilot studies.

Phase two of the Delpro project turned out to be much easier thanks to the comprehensive work the team had done at the start. The bureaucratic and legal environments were now relatively well known, as were the common agricultural crops and processes. Although there was more time required for travel as the pilot farms were further away, it was really a simple matter of transferring the methodologies defined earlier to a new set of subjects.

They discovered their work was further facilitated by a lack of any confusion or contrary information. The review of the new target farms provided a clean flow of data from start to finish; no difficulties to explain, no omissions or contradictions. On the ground they were exactly what they were on paper. A straightforward and amazingly clear-cut pathway to reviewing the selected operations, merging the results into a generic instrument that could be applied more broadly, and then drafting a plan as to how these wider assessments could be undertaken.

In stark contrast to the great difficulties Eddie had encountered when first trying to get his job going, the second half of the assignment presented no real problems in terms of collecting and analyzing the information. The high degree of correlation between the operations' official dossiers and their observed activities made the fieldwork a snap. However, the interpretation of these data along with the crafting of the overall plan and final report were much more trying.

Eddie's first reaction had been to develop a comprehensive report that underscored the potentially sensitive issues of the first phase. However, after consultation with the team members, they decided the best tactic was discretion—if Mr. Smith had wanted to know more, he would have asked.

So it was that the brief and orderly documentation presented by the team, while professionally inadequate from Eddie's perspective, was met with satisfaction and even a generous bonus from Mr. Smith.

Mr. Smith did, however, insist on a rather burdensome, and from Eddie's point of view, unnecessary set of appendices that identified each person they had interviewed, each farm they had visited, and presented the raw data from any surveying or other similar studies.

The bonus began to seem less like a bonus and more like due compensation for overtime as the team devoted several more weeks to getting the documentation into exactly the form required by Mr. Smith.

When all was polished and collated, Eddie met with Mr. Smith one final time to hand over the work. As no further discussion was needed and all final arrangements had been made, Eddie and Mr. Smith simply met at the marble-topped counter at the reception to complete their business.

It was a convivial, if brief moment. As Eddie was leaving through the frosted-glass main entrance, he turned to wave goodbye to Mr. Smith. However, he saw his now former employer had left the reception and was further down the hallway, handing what looked like his report to a man whom Eddie did not know, but who, even from a distance, was remarkable for his mane of alabaster hair that offset a pink complexion that nearly glowed in the subdued florescent lighting.

Due to the considerable extra time spent in carefully finalizing their product, the team reached the end of their assignment at nearly the same time as Samantha reached her first anniversary at AMORE.

With a now unemployed husband to help in making decisions, and with excellent marks during her probationary period, Samantha discussed the next steps with Eddie. They decided, while the learning processes had brought no small dose of angst, they were on a good trajectory and should continue. Samantha accepted AMORE's offer to head-up their small office in Chipata, Zambia.

AMORE had a modest presence in the capital of Zambia's Eastern Province; sitting on the country's far eastern border on the T-4, the Great East Road, bridging to Malawi and Mozambique, AMORE had made a meaningful space for themselves. This was a hub of a good deal of undocumented immigration between the three countries—prompted by civil unrest in Mozambique and magnified by people moving in search of greater economic opportunity. Between copper mines in Zambia, tea and coffee plantations in Malawi, as well as fisheries on Lakes Cabora Basa, Tanganyika, Kariba, and Malawi, there was considerable seasonal and short-term employment to be sought by the peasant and subsistence farmers who occupied two-thirds of the total population—employment that, although menial, inevitably offered greater remuneration than trying to feed one's family soley from tilling their homesteads' stony and worn soils.

Migration increased greatly in years of major drought, which seemed to be coming all the more frequently. Parched months for farmers relying on rain prompted the movement of more and more people off the farm and on the road in search of any means to survive.

But the economic refugees were dwarfed by those fleeing the Mozambique Civil War. Since 1977, the party in power, FRELIMO, had been battling South-African-supported RENAMO. Fighting had resulted in an estimated one million deaths and over five times that number of people displaced—some internally, others seeking safety in neighboring countries like Zambia. For over 300 miles, the T-4 ran along the Zambia-Mozambique border between Chongue and Chaduza. The south Mozambican side of the road looked like a continuous serpentine village—families huddled along the country's fragile edge, receiving food aid from donors and hopefully being unseen by the warring parties. It was as though they were in suspended animation, just one step away from Zambia, held in place by stout treads to home in Mozambique.

As families moved across porous administrative lines that divided clans and tribes, there could be disruption and even considerable chaos when authorities adopted stricter controls on travelers. One of the results of this fluidity, this ebb and flow through the Luangwa Valley and the upper reaches of the mighty Zambezi system, was that children would be separated from their family. Children were all too often the victims—whether parentless youth searching for security and the ways and means to become adults, or younger children adrift, severed from their families as they tried to avoid border agents and thugs during their migration. These were the children Samantha would try to help while at her new AMORE post.

For Samantha, managing an office, even if in a relative backwater, would not only be a big step forward, but also was a means to at least mitigate some of her soul searching. As the boss, most of her time would be spent on administration, freeing her heart strings from the constant direct pull of those in her fold. This was a rare opportunity. She and Eddie decided they could not let it slip away.

As they prepared for yet another move, Eddie went by Delpro to say goodbye to Mr. Smith. He still had mixed feelings about the work he had done. Nonetheless, Mr. Smith had been supportive—an excellent employer—and, Eddie had had quite a few.

Once again, Eddie was surprised as Mr. Smith heartily endorsed their move to Zambia, giving him the personal contacts of the head of the Delpro office in the capital, Lusaka—promising to send his colleague and personal friend a note immediately, so that the door could open for Eddie when he arrived south of the Equator.

Eddie was grateful, although he felt somehow like a fish being played on a line. He had worked hard for Delpro. He had been well compensated for his efforts. Yet, as he exited one last time over the dirty Moorish tiles and left the drab ground-floor reception, he felt somehow like someone who had tasted a meal without ever having the chance to really eat it. He had not been able to say goodbye to Maria Helena, David, or Alberto. After presenting their final write-up, his erstwhile colleagues had vanished. It seemed so unusual to Eddie—but what did a bucolic kid from, as many Europeans saw it, the rough-and-tumble American west know about usual?

Nevertheless, things looked strange. Not only had the team evaporated, there had been no questions about their work. He had no idea if Delpro had, or ever would implement the plan they had worked so hard to craft.

But now on a bustling Granada thoroughfare, Eddie took a deep breath of the spicy air, filled his head with the cantata of the street, and tried to absorb the Moorish aura—knowing the senses would soon be enticed with new scents, sights, and sounds. This was Samantha's time. She had worked so hard, both at her job and at her inner self, to find the right way forward. She felt she was—*they* were—now moving in the right direction. So, uncertainties aside, they would move on.

Although they could have flown from Granada, they chose to take the train to Madrid to see more of the country that had been their home for just over a year. They then took an Iberia Airways flight from the national capital to Johannesburg, continuing to Lusaka on South African Airways. AMORE put them up at the very nice Pamodzi Hotel while they went through orientation and took care of all their administrative matters.

Soon after their arrival, as Samantha was learning how to fill in payroll sheets and maintenance forms, Eddie took a robin-egg-blue city taxi to the Delpro address given to him by Mr. Smith. The offices were in an industrial area south of town, on the T-2 Highway, almost to the suburban village of Chipata. The aluminum and glass structure put the old edifice in Granada to shame. Yet, inside, it was in one way or another almost a mirror image of its northern sister. There was the same modish and youngish, well-groomed woman, although she was not a blonde. There was the same leather divan, but this time, rather than a rotund late-middle-aged gentleman with an impeccably tailored suit, he was met by a slender, even muscular, casually dressed gentleman only a few years his senior who introduced himself as Monsieur Van Houtte. Eddie, based on the name and the accent, had guessed his new contact was Dutch—only learning later he was Flemish, and had been raised in a small village along the Scheldt River, south of Antwerp.

Mr. Van Houtte lacked Mr. Smith's effervescence—more reserved and soft-spoken. Nonetheless, he had received Mr. Smith's communication and expressed his satisfaction at meeting such an accomplished technician as Eddie who had already been such a help to Delpro. He was sure that, once Eddie was established, he would want to avail himself of Eddie's talents. They separated with a promise to get back in touch in the coming months.

When Samantha was out of her management class, Eddie briefed her about the possible Delpro/Zambia link as they enjoyed a fragrant curry at one of the several local Indian restaurants they frequented. They found the spaciousness of Lusaka to be a pleasant change from the almost claustrophobic medieval conditions of southern Spain.

They enjoyed the spread-out city with a subtropical climate that was cooler than Granada in summer. They found their AMORE colleagues helpful and attentive. They found the people friendly, even gracious. They found the city congenial—overall, more open, both physically and socially, than Granada. But they were in a hurry to leave. They were in a hurry to explore their new home.

When the long-chassis Land Rover that had carried them for almost seven hours along the T-4 passed under the green, red, yellow, and black arch topped with crossed elephant tusks, greeting them with "Welcome to Chipata," they were ready to dive wholeheartedly into the next chapter of their lives. Eddie, who had spent his time reading about Zambia at the Embassy's Information Agency while Samantha was indoctrinated into AMORE operations, wondered how Zwangendaba kaZiguda Jele Gumbi had felt when he had arrived in this area more than a century and a half ago. This Ngoni King and his people, defeated by Shaka Zulu, had had to flee their home in kwaZulu-Natal—spending twenty years migrating a thousand miles north. The progeny of Zwangendaba now spread through the present-day Ngoni people in Zambia, Malawi, Mozambique, and Tanzania.

Eddie, however, did not romanticize about Zwangendaba. Though like Moses, he had led his people to the promised land, he had done so fleeing utter destruction. He thought more about his successor, Mpezeni, called a "warrior-king," who was a son of Chipata, born just a few years before Zwangendaba's death. Mpezeni had tried to fight the system. When his lands were threatened by Cecil Rhodes and his British South Africa Company, Mpezeni first tried diplomacy, negotiating with both Rhode's people and the Portuguese to try and find an equitable solution. When talk failed, at the age of sixty-seven, he tried to rise up with a force of thousands, but he could not dislodge the British. He finally signed an agreement with the foreigners but keeping him as Paramount Chief of the Ngoni in Eastern Province. Even today, nearly a century later, successors of Mpezeni are called "Paramount Chief Mpezeni" when they take the throne. Somehow, even in defeat, he had succeeded.

Eddie hoped that here, on a new continent, in a new culture, in a completely new environment, Samantha and he would succeed. Everything was different. So much had to be learned. Would they succeed in making Chipata the first real home for themselves?

Founded in 1899, Chipata, initially called Fort Jameson after Rhode's contemporary Leander Starr Jameson, was named after the Ngoni word for "large space." Through time, this space had transformed into a modern town with a major hospital, a university, and a golf course. The town was hillier and more compact, and certainly much smaller than Lusaka. It had almost a cozy air, making Samantha think that nearly anything of any importance was right here at her fingertips.

There was pretty much a parade of expatriates in many African communities. Bi- and multi-lateral agencies, NGOs, international businesses, and just plain want-to-do-gooders passed through with a predictable rhythm that embraced the departure of the predecessor as well as the arrival of the successor. Houses, furnishing, vehicles, and even household helpers were conveyed from the outgoing to the incoming. The merry-go-round seemed never to stop—often, with no trace of the riders to be found.

AMORE offices were located, appropriately, so Eddie thought, at the center of a triangle connecting the Mosque, the Cathedral, and the central market. Perhaps such an almost indiscernable geographic phenomenon would only be caught by the ever-searching eye of a surveyor-*cum*-agate hunter.

The office itself, in basically a residential area, was a repurposed largish house. In the front, the former roomy residence had been tastefully remodeled into three offices and a reception as well as small meeting room that doubled as a compact library and coffee room complete with a hotplate and kettle along with a small fridge. The back of the property had been transformed into a comfortable, if somewhat crowded two-bedroom apartment with a nice sized full kitchen and a comfy combination living-dining area—Samantha and Eddie's new home. The large window in the dining room looked over a small neat garden anchored by a frangipani tree offset by roses and birds of paradise on one side, a narrow stand of banana and papaya trees occupying the other border.

Across the garden was a pair of guest rooms that had originally been the quarters for the household staff. With lots of visiting staff, AMORE had wisely modified these into two comfortable bedrooms with a large shared bathroom complete with a small laundry area and a kitchenette.

In the spirit of what Eddie's mother would have called, "Many hands make light work," AMORE included in their operational arrangements the employment of two part-time staff to take care of all the premises, including the front and back yards.

As it turned out, these jobs were done by a couple: Paulo and Beatriz. They were Mozambicans who had fled across the border at the onset of the war. In the turmoil, they had been separated from their son, Adao. AMORE had been instrumental in their reunification as a family and, when they decided to settle in Chipata, the program head at that time had engaged them to take care of the property. Although they had their own small home a few miles away, they seemed to always be around the office, Paulo at the ready to jump on his bicycle and run an errand any time of the day, and quite possibly even at night.

Samantha was very pleased. Eddie was supportive. Internally, he was less enthusiastic about living virtually in the same building as the office. He had visions of a twenty-four seven job where his cherished Samantha would be a stranger, albeit only a dozen feet from their bed.

But these thoughts did not deter him. As the house was nearly fully furnished, they were able to jump into bed at an early hour and consecrate the house and its spirits with a night of lovemaking. Eddie could tell from the passion of their union that Samantha was both satisfied and determined—Chipata perhaps being the transformation between a malleable young lady and a skilled mature woman.

Samantha had her hands full. Running the office was time consuming, but she felt she had good training and a good staff. There was a secretary/receptionist, a bookkeeper, along with senior and junior field officers—four full-time staff in all. She found her squad to be motivated and qualified. At busy times, the core team was assisted by up to three consultants who would set up in the library—sometimes, overflowing into the garden.

Samantha could not complain about not having enough people for the job. Nor could she complain about not having enough funding. Her office was well supported. If there was a complaint, it was that the job was quite simply much larger than she had imagined.

The drought of 1983 had pushed people off their lands, in all directions across southern Africa. Yet, the famished children who found themselves in AMORE's care were lucky by comparison to the ravaged and wounded coming from the Mozambique war. The impacts of the war could only be described as terrible.

AMORE was really a clearinghouse. They had arranged with several churches and mosques to take the needy children temporarily, lodging them with members' families while they tried to concentrate on each child individually. AMORE staff would focus on finding parents for those they could, urgently sending the ill and wounded to Lusaka for treatment and keeping the others long enough to try and dissect their biography sufficiently to understand how best to help. Inevitably, most of this latter bunch was ultimately also transferred to Lusaka where they would be introduced into larger groups—in camps really, where, with the help of UN agencies, AMORE staff and partners would try to find a place to put each child. It was a daunting task.

The children seemed to come in waves; sometimes several dozen at a time. The field officers would start interviewing them one by one. Between the two of them, they spoke most of the key languages in this part of southern Africa—Chichewa, Nyanja, Tsonga, and Kiswahili—so detailed discussions were possible with those children who were not simply too traumatized and too locked-up by their current misadventures. Most were, very understandably, so terrified they shut down, saying little.

Samantha's role was much more in the background. Having been at the forefront in Granada, she was happy to take a seat in the second row. In addition to paying the bills and keeping the office moving administratively, she was responsible for providing the food and incidentals the churches and mosques needed to take care of their new charges as well as, in close collaboration with the central Lusaka office, arranging for the transport for children moving west. Her direct contact with the children was generally limited to random exchanges she would have with those she would find in the office during a moment when she had a few minutes to chat. From these disjointed pieces, she was able to assemble in her mind a rather complete picture of the horrors many of these children had faced for far too long.

Eddie seriously considered trying to just help out; he volunteered to assist with logistics and ferry staff and children about the community. While Samantha immensely appreciated Eddie's offer, she knew her spouse too well. He was like a dog chasing a ball when a squirrel cuts his trail—off he would go into the bush after the rodent. With the best of intentions, Eddie would start something only to end up far away doing something completely different, having found a squirrel he just had to chase. It was best if each followed their own separate assignments.

Accordingly, in accepting Eddie's kind offer to help, she gave him his first assignment to take a group of kids to Lusaka and, while there, instructed him to make sure he checked in with Delpro. Fingers crossed, he would come back with his own new job to absorb his energies and occupy his time in an area more suited to his skill set.

Samantha seemed to be more than a little savvy about persistence when seeking opportunity. The trip to Lusaka had achieved its twin aims. The kids arrived safely and, as she had hoped, Eddie returned after three days in the capital proudly proclaiming, he had a new job with Delpro.

---

The South Luangwa National Park was a hidden jewel—the embodiment of wild Africa and the drama of big game. The 3,500 square mile area, established in 1938, was home to some sixty species of mammals and 400 species of birds. Roughly halfway along the 110-mile journey that separated Chipata from the park was the Ngoni Reserve and, near the midpoint between the Reserve and Chipata, thirty miles west of the town, was the Msandile River. The River passed through sparsely populated rolling savannah. It was here that Delpro was seeking to lease 150,000 acres to grow maize and soybeans. The initial request had been received by the government and it was now necessary to prepare a formal dossier proposing the lease. To be able to do this, they needed a comprehensive survey of the property; hence, once again seemingly purely by chance, this was a job opportunity for Eddie.

Mirroring Mr. Smith's arrangements for the Granada assignment, Mr. Van Houtte efficiently and promptly organized materials, transport, a driver, and an assistant to be assigned to Eddie in Chipata. In less than ten days he was bouncing down nearly deserted lanes along the banks of the Msandile in a sturdy Nissan Patrol with his talented driver Isaac and his apparently even more talented and hardworking assistant Gideon.

Gideon had made arrangements with the kitchen of the local Government Guest House where he stayed and every morning at sunrise Isaac would pick him up with a big lunch hamper for three. They would stop at the AMORE office for Eddie and head out with their backs to the rising sun, returning well after sunset.

Eddie was in his realm. When the early morning shadows covered the dewy plains, it easily could have been southern Montana or northern Wyoming. A great gulp of fragrant fresh air, the breeze rustling his hair, and a good job at hand—he could want little more—especially when every evening he was able to go home to Samantha.

The days went by quickly. It was dry season. The mornings were cool. The afternoons were hot—but not burning-hot. It was mostly open terrain and they covered the ground at a fast pace. The plot was over 230 square miles, but it comprised only slightly more than six hundred smallholder farms—one-fifth the normal rural population density for the province.

For each farm, they created a separate file similar to those he had done for Delpro in Spain. While these farms were much smaller and simpler in operation, Eddie's work, he understood, was most important both to Delpro's aims and the farmers' wellbeing. The information he garnered, farm by farm, was critical if Delpro was to succeed in securing the use of the land. If Delpro was awarded the lease, each farm family would receive a significant cash indemnity as well as assistance in relocating to another part of Eastern Province, as close to their traditional homesite as possible. It was never easy when people had to be moved off their land. And, it was always about the money and not the people.

Samantha had challenged Eddie's work from the onset. She had said the lease was a foregone conclusion: money talks. In a dollar-a-day economy, even a generous payment to the families would be insignificant to a transnational like Delpro. If the father did not drink the money away, and that was a big if, they would have a chance at resettling and restarting—all this so Delpro could make even bigger profits. But there were almost equal chances that within a year the family would turn up landless and homeless in Chipata or even Lusaka. How did Eddie feel about forcing families to take these chances, so outsiders could benefit?

Eddie was in fact very sympathetic to Samantha's concerns. Not only did he share these because of his deep love and respect for her, but he still had a nagging suspicion that the work they had done in Spain had not really been all that aboveboard. He was convinced there had been other agendas in play and he had been intentionally kept out of the loop—a tool, not a player. He thought again of Mpezeni and how to achieve some degree of success despite the odds.

Yet, he knew he was maybe rationalizing, most things seemed to run on multiple agendas. Show me an honest politician or businessman. It was all a shell game where the rich and powerful became more rich and powerful at the expense of the common man. It was like the proverb he had learned recently: when the elephants fight, it is the grass that suffers. He could not deny that he was probably a tool in the toolbox of the powerful. However, again rationalizing, the box had many tools—if they did not use him, they would use someone else—perhaps even someone else with less of a conscious. In his own defense, he did not feel so much he was joining or even abetting the enemy as he was interjecting some humanism into an otherwise harsh and insensitive environment.

Samantha did understand her husband's convoluted reasoning and finally agreed. Nonetheless, she was troubled by her acquiescence since she was honestly unsure if it was motivated more by her spouse's possible good-doing or by the fact that it gave him a much-welcomed activity that he not only enjoyed immensely, but that helped put food on the table.

Eventually, as always, the work became routine; the apprehensions were pushed back into the shadows. They fell into a comfortable pattern and Chipata became home.

Samantha knew, of course, of Eddie's interest in the life of Mpezeni. Sometimes, when she was frisky, she would tease him with "the word." It was almost but not really the same Mpezeni. It was *mpenzi*. It was her romantic effort at a special double entendre with her spouse. From her Kiswahili-speaking wards, she knew this to be the word for lover. He was her *mpenzi*.

✸

While Samantha tried to keep from being totally inundated with children and overloaded with need, Eddie had advanced well past the midway point of his assignment. As he stepped out of the Nissan in the morning, he watched a kite spiral upward in a bluing sky, and felt his boots squish into the good soil like someone falling on a favorite mattress. He had just left his own, dampened by the sweat of lovemaking, and he thought about being Samantha's *mpenzi*. He almost felt guilty. He had that gut-tickling good feeling. He was a lover.

He loved his work, too. He knew this was not the same love as for his wife. And, he dearly loved Samantha. But he loved his work a lot. He was free to plan his day and to drink up nature at its purest. While the tasks that consumed the day itself were, after years of practice, frequently mechanical and rote, the soaring of his mind was anything but an old recital. There was newness everywhere.

While he was at times concerned about the uses to which the results of his efforts might be put, he had no moral or emotional turmoil as he walked across the savannah. He simply felt he was at the right place at the right time.

He also knew his *mpenzi*'s day was very, very different. She was not looking at the gray and gold band where the horizon merged with the heavens, she was gazing into children's eyes—troubled and suffering eyes. He had it easy.

Ease was, of course, relative. Eddie's work always got more difficult toward the end when he tried to weave all the numbers into a meaningful tapestry that satisfactorily reflected the chunk of Mother Earth that had been the object of his attention. In this case, the sheer magnitude of the task made crafting the needed images all the more challenging; hundreds of smallholder farms were scattered over thousands of acres. All this needed to be visually and spatially described for his overseers at Delpro.

Nevertheless, to a large extent, handling a really big project was just a question of calling up the experiences of a number of small assignments—the same tools and processes applied. Isaac had proven himself to be a very apt communicator and down-right good helper. With him as intermediary, Eddie felt they had been able to get all the necessary data from the farms in the lease area. Additionally, Gideon had demonstrated an exceptional high-energy work ethic; the days were never too long, the morning never too early, the dust never too much. He was always ready to go. Not only was he ready to go in the field, and not only did he make a major contribution in the field, he showed himself to be very good at organizing and assimilating the data. Eddie had, once again, been very lucky in having an excellent team at his side.

In just over six months, they were able to present Mr. Van Houtte with a first draft of a very comprehensive study of what Delpro hoped would become their eastern complex of Zambia Farms, Ltd. Unlike his experiences with Mr. Smith, Mr. Van Houtte assembled a group of his senior staff and, with Eddie and his team, reviewed the work, page by page.

The company's assessment was thorough. Eddie and the team had to return to the field on three occasions; the first alone required almost a month to collect supplemental information and a fortnight to integrate the analyses of these data into the report.

Mr. Van Houtte then asked for a series of annexes, mostly background and administrative details gathered through interviews in Chipata or Lusaka. All told, from start to finish the work required a little more than a year.

At times Eddie was frustrated as it seemed as though he would never be able to satisfy his boss. But he was handsomely paid throughout, so he really had few complaints.

When the Delpro job was wrapped up, he returned to his role as Samantha's gofer. However, as was unavoidable, his desire to help proved to add and not subtract from Samantha's considerable workload. She had sculpted a system for her office that worked well, and Eddie's overzealousness most frequently made her work harder. She planted a seed she hoped would divert those high-level energies she so loved, leaving her office in the peace and quiet it required.

Since beginning with AMORE, her emotional and professional responsibilities had required her full attention. When, after they were settled in Granada, Eddie had suggested they should organize a visit by their parents, Samantha had balked. She had known her parents would have truly enjoyed visiting southern Spain, not to mention seeing the two of them, but she felt unable to undertake such a task. She simply did not have the extra verve to take care of her parents.

She had suggested Eddie arrange for his parents to come and they would deal with the Montana family at another date. But Eddie's schedule was full and, more to the point, he knew that even if it were only one set of parents, this would still be a probable encumbrance on both of them since their careers were on rather fragile footings.

Accordingly, they had left Granada without ever having a visit by their parents and had come to Zambia without returning to the US. They had both accepted this as one of the requirements of their situation—so be it.

Now, with Eddie taking a break from work, why not arrange for his parents to come to Chipata? He had made good money. Even with his contributions to their costs of living, there was plenty left over, and he could pay for his folks to come and they could visit South Luangwa Park—an opportunity of a lifetime.

Eddie immediately warmed to the suggestion but thought they should still try to get all four parents there—do it once for all. It took Samantha considerable effort to convince Eddie that she was really not ready for her own parents to come—they would visit, just not now. Nonetheless, he could fully concentrate on his parents without posing a burden on her or her work.

Sold.

Eddie checked with a travel agent on his next trip to Lusaka. His folks could fly from Portland to New York, getting a flight from there to Johannesburg. From South Africa, it was just a short hop to Lusaka. And, if he booked ninety days in advance, he could get a good reduction in fare. So, he made tentative bookings for Valentine's Day. This would be the southern hemisphere's summer, with temperatures ranging from the low sixties to the high eighties—a real delight from the middle of a wet Pacific Coast storm season.

Taking into account the nine-hour time difference, he called his parents to see how they would react to an offer to fly almost halfway around the world—to Africa!

He had learned not to double guess his family. Though so often so predictable, they could come up with totally unimaginable things often enough to make any prediction impossible. Foreseeing no specific reaction, he was very happy to hear the nearly immediate and wholeheartedly enthusiastic acceptance of his proposal. It was a go.

As Eddie began firming up the arrangements, he was surprised with a late-night call from his mother. He immediately assumed they had thought long and hard and decided they were too old to go trekking about Africa. He was, therefore, happy to hear his mother's continued eagerness to come and see her children in Zambia. She was calling, though, to ask her son's blessing on a slight change. They would, if he agreed, be coming with Uncle Hal.

*The enigmatic Uncle Hal surfaces again*, Eddie reflected, still unsure of how he fit in the family. Nevertheless, as his mother had assured him that Hal would be paying his own way, why not? This would likely be the last big adventure for his folks and, if Uncle Hal was the catalyst needed to get them across the Atlantic, it was OK by him.

---

It was a lukewarm Lusaka morning when Eddie picked up his family at the airport, fifteen miles northeast of the city center off the T-4 (360 miles from Chipata). They were tired as they had left their home on the wave-washed shores of the Pacific two days earlier. It was a long trip.

They went into town rather than attempting the fatiguing drive to Chipata. He took them on a long tour of the city, not wanting them to crash too soon. They needed to adapt to the time difference. After a light lunch, they all checked into the Pamodzi, and he was able to convince them to rest by the pool as opposed to in bed. High tea was served in the piano lounge, so they had some strong refreshment with lovely sweet cakes that kept them going for a few more hours before falling into a deep sleep in their rooms on the fifth floor—far from the noise of a city that was still wide awake.

Sitting in his room, still lit by a waning summer sun, Eddie could almost feel the city's vibrations, but, his thoughts were far from the jacaranda-lined streets of the former Northern Rhodesia. He was thinking back to that last visit home; that Fourth of July when he had last seen his parents and when he had first seen Uncle Hal. Back then he had remarked his parents were older, bent, and shrunken, no longer moving with the fluidity he remembered from his childhood. Today all these things were more pronounced. His parents had really aged. Although they seemed to have done so nobly, there was no other way to say it, they were old. It was funny though, thinking back to the fireworks at the river, he had thought Uncle Hal looked muscular, noting his good posture, short hair, clean-shaven face. Today Uncle Hal looked exactly the same.

Hal was supposed to be just a few years younger than his sister, but now he looked decades younger. Was it just fate? Was he one of the rare un-aging, while Irene and Earl, just common folk, kept plugging down life's path with but one certain outcome? Hal looked more like Eddie's older brother than his uncle. Was he a Phoenix spawned in his family by some quirk? Or, did he just look a helluva lot younger than he really was? Eddie was perplexed. He was also tired and could not devote any more energy to Hal. He had to take care of his parents and get them safely down the T-4 to Chipata. This meant leaving early in the next morning, just after a daybreak breakfast.

The vibrations of the city continued to bounce off the bed's mattress as Eddie joined his family in slumber, dreaming of waves crashing on rocky beaches as sandpipers cried in warning.

Eddie was greeted by a bright cobalt sky on a calm and stunning morning as he hurriedly got his kit together and went to the restaurant to meet his family as arranged before they all retired last night.

On the margins of the large dining area, next to big sliding glass doors with a clear view of the manicured gardens, he found his family already seated around overflowing plates. The hotel offered a full buffet English breakfast with everything from steak and kidney pie and kippers to savory South African Boerewors and a large collection of tropical fruits. Earl could not resist the dramatic change from his routine of All Bran and skim milk. His plate was literally seeping onto the placemat as local honey oozed across a pancake that unsuccessfully tried to cover scrambled eggs, a rasher of bacon, hash-browns, grilled tomatoes and mushrooms, and even a nice sized T-bone steak with a healthy chunk of spicy sausage at its side.

Eddie's immediate thoughts were, "I hope he doesn't get car sick."

They all ate their fill, and then some, and were soon checked out, heading east out of town against a nearly unbroken line of traffic slowly filing into the city to carry civil servants to their jobs, shoppers to the market, and students to schools. The four of them, along with their luggage, were able to fit not too uncomfortably into Eddie's 1984 Mazda Familia Wagon. Eddie thought the car looked too much like the more expensive Peugeot 505 (recalling the 1980 wagon he and Samantha had had that had served them so well), and he only hoped this vehicle was half as tough as its French counterpart.

When his work at Delpro had finished, he found himself transportation-less. Samantha had an aging, most would say aged, Volvo wagon that was assigned to AMORE and, as the head of the office, was available to her to run errands and do other personal business. However, it was not available for her spouse to go to the capital to pick his parents up at the airport.

The Mazda had become available when a Polish ag advisor had fallen ill and had to be repatriated from the verdant fields of Eastern Province. She, Eddie knew all vehicles were feminine, was far from her prime, but seemed to have been well-maintained and still possessed some inner gumption that convinced Eddie she was worthy of travel along the T-4. She had done well on her maiden voyage into Lusaka. Eddie trusted she would do equally well on the long haul back to Chipata.

By the time they cleared the amoeboid urban sprawl of Lusaka, his visitors began to settle into the rhythm of the road and really absorb their surroundings. For his parents, he knew things could not have been more different. He imagined it was only a deep sense of decorum that prevented his mother from shouting out, "Everyone's black."

Irene and Earl sat side-by-side in the back seat, oohing and aahing the blurry cinematography displayed through the Mazda's rather dusty windows, as they passed through villages and roadside communities where people carried on as they had yesterday and as they would tomorrow.

When a longhorn cow, called Ankole-Watusi by some, disinterestedly eyed their passing, or a young mother appeared on the shoulder, dressed in all her finery, going to some sort of celebration with a baby on her back, Irene would elbow Earl hard in the ribs and, somewhere between a whisper and a cry, utter, "Look, look, look."

Throughout all, behind large aviator sunglasses, Hal was stoic; at times, Eddie thought he was dozing.

They stopped a few times to stretch their legs, a few times to heed the call of nature, and once to get some snacks and drinks at a petrol station. It was tea time when they pulled into the parking at the rear of the AMORE office. Each was immediately met with a warm embrace from Samantha who had prepared a smorgasbord of bites, as she called them—salads, cold meats, fruits, and sweets accompanied by strong Malawi tea, that could tide them over until the morrow as the combined effects of time and travel would likely push them quickly into their beds in the detached guest rooms which Samantha had knowingly readied for them.

The next morning Eddie got everyone up and going by eight o'clock; he knew the best cure for what ailed them was to quickly get into an established routine and reset their internal clocks to a new diurnal cycle. Breakfast was a simple affair. Nothing like the Pomodzi buffet. Mazuzu coffee from next door in Malawi, cheese from the Kalundu Dairy, toast, and passion fruit-pawpaw salad.

Midmorning, keeping to a slow-motion schedule to allow his guests to unwind, Eddie took them for a drive around Chipata, mixing the highlights with dabs of history he had slowly assimilated. Samantha took the afternoon off to host her visitors for a braai (barbecue) in the backyard. She had amassed riches to bring salivary overflow to the keenest carnivores: *karoowors*, a specialty South African boerewors, chicken breasts marinated in heady pilipili sauce, steaks from Boran cattle raised in the southwest of Zambia, goat cutlets steeped in garlic and ginger, and to top it all off, fresh two-pound tilapia from Lake Malawi—called Lake Nyasa by most outside Malawi, as she would later explain. It was an epicurean offering selected and prepared with meticulous loving care.

When the family was seated around the table Paulo and Beatriz had helped move from the meeting room-*cum*-library into the yard—the couple agreeing to stay the afternoon to help with clean-up with payment in the form of their own heaping plates of gourmet barbecue—Samantha inspected all with satisfaction. It was a repast suitable for her in-laws whom she loved dearly.

As heavy platters were passed from one to another, she watched Irene help Earl choose the tastiest pieces coming from the half-fifty-five-gallon drum that served as the charcoal grill. Her mother-in-law was intelligent, gracious, empathetic, and a sentimentalist. She was even classy in a homespun way, but with a backbone of wrought iron—not someone with whom to unwittingly trifle. In many ways, she was the yin to Earl's yang. Her husband was quiet, often pensive. Occasionally, he could even be brusque. At the same time, he was open and honest. While very astute in a wide variety of matters, he chose to appear as just a simple millworker, the facade masking a profound questioning of the world around him. Samantha watched as Irene and Earl literally and figuratively leaned on each other, knowing the other was always there. She hoped she and Eddie had an equally strong and shared presence.

Eddie watched Samantha watching his parents. He saw the silent change in her expressions that he so loved; her nose wrinkling, lips slightly parted, eyes wincing in the corners as she concentrated on something she valued. He felt, and was so grateful for, the strong bonds his wife had with his parents. In many ways, Samantha looked more to Irene than her own mother as the light that illuminated her path. She felt an almost spiritual link to her mother-in-law that prompted an inner glow in Eddie's soul.

Samantha was such a unique person. Eddie watched as she oversaw the serving of the choice meats, nearly as a conductor guiding an orchestra. She had moved her arms with grace as she had gestured to her guests where to sit or where to find a knife or fork. She now stood at the center of her visitors caring for their every need, dressed in a simple tie-dye dress, with almost an exquisiteness that turned Eddie's inner glow into a flame. She was amazing.

He found himself staring at his parents as they used their fingers to pick up savory pieces of goat and succulent parts of tilapia, his father unabashedly having a red checkered napkin stuck in his blue work-shirt collar to soak up the dripping juices—how different from those sedate dinner tables growing up. His parents were already enjoying their adventure. He was glad they had come. He wondered, however, if they would have made the effort if it had been just for himself. They adored Samantha, after all, almost as much as he did. She touched all their lives.

Then, as he scanned the garden, his eyes fell on Uncle Hal. He had already unceremoniously served himself and was sitting quietly at one end of the table, tasting tiny morsels of his meats, still wearing his aviators, and apparently in his own separate world. As Eddie watched, Samantha, ever the attentive hostess, stooped over Hal's station to make sure he had all he needed. He offered a hooded half smile, but almost shooed her away with assurances that all was fine. The more Eddie saw, the more questions he had. He wondered where he would find the answers.

The braai was an unbridled success, the guests somehow waddling off to their rooms in the early evening—the scent of roasted meat emanating from their pores like an earthy perfume. Eddie and Samantha, with the able assistance of Paulo and Beatriz, quickly dispatched the dishes and any other cleanup—the Mozambican couple returning to their own home with a large basket filled with meats that would last a week.

The seared meat aroma seemed to have an ardent effect and, after a deep sleep that was preceded by intense amorousness, Eddie awoke early the next day to finalize all the plans for their visitors.

They had one more day of low-key activities before driving to South Luangwa National Park as Eddie described in horrible detail all the abstruse work he had just completed in that area. They had booked rooms at the Mffuwe Lodge, just a few minutes from the park's main entrance. The lodge had a large pavilion where meals were served, with a bar and lounge. Guests then stayed in one- or two-bedroom chalets that were arranged in concentric circles around the central longhouse.

The evening of their arrival, after a filling meal of venison stew accompanied by a crispy salad of local greens, professing real fatigue after a day on the road, Earl and Irene went back to their half of the chalet to get an early start on much-needed sleep. Eddie and Hal sat on the wide veranda of the pavilion, listening to the night sounds of the park as they sipped good single malt.

Eddie felt he would never get a better chance than the present to try and dig out some answers to the box full of questions he had regarding his Uncle Hal. The discussion turned out to be like trying to pick a crab out of the trap, you knew there was only one way to hold the critter without getting soundly wounded by those big pincers. Eddie tried a variety of handholds to be able to grasp Hal's story. Hal was an experienced and skillful defender who could parry most of Eddie's rhetorical thrusts. Yet, even with his keen ability to deflect, as the conversation expanded and the level in the bottle of malt fell, Eddie was able to pick up small pieces and assemble them as a jigsaw puzzle.

Hal was considerably younger than his sister. Eddie did not know an exact number, but Hal was finishing grade school when his big sister was wrapping up college. He must have been a good student because, when he finished high school, he got a full ride to Georgetown University. He had gone east and never looked back. When he had finished at Georgetown, he went on for a master's at Columbia and from there into a variety of government positions—here becoming even more obtuse as to the where's and what's of his public service.

It wasn't much, but it was a lot more than he had had yesterday. He could now at least put some sort of a frame around Hal; well-educated, youthful, and accomplished. He was clearly extremely guarded with all his discourse, making Eddie imagine even more secretive and dastardly events at Hal's hands than he had first conjured. He hoped with time some more pieces would take shape and he would be able to feel as though he were interacting with a real member of his family and not a performer.

An incomplete picture notwithstanding, by the time they finished the bottle, Eddie and Hal were leaning upon each other to reach their chalet and the bedroom they shared; both collapsed nearly fully clothed and were soon a duet, snoring the refrains of the inebriated.

Morning came far too early for the two tipplers. They emerged blurry-eyed to find Earl and Irene enjoying the morning's fresh gusts coming off the river—ready for a hearty breakfast and a trek—both revolting thoughts for the evening's boozers.

Eddie and Hal found the solution to their dilemma: a Bloody Mary with breakfast. With the help of the hair of the dog, they were able to make considerable inroads into the lodge's bountiful buffet. The foursome then piled into the long-wheelbase Land Rover which, complete with a guide and a large picnic basket, were part of the package they had arranged for their three-day stay at the lodge.

On the morning of the fourth day, they were elated to get into Eddie's Mazda, now feeling it to be one of the most comfortable cars on Earth, and head east back to Chipata. They had spent hours meandering over the undulating terrain; through the peaks with Miobo woodlands, the troughs covered with Mopane woodlands, and along the banks of the Luangwa. They had seen Cape buffalo, elephants, zebra, giraffe, lions, antelope, crocodile, hippos, and even a leopard. It had been breathtaking. It had been taxing. It had been a once-in-a-lifetime opportunity.

Back at AMORE, they were delighted to see Samantha, find what they now saw as their rooms, take hot soapy showers, and enjoy a chilled Mosi lager in the back yard. Fortunately, Eddie had built in a bit of a reprieve into the planning of their odyssey; they were able to laze about for several days before the next leg of their, what Eddie now called, walkabout.

The next step involved traveling further eastward into Malawi. Eddie had fortunately foreseen this eventuality and all three Stateside guests already had Malawi visas—Eddie himself having a year-long multiple-entry visa.

Eddie had hoped Samantha could join them, but the surge of Mozambican refugees seemed to only be increasing and she felt she could not leave the office to go sightseeing. So, Eddie again loaded the Mazda and they went as far as the capital of Lilongwe the first night, staying in the expansive Capital Hotel. The next morning, after another sumptuous hotel breakfast offering, they drove the 140 miles, and descended nearly 1,800 feet in elevation, to the shores of Lake Malawi, alighting at the Monkey Bay Beach Resort.

They spent two nights on the lakeshore, enjoying the warm sandy beaches as they thought of the cold inhospitable storm-ridden winter coast of Oregon. They marveled at the lake's size, taking canoes offshore to see how the fishermen fished—quite a difference from Pacific Northwest salmon trawlers. They then drove to the older, more commercial Pre-Independence Center of Blantyre for another night before spending the final day driving back to the Zambian border and on to Chipata.

There was then a lull in the otherwise hectic schedule, with a week to just lie about before heading back up the T-4. However, rather than flying out from the capital, Eddie had devised a different return leg—a kind of special dessert for their stew of African travels. They would, he proposed, go back to Lusaka, but, after another night at the Pomodzi, they would then continue south through Kafue to Saivonga and cross the Zambezi River at the Kariba high dam, spending the next night at Kariba before continuing south and west to Harare, Zimbabwe, where they were already booked at the Bronte Hotel.

Eddie's itinerary was endorsed enthusiastically by all.

Samantha took annual leave to accompany the family on the Zimbabwe safari. As most of her time was spent indoors, she was as exhilarated as her in-laws at all the passings-by from the simple things like a small boy herding a flock of goats to the massive things like the water thundering over Kariba dam that, she felt, shook her from her toes to her earlobes. She became completely absorbed in the sparsely populated, at times desolate, countryside through which they passed—often thinking she was back in Montana. So different, yet so similar.

Harare was another memory-jogger. As they spent a few days enjoying the city's sophisticated ambiance, they all felt they had taken a step back to a mid-sized American city like Portland in the 1950s. The clean and well-engineered municipality had a compact city-center with department stores with elevator, they called them lifts, operators who called out the floors. There were tailors creating elegant three-piece suits. There were linen shops and flower vendors. And, sitting on the crest of tropical and subtropical agricultural zones, there were greengrocers with baskets of grapes and apples next to papayas, mangos, and pineapples. There were cauliflower, green beans, and beets competing with more typical yams, cabbage, and cassava. There were butchers with aged beef, sausages, and ham. There were bakeries with a mouthwatering mix of European and African sweets. Everything seemed to be there; and, at prices that made one almost embarrassed to pay—a fraction of what Samantha would pay in Chipata, if she could even find the item.

They had dinner at Meikles Hotel where the gents had to wear a tie, the liveried waiters wore spotless white gloves, and the food was scrumptious all the way to the flaming crêpe suzettes. They had beer and biltong at the Jamison Hotel. They had bush meat accompanied by local wines and jazz at the Amanzi. They had a great time.

Then it was over. Samantha and Eddie accompanied the trio to the airport for the afternoon flight to Johannesburg. Irene and Earl would retrace their steps, taking the night flight to New York and then on to Portland. For reasons he felt no need to explain, Hal was separating from his sister in Jo'burg and taking VARIG to Rio.

After hugs and a few tears, Eddie and Samantha went back for one last night at the Bronte. They both felt this sweet-sorrow in the pit of their stomachs. They were grateful the visitors had come, sorry to see them leave—remarking they felt Earl and Irene were walking more erect as they departed than when they had arrived. They felt their guests had had a genuinely enjoyable stay and hoped the Stateside trio felt the same. They were also keenly aware this may have been the last relatively unencumbered time they would spend with the aging Irene and Earl. While in general good health, as they themselves had often noted: they were old.

In the cool of the night, Eddie and Samantha were intertwined on crisp sheets, overlain by a woolen blanket that created almost a swaddle weaving the pair together. Samantha was soundly asleep, making little murmuring noises Eddie so loved as her breath dribbled from her half-open lips—lips he wanted to bend over and kiss at that moment.

Sleep had eluded him, but he did not want to disrupt his wife's well-deserved slumber. He had been thinking of his parents, getting to the ever-bustling Jan Smuts Airport, having to wait six hours before their flight west across the Atlantic. It would take them over sixteen hours to reach JFK. They would then have long waits at immigration and customs with a five-hour layover before they could board their flight to Portland.

For people of their age, to say it was exhausting was to seriously underestimate the real hardship his parents had accepted to be able to visit their son in a far-off land.

He hoped they were now as happy making these sacrifices as he was that they had come. He had never been an easy child. He knew his father had had a vision of his son going to university and becoming a doctor—rising from the sweat and sawdust of the mill to higher ranks. In many ways, he felt he had let his father down. He had followed his heart. Yet, at the end of the day, he did not feel he had done too badly. He hoped his parents felt this way, having seen him in action in Zambia.

He knew his parents loved Samantha—often joking about how astonished they were that their errant offspring had so surprisingly done so well in finding the perfect spouse. He knew the agony of the voyage had been just as much to see Samantha as to see him. He trusted they—Samantha and himself—made it all worthwhile.

Finally, like a Pacific wave, sleep swept over him and his soft snores were mingled with Samantha's cooing.

The next morning, they left Harare, driving north to Victoria Falls where they had rooms for two nights at the much-lauded Victoria Falls Hotel.

The hotel, living up to its luxurious reputation, was only a ten-minute walk from the falls, reportedly first seen by a white man, David Livingstone, in 1855. The falls themselves were nearly heart-stopping. At a mile wide and over 350 feet high, they were proclaimed to be the world's largest in terms of a single curtain of falling water. When Samantha stood by the side of the torrent, her throat tightened. If she felt the river had shaken her body at the dam, here she felt it shook her soul.

That night, after long and tender lovemaking, she and Eddie held hands in bed, listing to the river as sleep fell upon them like the mist from the falls. It was a magical place.

After another night under the mists, they crossed the border back into Zambia, feeling thankful and refreshed.

Back in Lusaka, it was back to work. Samantha had a full day of meetings at AMORE so there were two more nights in a hotel—this time the more familiar Pamodzi. While Samantha discussed how to deal with the growing tide of refugees, Eddie decided to see if he could get an appointment with Mr. Van Houtte—thinking that maybe Delpro had something new to offer.

It turned out, according to Mr. Van Houtte, to be amazing serendipity. He had just been thinking of Eddie. There was some work in Southern Region of Malawi. Delpro had quite some investments in commercial agriculture in Malawi—tea, coffee, other crops. About twenty miles south of Blantyre, at Thyolo, they owned a tea estate where there was a heated dispute with the local population as to the exact boundary of their land. They had a similar problem twenty miles northwest of Blantyre, near Tedzani, where they had a chili pepper farm that was irrigated from a nearby forty-acre dam—a dam they owned, but that the local community was now saying was theirs.

Delpro needed to deal with these two unfortunate matters—matters that could fester if not quickly cauterized.

Resolution required preparing a pile of documentation for each case—documentation based upon current, objectively sourced facts—evidence.

Herein lay the role for Eddie the mapmaker.

Mr. Van Houtte figured the two assignments would require five or six weeks in the field to collect the raw data and interview the concerned parties. Official documents would have to be sourced at local administrative offices. In some instances, related documents may need to be found at the regional or national capitals. Property lines would need to be surveyed. Discussions would be required with people from both sides of the arguments. Mr. Van Houtte then calculated that the collation and transcription of the information garnered in the field would take another three or four weeks. So, to allow for the inevitable unforeseen circumstances, Mr. Van Houtte was willing, on the spot, to offer Eddie a three-month contract with a twenty-five percent increase in his rate compared to his first assignment.

Eddie was not stunned but he was pleasantly surprised. They agreed that in a fortnight he would return to Lusaka to collect all the background material and then head directly to Malawi.

※

Eddie and Samantha thankfully returned to their own bed, although Eddie would be leaving all too soon. Samantha, as always, was grateful for Eddie's work—not only for its contribution to their budget, but also for the engagement and opportunity for professional growth that it provided her dear husband. She did not want him to stagnate and then ferment into blandness as so many seemed to do with the passing of time. She loved his enthusiasm, his energy, his ups and downs—he was her *mpenzi*.

Eddie grounded himself in home and the passionate radiance of his wife before heading back up the T-4 to the capital and to Delpro. He was briefed—this time by Mr. Van Houtte and his team—with basically a more detailed rehash of the scenarios initially described by Mr. Van Houtte at their previous meeting. He was given voluminous documentation. Eddie had assumed he would also be given a vehicle and the good services of Gideon and Isaac. Assumptions are, of course, dangerous. He was informed Delpro had a small office in Blantyre and all his logistical and staff support would come from there. All was settled. He was back on the T-4.

They had one all too brief but romantic night in Chipata before Eddie crossed the border and headed south to Blantyre—the travel expenses liberally provided by his employer being more than double the costs of keeping his old Mazda on the road. Maybe, he thought, he could use the extra to buy a nice gift for Samantha in the very cosmopolitan Blantyre.

With few delays, he reached the Malawian commercial capital, the city named after the birthplace of David Livingstone, just after tea time. He went directly to the Delpro offices which were situated on the third floor of a venerable brick structure near the city's center. They had been forewarned by Mr. Van Houtte and had booked Eddie in the expansive Mount Soche Hotel and made an appointment for the next morning to start work.

As promised, the first thing in the morning the Delpro office manager, Mr. Singhe, mustered his modest staff of one, Fritz, a do-it-all field hand, and ushered Eddie into a small meeting room where there was already a middle-aged man seated at the rather cramped table.

Mr. Singhe was matter-of-fact. He introduced the fourth person as Simon, quickly encapsulating his varied background ranging from work at Chancellor College in Zomba to a position with the Malawi Timber Company in Mzuzu. Simon would act as driver, interpreter, rod-man, and all else required for the completion of the assignment. His office, Mr. Singhe added, would provide transportation, recalling Eddie had received all the necessary guidance from Lusaka. Finally, he confirmed that, although Kacchi was a common language in Blantyre and Kakole in Thyolo, Simon spoke truly excellent Chichewa which was the *lingua franca* of the entire region, if not the country. Mr. Singhe then provided a single sheet of paper with the telephone numbers of the office as well as the residences for Fritz and himself—assuring Eddie that they were there any time, night or day, to provide any needed assistance.

The briefing was indeed brief. As Simon led Eddie to the street, he thought about Mr. Singhe's attitude. It was too soon to jump to any conclusions, but it certainly appeared as though Delpro's man in Blantyre felt he was generally out of the loop for an assignment that was taking place on his turf but managed from Lusaka. Or, was Mr. Singhe opposed to the work all together? Or maybe he was just overworked? Eddie was sure that as his work progressed, the larger operational environment would become clearer.

He brought his thoughts back to the present as he followed Simon around the corner to a side street where a well-worn, if not dilapidated, Russian Lada Niva four-by-four station wagon was parked. The car seemed emblematic of his relationship with the Blantyre Office—he hoped Simon would work out well.

In defiance of its appearance and rough interior, the Niva seemed to have good power and, importantly, a smooth suspension. As they headed out, going first south, Simon pointed out a local BP petrol station, saying Delpro had an account there for fuel and any repairs. With the twenty-liter jerrycan affixed to the tailgate, Simon guaranteed they could easily spend a full day in the field and come back to fill up with a quarter of a tank remaining.

They drove through low hills, the slopes covered with *Camellia sinensis*, the tea plant. Since the colonial period, this had been a large tea producing area—many of the plantations little changed over more than a century. A bouquet of color moved slowly among the flat-topped, jade-hued plants. These were the workers—most often women, but numerous children, and no small number of men. They were all dressed in an amalgam of secondhand clothing, layered against the cold and dampness, much of it in tatters. In some strange way, they reminded Eddie of Raggedy Ann and Raggedy Andy dolls floating through the tea leaves. They had great baskets harnessed to their backs to receive the leaves they methodically selected from the garland of sprouts of different ages that adorned the tops of the pruned plants. They worked long hours, to close the day at a weigh station where they were paid pennies a pound for the contents of their baskets.

Interspersed between the lush expanses of tea were ramshackle hamlets of adobe block and corrugated roofing sheets. This was the company-provided accommodation that justified even lower than normal wages. These quarters were without electricity and generally only with one community well for potable water. Several communities banded together to have a common weekly market, school, and church. It was, at the very most, a rustic existence.

They continued a few miles beyond Thyolo to the estate that was the object of their work. Here a group of smallholder farmers were accused by Delpro of encroaching on estate lands; maize and bean fields were where tea should be. The social justice aspects aside (Eddie was glad Samantha was not here), technically speaking it was a straightforward question. They needed to review the maps, titles, designations, and overall formal status of this area. They could then survey the official boundary and answer directly the question of who was right and who was wrong.

The next day they went north to Tedzani. Here the terrain was totally different. The topography was nearly flat and the climate dry; no wonder the issue of a dam was of so much importance.

The dam in question was located no more than a mile north of a village with 250 inhabitants. Less than a mile to the south of the dam was a commercial farm of 20 acres of chili plants—a Delpro farm. Delpro maintained the dam was theirs and that the village had no user rights—offering to help the village drill a well for their water needs. The chief of the village insisted the dam had been built for them and that they had guaranteed access in perpetuity. As with Thyolo, the humanitarian dimension notwithstanding, a solution seemed rather straightforward. Once more, they had to start with the historical documentation.

Both cases required considerable research. Simon proved most helpful—Mr. Singhe stayed out of the way. Slowly, the pictures of each location came into sharper view. It was, nevertheless, a slow slog to get all the pieces documented and verified. It took weeks. Pangs of separation grew too great for Eddie and he went home to Chipata and Samantha after three weeks. When he re-entered Malawi, he spent four days in Lilongwe validating their data and basic operating assumptions. By the end of week four they were ready to get their boots on and start the actual surveying which, from all appearances, would be the easiest part of the assignment.

As Eddie had initially surmised, the Thyolo site was clear-cut. Delpro leased large tracts of tea estates that had been under private ownership prior to independence but had reverted to the state at the end of colonial rule. Copies of the original agreements were on file, as were the precise maps of those parcels currently allotted to Delpro. Eddie and Simon engaged a few day laborers and were able to mark for all to see the delineation of the officially established and leased tea estate—extending some 100 yards into the smallholder fields. Otherwise put, the smallholders had indeed encroached on Delpro land—albeit probably unintentionally as the strip of land in question had never been planted with tea. It was now up to Delpro to either cede the small contentious area to the local community or find the means to make them leave without stirring up too much anger. This was far beyond Eddie's remit.

Tedzani was less straightforward. According to a variety of records, the dam had been built by the Ministry of Agriculture a decade earlier to, among other functions, provide water for the nearby village—water for both domestic and agricultural uses. The chief was right, according to the archives, the village had the right to use this water for as long as it wished to do so. However, the agreement stipulated specific parts of the dam that could be used for watering livestock, washing clothes, or even fishing. Indeed, a comprehensive management plan had been drafted at the time the dam was built to try and provide as much water as possible for as many uses as possible. Over and beyond the various uses by the village, there had been provisions for use by farmers—both commercial and smallholder—for irrigation should the lands around the dam be developed into farming areas. Thus, Delpro had a right to share the resource, but the dam was definitely not theirs.

Again, the implementation and updating of the existing agreements was not part of Eddie's job. He did, though, refer to the original management plan and stakeout the areas assigned for various specified activities.

Eddie had gone back to Chipata again between the field work at the Thyolo and Tedzani sites. He was surprised to hear from Samantha that Mr. Van Houtte had called her office and asked that Eddie call him the next time he was home.

Essentially Mr. Van Houtte wanted a briefing which Eddie readily provided in suitable detail. Mr. Van Houtte seemed to take particular interest when Eddie said the Malawi part of the work should be finished in a week or ten days.

When he was back in Blantyre, Eddie and Simon briefed Mr. Singhe, who seemed as disinterested or sidelined as always. They then collected all their materials, both the historical documentation and the work they had generated themselves and retuned to each of the sites to double check everything—making sure there were no accidental omissions or inaccurate insertions that could have to be rectified later.

As they were preparing for their final departure from Thyolo, a lady in a patchwork quilt of clothing, with a large straw hat covering a soiled once polka dot bandana, approached Eddie. She said someone had told her that Eddie was from Chipata. Eddie confirmed her information was correct. The lady then seemed to gather her inner strength to address Eddie again. She told him she had two teenage children who had simply gone missing. She was stunned and had no idea how this could happen. Then, someone had said they had seen her children in Chipata. She reached between several layers of clothing and extracted a large but ragged envelope. With nearly clenched fingers, she fought to remove the envelope's contents: pictures of her two children along with a sheet of school notebook paper written in a rough hand with the names and birthdates of the two. She curtsied as she handed Eddie the envelope and its contents. She simply said, "Please find my children."

Eddie looked into the pained and suffering eyes. He did not want to mention Samantha and AMORE. He did not want to create any false hope. Living on the tea estate was, as he had seen over the past weeks, difficult at best. It did not seem too strange to him that teenagers would run away in the hopes of finding anything else over the next hill—for, almost anything could be seen as better through the eyes of a teenager.

Eddie said none of this. He simply solemnly took the offering, saying he would pass it to colleagues in Chipata. He hoped he could be of some help, but obviously this was an outside chance.

The teenagers' mother seemed to have no idea of what an outside chance was. But she showed, with her bowed head and slumped shoulders that she clearly knew what it meant to be out of luck.

Driving back to Blantyre, Eddie and Simon could not forget their last image of Thyolo: a woman old beyond her years crying as they left. Hopeless. Crushed by loss.

When Simon dropped him off at the hotel, he was taken aback to find Mr. Van Houtte waiting in the lobby. His employer greeted him with a broad smile and a warm, if doughy, handshake. He informed Eddie that, as the field part of the assignment was wrapping up, he thought it a good idea to drop in and see for himself the situation as, confidentially, Mr. Singhe was not all that interested. He added, for uncertain reasons, that Mr. Singhe was, indeed, the epitome of the foreign businessman in Africa: it was all about profits. Such profiteers felt collateral damage was unavoidable, especially in fragile economies. By comparison, he, Mr. Van Houtte, was a holist. There were too many moving parts to focus on only a few that most affected one's self interests. The whole was greater than the sum of the parts.

Eddie felt he was in a pitch-black room feeling awkwardly for the light switch. His mind, if not his hands, was flailing about. Mr. Van Houtte's presence seemed totally incongruous. But here he was, right now proposing Eddie go up to his room to freshen up and then they would go out for a good dinner at the Casa Mia—his treat.

He was, after all, being visited, even if unannounced, by his boss. He had few options. Dinner at Casa Mia it was.

Over plates of homemade pasta and carafes of imported Italian wine, Mr. Van Houtte regaled Eddie with his thumbnail sketch of recent southern African history in general, and Malawian chronicles in particular. These were times of turmoil. It was not that long ago Rhodesia had become Zimbabwe, with majority rule. South Africa was aquiver with all signs pointing to a transition similar to that of Zimbabwe. The Life President of Malawi, now in his late eighties or early nineties (no one seemed to know), a lifelong anglophile, was presently seen by many as a *collaborateur* with white nationalists. From one day to the next, things were changing—drastically.

Delpro was big (Mr. Smith's words ringing in Eddie's ears). Delpro, by the very nature of their varied investments, had to be malleabile—adapting to different circumstances as they arose. The heavy-handed days of the white bosses in Africa were disappearing—this was not to say, he inserted, that they were replaced by anything better. Maybe not better, but different. And Delpro had to adjust. Some of Delpro's investments in Malawi were practically functioning as they had during the colonial period. This would likely have to change. Not necessarily because the company wanted to change. Change cost money. But survival was often based on change.

Ordering tiramisu and cognac for them, after wiping his plate clean with a piece of crusty Italian bread, Mr. Van Houtte appeared to wind up by assuring Eddie he was here to make sure, based on Eddie's work, Depro would be able to change in the right direction.

Mr. Van Houtte was also staying at the Mount Soche. After breakfast, Simon appeared to pick them both up for what had heretofore been unplanned visits to the two sites. The arrangements had apparently been made quietly by Mr. Singhe.

More revelations were to unveil themselves as Simon pulled up in one of the hamlets in the estate near Thyolo, not far from the contested boundary. They were greeted by a large crowd, certainly larger than the residents of the settlement. The exceptional size and buoyancy of the gathering became apparent when Eddie, exiting the Niva, saw long tables heaped with platters of nsema, meat stew and other relishes, bread, fruits, and cases of Carlsberg Green. Free food and drink. Delpro, Eddie thought.

Indubitably, someone from the company had been here early with a pickup load of goodies while arranging for a day off for the tea workers. This had all the trappings of a political rally with Mr. Van Houtte at its center.

Unabashedly, Mr. Van Houtte addressed the group with Simon translating into Chichewa. He extolled the efforts of all those hard workers from the estate, sympathetically, if a bit overly-theatrically, linking their tireless toil in the cold and damp to fine cups of tea, served in fine china, at fine homes around Europe. He pledged Delpro's commitment to their wellbeing. He regretted profusely any misunderstanding about who could farm where, pointing to Eddie and highlighting that Eddie's work would surely solve all their problems.

Eddie felt betrayed. He was only a tool, a collector of facts and numbers. Whatever did or did not happen was a direct consequence of how Delpro reacted to his results. He was not a solution. He just hoped he was not part of the problem.

He gazed at the crowd; his eyes almost magnetically drawn to the lady who had addressed him yesterday. She was standing on the fringe with a six or seven-year-old girl holding her hand—perhaps another daughter. He could see the sorrow in her eyes. He could see her plea for help. He could see her incredulity at Mr. Van Houtte's words. She had seen and heard too many politicians. She had been bathed in too many promises. Regardless the speaker, regardless the pledge, she remained a tea picker. Pragmatic fatalism led her to the conclusion she would die a tea picker. But she hoped, she so hoped, her children would escape the same fate.

All of this Eddie understood as his eyes looked across the crowd. The spectators were more engrossed in guzzling beer and devouring corn dumplings with spicy sauce than in filtering and digesting Mr. Van Houtte's monologue. The words were stale. The food was fresh, the beer chilled.

When his boss had finished speaking, Eddie somewhat guardedly took him to the exact spot where he had staked the limit of the plantation. He pointed out the fields that were on estate land, emphasizing it was he, Mr. Van Houtte, or perhaps Mr. Singhe, who would have to deal with the resolution of the situation. He could only show them where their land ended and confirm that certain portions were being used by other parties.

The task having been accomplished, at least for the moment, they promptly left the soggy tea estate for the much drier chili farm. Here there was no fanfare. Evidently, Eddie thought, Delpro did not want to pop for festivities at two villages at a time. Here, in fact, they did not even make the expected courtesy call on the Chief. Eddie indicated the different use areas around the dam, summarizing his findings; after which point, Mr. Van Houtte briskly inspected the chili farm before they headed back to Blantyre.

That evening dinner was at the hotel. Mr. Van Houtte reiterated his satisfaction with Eddie's efforts, confirming he would fly back to Lusaka the next day. Eddie, still thrown off by Mr. Van Houtte's theatrics and more, signaled in a reserved tone that he too would be spending a few days in Lilongwe before returning to Chipata.

He needed to make sure he had copies of all the official documentation he required while still in Malawi. Lilongwe, as the capital, was not only the repository for all formal papers, but also provided many more services than Chipata. He wanted to work on his maps there where he had the support he needed, before he went back across the border. Mr. van Houtte offered to make contacts for him with Delpro's Lilongwe office to facilitate his work—an offer Eddie respectfully declined.

Eddie verified he would be in Mr. Van Houtte's office within the month to submit his report. After coffee, each went his own way.

Later that same evening, Eddie went down to the reception to ask them to prepare his bill as he would be leaving in the morning. When he turned from the night clerk to go back to his room, he spied Mr. Van Houtte sitting in the lobby, engrossed in conversation with another white man—remarkable for his mane of alabaster hair that framed a pink complexion that nearly glowed in the dim lighting. Strangely, while he was sure Mr. Van Houtte, looking startled and uncomfortable, had clearly seen him, his boss made every effort to ignore his presence. Taking the not too subtle hint, Eddie returned to his room wondering who the mysterious pink-and-white man was—this now the second time he had seen him in the shadows.

Eddie's stay in Lilongwe was even shorter than he had planned. They had done thorough research from the onset, so validating their documentation was relatively quick and easy. He was also able to rapidly plot his data and make copies of relevant maps. In less than seventy-two hours after arriving in Lilongwe, he was parking his Mazda behind the AMORE office in Chipata.

Telephone communications were undependable at best, and Samantha did not know he was coming when he walked into the NGOs front door. She flew from her office into his arms, oblivious to the stares of her staff who generally believed in more reserved emotions in public.

That night was truly special and tender—it was as though they had been separated for years.

The next day, with the help of Paulo, he set up a makeshift office in one of the detached bedrooms. He carefully collated and classified his sheaves and sheaves of paperwork. He unrolled his own maps as well as the topo maps he had copied. He brought in an Olivetti he had borrowed from the office (the age of the computer was something only to read about in the newspaper, a distant sketch on a far-off canvas).

Over the next two weeks, he divided his time between pampering his wife and writing his report. He scarcely left the compound. He felt he had traveled more than enough as of late. And he was now more uncertain than ever of where he stood. He began musing more and more about Delpro and their real role in all the spectacles he had witnessed.

During this time, he did share with Samantha the envelope the lady from Thyolo had given him. This immediately piqued her interest. After all, this was AMORE's mandate: help the children and their families. She prepared a brief AMORE dossier for the two teenagers with photos, personal details and contacts. She posted this in her office as well as at the various points around town where other children were staying. She also faxed the dossier to AMORE offices around Africa and in Europe. This was a routine she had done so many times before. It was so often so frustrating, so futile.

She was, therefore, amazed to get a prompt reply from her old office in Granada. About six months ago they had had contact with a girl, a teenager, who called herself Angel. She was anglophone, saying she was Nigerian. But she seemed to have little knowledge of Nigeria or Central Africa. Moreover, she looked exactly like the photo and she gave the same birthday. She had been picked up on the street by the *Guardia Civil* and was not what one might call a willing guest. In truth, before they could completely process her paperwork, she disappeared.

Samantha replied with thanks, asking if they had any more information.

After a short delay, her old colleagues from Granada replied saying they had dug as deeply as they could, investing extra effort as this was for Samantha. The only additional piece they could offer was that a few days before the girl vanished, some staff believe, but could not confirm, she had been visited by a young male. When shown the photo of her brother, they thought this was the visitor, but they were not 100 percent sure.

With Eddie pushing her hard, the vision of the teenagers' mother vivid in his mind, Samantha convinced her old workmates to prepare some handbills in Spanish with the photos of the brother and sister to be posted all around Andalusia.

Sadly, this was nearly a dead end. The only follow-up came from a village social worker not far from some of the farms where Eddie had worked. She had seen a couple of black youths, obviously standing out in rural Spain. They looked forlorn. They looked hungry. She had reached out to them and they had agreed to meet her at a café to at least get something to eat. But they had never showed up. They were not seen again.

Samantha could do little more. She asked her northern friends to let her know if there were any new developments, and she filed the dossier in the drawer of her file cabinet marked "unknown."

Eddie felt as though he had let the mother down. Samantha assured him they had done all humanly possible.

Eddie made better progress with his report to Delpro. After a little over two weeks, he had a product of which he was proud and that he could present to Delpro. He felt he had managed to get down on paper what he had discussed with Mr. Van Houtte: he was a tool. He did not offer solutions or even actions to take. He simply described the situation past and present in minute detail. Remedial measures were at the discretion of Delpro.

Eddie telephoned Lusaka to let Mr. Van Houtte know he had finished his assignment. His boss, for whatever reason, was not his charming self. He seemed truly to be in the throes of some unseen calamity. He wanted Eddie's report posthaste.

The weekend was approaching, and Samantha had a trip planned for Lusaka the following Tuesday. He had planned to accompany his wife, getting his document to Delpro while she was in meetings at AMORE.

This would not satisfy Mr. Van Houtte. Eddie needed to come now. There was almost a bitterness in his tone.

Begrudgingly, with no small dose of ire, Eddie informed Samantha he had to quickly go up to Lusaka and would, accordingly, not be accompanying her the next week as he was not sure how long he would be—adding that Mr. Van Houtte seemed to be in a foul mood.

It was Friday just at the close of business when Eddie had made it up the T-4, across Lusaka, and was entering the Delpro offices. Mr. Van Houtte was nowhere to be seen. There was, however, a note from him with his secretary. Eddie should leave his report with her and then come to the office on Monday morning for any debriefing and final payment. This only flamed Eddie's exasperation. He went to the Pamodzi, making sure the room was charged to Delpro and called Samantha. She was nearly as vexed as he. She had planned a braai for them on Sunday, complete with post barbecue amorous gymnastics to aid the digestion. She would now have to postpone everything until the next weekend. It was not fair.

Fair was one of the milder thoughts going Eddie's mind as he spent a lonely weekend in the sterile steel and glass of the hotel—ignoring the pool and the spa in favor of the solitude of his room.

Eddie's displeasure was only increased when he went to Delpro early Monday morning to find no Mr. Van Houtte, and another communiqué with his secretary. This time there was an envelope containing a curt note that, in as much as they had discussed in Blantyre, he had no questions regarding the assignment. The enclosed check represented the balance owed, reimbursement for any expenses submitted, as well as a bonus for a job well done.

Even the additional payment, which Eddie saw as outright baksheesh, did not lift his spirits. Quite to the contrary. He had lost an entire weekend. As Samantha had said, "It wasn't fair."

By the time he got out of the long queue at a busy Barclays, where he had deposited the check in their joint account, it was too late to head home. He had yet another night alone in the Pamodzi. Life definitely was not fair.

He brooded all the way down the T-4, hoping at the very least that he would cross paths with his wife for a quick embrace to stave off the frustration. What had happened? He did not know. But he made it all the way to Chipata without seeing her.

Alone again that evening, he called her from her office. Samantha was so apologetic. She too had looked forward to seeing her husband, be it only on the roadside. However, at the last minute they had had to change their itinerary, turning south at Katete on the T-6 to Mlolo, nearly to the Mozambique border, to collect a seriously wounded child they needed to transport to hospital in Lusaka. This was a thirty-mile detour, undoubtedly responsible for them not meeting on the road. With a smile in her voice, she promised to make it up to Eddie when she got home on Wednesday.

Wednesday Eddie waited anxiously. He had put fresh bouquets of flowers on the dining room table and in their bedroom. He had a bottle of wine breathing, but not as hard as he. A little before tea time he was surprised to hear the door open; he had expected Samantha only to get home after sunset. He turned to see Beatriz.

Her face was ashen. Tears streaked her cheeks. In a halting voice she tried to tell Eddie; she tried to describe what was indescribable. The police had just come to the office. At the airport junction on the T-4, a military Unimog at high speed had run a stop sign, crashing into a car and a bus stop. Two people were killed at the bus stop and three in the car—one of them was Samantha.

Eddie was destroyed.

*Book Six*

# Frozen Roots, Wilted Stems

I T was inexplicably difficult.
Eddie could never have imagined anything so difficult.

He tried to block it out, but it kept coming back. The excruciating pain of identifying Samantha's body, sending her home to Montana, leaving Chipata, and spending untold hours in airports and airplanes as if in suspended animation, tortured, in anguish, locked in his own grief, and nowhere to turn.

Her family had been stupefied. Their little girl gone, taken by a senseless accident in a place where she should never have been.

The funeral was held in Billings. Martin, aging and forgetful, tried unsuccessfully to comfort June, who was nearly always heavily sedated. Michael, now living in Salt Lake City, a sales manager for a sporting goods company and married with three children, came as did Earl and Irene. Earl leaned heavily on his cane and seemed far older than he had such a short time ago when they had separated under such happy circumstances in Harare.

It was a terrible time.

※

AMORE had had a generous accidental death policy for Samantha, as for all their employees. They had also threatened to take the Zambian Military to court. Probably a very tricky event if they could even pull it off, but it had triggered a response, an apology, and a large settlement—most of which AMORE passed on to Eddie. The irony of it was that, for the first time, Eddie had ample funds, even if he was not really rich.

This meant nothing in the absence of Samantha. It was only at Irene's vocal insistence that he had even accepted the monies. They were, as everything else, unimportant to him. Nothing mattered anymore.

The old adage—things are never so bad they can't get worse—proved to be so true.

After the funeral, Eddie returned home with his parents. It was here where his mother worked hard to persuade him to pick up the pieces and get on with his life. She encouraged him to use the resources that had so unexpectedly, if unfortunately, become available to do something that Samantha would like. It was here, as she began to see her son fight again for life, that she decided the time was suitable to tell him of death. He had, of course, seen Earl's deteriorated condition. Irene now told him his father had cancer—having only weeks, a few months at the outside, to live. As she had feared, this put her son back in a dreadful state. She only hoped all the awful things could pass and that Eddie, she with him, could get his feet back firmly on the ground.

※

Earl's funeral was six weeks after Samantha's. Eddie felt he was an empty shell—he had nothing more to give. But he could not abandon his mother. He had to be there for her. Together the two figuratively and literally leaned on each other to make it through their darkest days.

Irene found religion, going to mass daily—even though she had to drive almost ten miles to the closet church. Eddie found the void. He would stare at the ever-moving ocean, watch the waves break, feel the breakers crash into the rocks—thinking macabrely of the Unimog crashing into Samantha. The sea would hypnotize him. He hoped somehow the sea would heal him.

Eddie had kept little from their home in Chipata. There were so many in so much need. He did as he knew Samantha would have wanted—he gave all he could to the children and their families. But he had kept her favorite checked shirt that she wore, as she used to say, "While loafing about the house." As the waves pounded on and the rocks resisted, he would press her shirt to his face, inhaling her aroma, the coarse cloth absorbing his tears.

Things changed, as so often, due to the unexpected. A neighbor from up the lane came by one afternoon to see if Eddie had lost his dog. Eddie did not have a dog.

His neighbor had found a young female mixed breed cowering under his garage. If it was not from the neighborhood, he would call animal control.

Eddie knew the destiny of most entering animal control's cages—they never left. He could not let this happen. Not now. He would take care of the animal.

As best as Eddie could tell, she was a Chow-German Shepherd cross—one of nature's mongrels. She seemed to immediately bond with him, sensing the need they shared. Eddie named her Coco. She was a mutt, but he too felt he was a cur—not because he was a crossbreed, but because he was a phony. He had had so many grandiose thoughts, such high expectations. As Mr. Van Houtte has once said, "Don't fart higher than your ass." He had been pretentious. He had been arrogant. He had lost everything.

---

More for Coco than himself, Eddie began walking on the beach. Inescapably, his eyes involuntarily scanned the sand, pebbles, and stones as Coco raced ahead chasing seagulls. They were still there, the agates. After an outing, he found he would have six or eight nice stones in his pocket.

It was not only stones. Eddie began harvesting the things he had known so well during his youth that now seemed light years ago. He would get buckets of mussels that his mother would bake in the oven with cheese and wine—delicious if only his taste buds would taste. He would go to the river and spend hours with Coco dangling pieces of liver on strings to attract crawfish—managing to land quite a few despite those that Coco scared away. At the river delta, he would dig for clams. At low tides he would get piddocks—rock oysters. He would gather black and salmon berries for his mother's pies.

When the gulls would screech and circle high over the cove to the north, he would put on some cut-offs and old tennis shoes, whistle to Coco, and grab his squaw net—a unique A-shaped contraption he and his father had so often used to catch surf smelt. If the delicate little fish were really running, he could rush out into the surf, put his net down with the receding wave, and catch a bucket full of these local sardines which were ambrosia when lightly fried or pickled.

Soon he was bringing home so much food his mother had to ask him to put on the brakes. It had become, in essence, an obsession—thinking about what he could put on the table. Perhaps trying to create a distraction, trying to refocus. But he did not know. Could obsessing over fare for the kitchen help? Could anything help?

Slowly, very slowly, he felt he was not healing, he was getting used to living with the pain. The gaping hole where Samantha had been was still a gaping wound. The pain still throbbed through his body. But he was finding he could live with it. He had heard people say that great loss changed through time. The pain became less. The spirit of the deceased began to occupy the space where their corporal being had been. Their loved one continued to accompany them through their life.

He had heard this. This almost seemed to be the case of his mother who was trying to adapt, as well, to the loss of her mate. But for him, this was not happening. There was only pain, intense pain. There were not dreams, not even nightmares. There was simply excruciating pain.

※

Eddie, again with Coco as a crutch, haltingly began to expand his grasp on the world, going beyond the nearby beaches. Following old trails of his childhood, he took his dad's old GMC pickup, with his new chum seated beside him and a six-pack on the floor, and literally lost himself in the vastness of the woods. They followed aimlessly the meandering logging roads that crisscrossed the coastal mountains into the depths of their most distant arbors. They watched elk, deer, and black bear. They avoided the scattered human settlements as these, whether due to their cultivation of cannabis or just their reclusive spirit, seldom welcomed an outsider. They would find a small glen to disembark; Eddie would have a few beers while Coco chased a few squirrels or romped in a close-by stream. Eddie would stare up through the canopy of Douglas fir and incense-cedar, dancing in the breeze, the blue sky above twinkling through. The boughs would seem as though they brushed the sun. He felt he had a peephole to the heavens and he thought of Samantha, as always. This was not because he thought she was in Heaven and she could be looking down on him as he was peeping up. This was because she would know he would be having these very thoughts. In spite of all the suffering and toil she had witnessed, she was a devout believer; Heaven was real to her. When she would talk of her faith and her convictions, Eddie would lovingly chide her, asking if she also believed in the River Styx? How he now regretted anything he may have said that could have been interpreted as unkindness. He could never intentionally be unkind to her. But he could also never really control his speech—unlike her, he did not always say the right thing at the right time. She had deserved better.

He would finish his beer, not feeling some sort of emotional refreshment after having, in one way or another, communicated through his thoughts with his Samantha. He would feel as though the beer had opened the wounds and as he would get back into the truck he felt worse than when he had alighted. Coco, seeing him getting ready to leave, would jump across his lap onto the seat, wait for a pat, then satisfy herself with just being able to sit close to him—he, in his distraught state, not noticing the mud and briar she had brought with her. At home, Eddie would cry into the now very soiled checked shirt.

---

Irene moved on well before Eddie. She was ever the pragmatist. She had tried with little success to pull her son along with her. Meeting deep-rooted resistance from her scion, she mended herself. She began to go to church not only for solace, but to give solace. She volunteered long hours to help with church outreach.

These were rough years for coastal communities. Sawmills were closing, catch was falling; the time-honored community cores of forestry and fisheries were withering. People were frustrated. People were suffering. Alcoholism was increasing. Suicides were increasing. Despair was increasing.

Irene formed a close bond with Father Chris, a young Bostonian with his first parish, having a hard time making inroads into to what could be very closed coastal societies. As a member of the homegrown-sect, Irene added considerable credibility to Father Chris' words as he tried to comfort his flock.

Soon the pair were the nucleus of growing groups of community commiserators; the church providing means and even household goods to those in the most need. The commiserations, based on empathy, hopefully leading to positive problem solving. To get the work done, there were people and provisions to move about. Irene found her 1979 Chevy Malibu was really not up to the job, telling Eddie she would need to use his dad's truck from time to time.

It turned out "from time to time" was a lot. Eddie decided he really had to have, as they used to say when he was in high school, "His own wheels."

One day, when his mother was content to do God's bidding with Father Chris and her Malibu, he was winding through the tree-covered logging roads in the pickup. Reaching a barren hillock that had been clear-cut, he descended into the dell where the wooded stream bank gave way to an open pasture and a small dairy farm. Looking completely out of place, on the edge of the pasture was a 1987 moss green Ford Bronco with a "For Sale" sign on the windshield.

Eddie drove up to the farmhouse, feeling immediately an interloper. As the car crunched to a stop on the gravel patch in front of the aging home, a chunky middle-aged man in bib overalls came through the screen door and out on the porch with an enquiring, and none too friendly look. Eddie quickly said, "It's about the Bronco."

His host, although not really, bluntly quoted a price and added he had all the paper work if his really-not-wanted visitor was truly interested.

Eddie confirmed his real interest, with a strong accent on real. The man disappeared for a few moments and returned with a sullied manila folder which he handed to Eddie, offering nothing else.

Unsure of the next move, Eddie went back to his pickup; sitting inside, he studied the papers which were amazingly complete. Eddie did not even know with whom he was speaking, but he assumed from reading the pages that the vehicle had been owned by someone else—probably a family member. The Bronco had been well maintained, insured, and cared for from all the documentary evidence. He asked if he could drive the car.

His begrudging host again disappeared for a few minutes, returning with the keys.

Eddie and Coco drove over to where the Bronco was parked and, hopping in, noticed the clean interior as well as the quick spark of the engine. So far so good.

Not wishing to irritate the seller any more than his presence apparently already had, he spent about fifteen minutes driving about; this only reinforced his initial conclusion that this was a good deal.

This was an opportunity not to squander. Not wanting, so to speak, to put the car back on the auction block, he drove up to the porch where the owner was sprawling in a ramshackle swing that looked as though it would collapse at any second under his considerable mass.

Eddie signaled to the gentleman that he really wanted to buy the Bronco. Unenthusiastically, the seller informed Eddie he would hold the vehicle for one week, at which time he required full payment in cash. They shook hands—a deal was done.

That evening, over a plate of steaming mussels, Irene helped Eddie make the arrangements for the Bronco. His small bank was almost twenty miles away, so if he called ahead, it would still take a couple of days to get the cash together. Then Irene agreed to go with him to drive the pickup home. Examining her schedule with Father Chris, in five days she felt she would have the time to assist her son in getting the vehicle and starting the process of officially changing ownership.

With no major hitches, everything worked as planned. Within a fortnight Eddie and Coco were careening through narrow, shadow-drenched logging roads in the Bronco while Irene, in the GMC, the "jimmy" she called it, carried boxes of fresh vegetables, donated to the church, to some housebound members of Father Chris' congregation.

Things had, in fact, turned out well, Eddie thought. And, to his surprise, he was pleased. But this was only poking about the edges. The core remained immersed in anguish—wretchedness. With every bump and jolt of the rough tracks he followed, even if his body jerked and jounced, his mind was laser focused. He could think of nothing but his loss.

Not infrequently, he would come to a stop, having no idea where he was. His thoughts had completely left the present and flown to the past. His head ached. His heart fluttered. He knew not what to do. He was awash in pain.

※

During one such event, Eddie and Coco had roamed much farther than they had imagined. They were a long way to the north of their normal range—finding themselves on the east slopes of the coast range. Eddie had no clue where he was. He finally had to cave in; driving into the next compound he reached, he asked for directions back to the coast.

He was never sure if he had followed the directions correctly or not, but after about two hours on backroads, he came over a rise and found himself on a hill overlooking a sawmill complete with its own little community and even its own rail line.

Driving down to the village, Eddie was greeted by a sign saying, "Welcome to Vanduzer, Home of Diversified Western Forest Products." He pulled into the combination gas station and general store to get fuel for the Bronco as well as for Coco and himself. Unsolicited, as he paid for the gas and snacks, the bearded and rather disheveled storekeeper enthralled Eddie with the story of Vanduzer.

The town had been built around the railhead of a small line laid to penetrate the heart of the coastal forests during World War I to access old-growth Sitka spruce—the wood of choice for planes flying in the Allied forces. The rails had been laid between 1913 and 1914, chiefly using Chinese labor that had come into the area in the 1870s. Then, to bring the saws closer to the trees, Collier Lumber built a mill at the site in 1919. In 1920 the post office was built. A grade school was added in 1938; this enlarged six years later to include upper grades. The town grew with the sawmill. In 1947 Collier sold to Valley Timber. In 1959, Valley was bought out by Diversified. Throughout, the lumber operations followed the same general approach irrespective of manager. Most of the old-growth and approximately half of the smaller timber was sent by rail to other mills—the remainder of the cut was sawn at Vanduzer and trucked to markets in Portland and other centers. By 1970, most of the old-growth was gone. Log size had considerably reduced. Diversified tore up some of the rail line, expanded the sawmill, and processed all the logs locally. The storekeeper finished his tale, lamenting that it was increasingly hard to get people to come and work at the mill—adding it was just about as hard to keep villagers from eloping. Folks today were attracted to new ways—to shiny objects. Folks today wanted the city and the easy life. Living in a small burg nearly lost in the coastal forests did not appeal to many.

Like the folks excoriated by the backwoods merchandiser, Eddie moved on.

He had come into the valley from the east. He left on the other side of village, still heading west, aiming for the Pacific Ocean. On a knoll overlooking the mill, he stopped and got out to drink in the surroundings. The mill was located on a rather modest log pond formed by damming the small creek that drained into the valley. There was the sawmill itself—what the workers would call the head rig where the big saws of the sort his father used to sharpen would slice the trees into boards. There were the dry kilns, from this distance looking like steaming kettles, where the boards were dried. There was the planer shed where the now dry boards were polished smooth. There was the wigwam burner, looking like a massive funnel, where all the odd bits and pieces of the forest were burnt. All these parts were interwoven like something he might have concocted with his erector set as a child. From afar it created a sort of bizarre extraterrestrial silhouette steeped in wonderful aromas of sweet sawdust, pungent steam, and full-bodied woodsmoke. From this distance, it appeared he could pick the whole thing up in his hands and move it elsewhere, like a god.

After several hours, much of it on nearly impassable trails, Eddie and Coco finally exited from the western fringe of the Coast Range, regaining the coast highway eighty-five miles north of home. It was nearly midnight before they got to bed.

Over the next few days Eddie was pensive. He and Coco would walk along their favorite beach paths; he enjoyed the salt spray on his face and the gush of the tide, while she pursued shore birds and picked up pieces of driftwood. He felt he was in his comfort zone—as much comfort as he dared to anticipate. In truth, he had become comfortable with pain. He had become comfortable doing nothing. He had become comfortable expecting nothing.

He knew his sedentary state of dormancy worried his mother. She was carefully sculpting a new life for herself. She was learning how to live with horrific loss; how to adjust, but not forget. He had learned to vegetate.

It was unfair to her. He was a burden to his mother. She needed the freedom to craft her new life as it befitted her, without having to carve out space for a malingering son.

He had come back. He had, for better or worse, savored his old home ground. He had, in many ways, begun to heal. He now needed to move on.

But he was baffled. He knew he should move. However, he had no inkling of where. He had no thoughts of travel or surveying or of any of the other pieces of his former life. These were gone. He needed a new place, but a place that insulated him from himself and others. The answer came quite simply: go and work in Vanduzer.

※

Like many of his generation, he had spent his summer vacations working in the mills. Three generations of Halls before him had blazed that trail; spending their entire lives in sawmills. It was a family tradition. He certainly was able to follow in their footsteps. Physically, he was in good shape. There would be no reason he could not quickly integrate into the mill crew. And, to say Vanduzer was off the beaten path, was to put it mildly. It was a lost world. Nonetheless, it was very possibly the right place for him as a lost person.

As he had expected, his plans met with little enthusiasm from his mother. She hoped he would either go back to surveying where he had, she was sure, so much to offer, or go back to school to learn a new profession. Yet, regardless of her own wishes, she knew her son well. She realized all too well that surveying was a central part of his past life—a life that was no more. Moreover, he had had it with books or even abstract thoughts—he needed something that was physically demanding, mentally numbing, rote, and routine. She could see mill work as a suitable option, even though she was sure the future of sawmills was far from bright. She feared her son was signing on to become a dinosaur.

In the end, she gave him her blessings and helped him pack some meager necessities before he and Coco retraced their steps to Vanduzer.

Eddie had done all this having no assurances there was any job to be had; he relied solely on the storekeeper's story. Nevertheless, when he arrived at the mill offices, he found them ready to hire an able-bodied relatively young man who was willing to do anything. They even helped him get settled in a run-down mobile home on the outskirts of the village that had a small yard where Coco could run.

Being a *parvenu* at a sawmill was like being an upstart anywhere—you got the worst or the poorest paying jobs. Eddie started in clean-up, spending eight hours a day with a broom in his hand.

But it was not idle work, so there was little chance he would find himself in the devil's workshop. He had volumes of material to clean up, from sawdust and bark to planer shavings, and ash from the burner. He was always busy.

He had been pushing his big broom for almost a month before one of the old hands took him aside and started with, "Hey kid." For everything there was technique—even sweeping. After weeks of watching him make a hash of using a broom, the old-timer invested the effort in showing him how to really use a broom. With the right technique, the job was done better and more quickly. He realized he had been bungling what had appeared to be the simplest of assignments.

Nothing was as easy as it seemed.

He slowly adapted to days and nights in a sawmill camp.

During the day, he was drowned in the never-stopping cacophony of the mill: the hum of the saws, the slap of the boards, the shrill whine of the planer, the hiss of steam and hydraulics. It would change pitch and volume but, it was always there.

At night, there was the buzz of the forest. There were invariably regular gusts that caressed the trees ever-encroaching on the hamlet. The song of the woods was similar in many ways to the soothing nuzzle of the waves he felt at home—although he was no longer sure where home was. His days and nights seemed to merge into a slurry still waiting to take shape.

Eddie's improved sweeping techniques, combined with the overall high level of energy he threw into his work, caught the watchful eye of his supervisor. After several months at, what most considered, the bottom rung of the ladder, his supervisor asked him if he felt ready for a real job.

Eddie was happy to change the calluses on his hands for ailments in other parts of his body as long as they deadened the anguish in his soul. Yet, he was unsure he was up to what his boss was proposing: green chain.

Here green, freshly cut, boards were manhandled from a slow-moving chain and stacked in piles called "loads." Each load was of a prescribed size, based on the grade and length of the lumber. The planks were water-soaked heavy and they came nonstop for eight hours. It was a grueling job.

On his first day, Eddie noticed his co-workers all resembled more bears than members of *Homo sapiens*. At least six-foot tall and at the very least 250 pounds of solid muscle—all told, they were much heftier than Eddie.

Eddie had thought he was in good shape, but after a week pulling green chain, he hurt everywhere. Then, after six weeks, he was literally pulling his own weight and went home with nary a sore muscle. As his frame strengthened and hardened, it was almost as though the same happened to his heart—after all, it too was a muscle. At the mill, the only thing he could do was think of the next board coming down the chain. When he got home, the only thing he could think of was getting Coco's and his dinners and hitting the sack. There was no time for self-pity. There was no time for remembering. There was no time for what if's. It was mechanical. It was exhausting. It was what he needed.

After six months, he felt physically strong and mentally stronger. Life was not good. But it was worth living.

It seemed just as his muscles were permanently bending to the demands of pulling green chain, his supervisor again came with a query, "Would he like a different job that didn't make him old before his time?"

This seemed a convincing argument and he soon found himself getting on-the-job training in operating an edger—the machine that takes the rough planks from the head rig that still have the remnants of a tree along their margins, and slices off bark and cambium, leaving only a clean board.

In an amazingly short period of time, he was an edgerman. This was diametrically opposed to pulling chain. No forcing heavy timber to do your bidding as your body leveraged it off the moving links; here it was sitting in front of a control panel that operated a mishmash of machines that manhandled the lumber for you before it zipped into the multi-sawed edger. This was not to say he became a cyborg. He had to be on his tippy-toes—mentally and physically. Boards could easily jam if the feed mechanisms were not continuously monitored. Every so often, like at least once an hour, things messed up. The saws were not where the guidelines said they should be. He had to hit reset. A proactive action could save a very chaotic reaction.

He often felt he was a kestrel on top of a fir snag, looking for a mouse, his agate hunter eyes always on alert.

These were all simple mental challenges that probably compensated for the physical damage maneuvering heavy boards for a lifetime could wreak. They did not, however, take into consideration the scarred eardrums he would have if he became a career edgerman. The combined howl of the headrig and his own saws was horrific. His ears loudly hummed for several hours after returning home.

It was, therefore, with mixed emotions that he received a letter from Father Chris saying his mother had slipped when moving folding chairs in the vestry hall—something she should not have been doing at all. She had fallen down the three steps joining the hall to the nave, landing badly, and cracking her pelvis. Father Chris added that she had not wanted to contact her son to upset him even more, but that he, Father Chris, felt it was important that Eddie know and that he should understand his mother probably needed help.

Nothing to do. Eddie informed his supervisor he had had a family emergency, loaded up the Bronco, and was off. He and Coco were home by the next evening.

※

Eddie still had his front door key. Figuring his mother was, at the very least, unable to move about as normal, he and Coco went straight in, without ringing the doorbell, and headed to Irene's room. He expected to find the room as he had last seen it—as his father had left it. He was surprised to see some sort of jungle-gym, jerry-rigged from three-quarter-inch galvanized pipe, suspended over the bed where his mother was partially reclined, her upper back supported by pillows against the old oak headboard. She was in rapt discussion with Elsie, her chum and long-time up-the-street neighbor, who was sitting on a dining room chair at the far side of the bed.

Neither of the elderly ladies heard him enter, so he cleared his throat loudly.

The ladies started, nearly in unison; his mother recovering first, opened her arms for him to come and give her a hug. After a bit more emotion than he had anticipated, from both women, he sat on the stool in front of his mother's dresser and quickly explained Father Chris' convocation.

Irene proclaimed she was a bit vexed at the good father's, as she saw it, untoward outreach to her son. She declared he had crossed some sort of a line, which disturbed her, but the twinkle in her eye showed she was truly glad someone had found a way to get her son to her bedside.

After a few pleasantries and the briefest of reviews of Eddie's sawmill pilgrimage, Irene demonstrated unintentionally the function of the pipe frame that wrapped around the bed she had shared for so long with Earl. She grabbed a strap encircling the pipe and, with its help and a big assist from Elsie, she managed to swing her legs out of bed, whereupon here neighbor helped her stand and the two hobbled to the toilet. They shooed Eddie and Coco from the room and shuffled together like two kids in the three-legged sack race.

Eddie once again regained his old bedroom and picked up his old habits of walking about the so-well-known rocks and coves that made up the domain he had known since his youth. He and Coco would come back, tracking sand onto the back porch—he with a pocket full of agates or other treasures, she with a carefully selected piece of driftwood, her favorite toy of the moment.

Irene welcomed her son, secretly happier than she dared show at what she saw as his healing. She too, having healed emotionally as much as she could, was now healing physically. Elsie was literally the strong shoulder upon which she leaned. While trying to be tactful and grateful, Eddie's mother did not encourage her son when he offered to help her out of bed and assist her with the chores around the house. She was old school. She had her own boundaries as to how intimately a son should interact with his mother. She needed her privacy. She needed cover, too, as she was quietly ashamed of the dumb fall that had put her in this condition—it was just plain stupid.

Eddie was more of a passive presence than an active caregiver. Nevertheless, this presence energized Irene and her mending accelerated. She was getting better.

Eddie was not someone who quickly tuned into more subliminal messages (as Samantha could have attested). He was always the "go head-on guy." At first, he was almost angered by his mother's reluctance to accept his helping hand. After all, he had quit his job, at the good father's prodding, to come and do just that—be her shepherd.

Irene was unwilling, albeit she probably would not have admitted it, to sit her son down and spell things out. She felt he should be mature enough to sense things, to know things.

Tensions slowly grew like bread rising in the oven.

Ultimately Elsie, the mute spectator in this mother-son silent ballet, decided she needed to intervene to avoid a completely unnecessary clash. She explained to Eddie that his mother was just being his mother—she had her, perhaps old-fashioned, views and only wanted him to respect these. It was really quite simple.

Eddie understood. He realized abashedly he should have understood from the onset. He was not trying to assume the role of his father. His mother had strict lines that should not be crossed. He understood.

He realized now he was more of an indirect influence. He was someone sitting in the bleachers, ready when needed, but otherwise, staying on alert. Through this lens, he recognized he had a lot of free time to do more than roam the beach with Coco. What to do?

---

Before he could answer his question, the routine was interrupted by a visit from Hal coming to see how his big sister was doing. Always the enigma, Hal just showed up one day unannounced.

Deliberately, he verified that his sibling's care met his high standards and that she was on the mend; he too realizing that his sister was healing physically and emotionally, as ever, on her own terms.

His visit was much appreciated, but Irene would not allow it to interrupt her routine.

Hal, for his part, was sensitive to his sister's needs. He tried not to be too disruptive but seemed determined to stay a while. This meant he and Eddie, at the same place at the same time with, in fact, time to spare, ended up spending a good deal of this time together—on the beach, in the village, or in the local bar.

While in many ways Hal remained a shadowy figure, never really saying what he did nor where he lived, he was a good communicator—basically a good guy. He and Eddie were able to talk about many topics from the cost of gasoline to the happenings in southern Africa. Hal seemed more than well-versed on a multitude of subjects.

One afternoon, watching the breakers smash into the basalt outcrops, Eddie was recounting to Hal his stay at Vanduzer and work with Diversified Western Forest Products when Hal started chuckling. Seeing no humor in working in the middle of nowhere, Eddie asked his uncle about the source of the comedy.

Hal replied, congratulating Eddie on "keeping it in the family."
This baffled Eddie.

Hal finally felt obliged to dig deeper: Diversified Western Forest Products was a part of Delpro—Eddie was still working for the same folks who had been his boss in Spain and Zambia.

Eddie had no idea how Hal knew what he knew. But Eddie knew enough to know that Hal was nearly always spot-on. He accepted this news unquestioningly, not really knowing what to do with it.

Hal spent another week with them—always helpful. Always exuding a kind of dour cheerfulness; Eddie was unsure if the geniality was due to an innate optimism or an accepting pessimism. Then, as spontaneously as he had come, he was gone.

---

Several months after Hal's departure—weeks during which Eddie felt he was chasing his tail, following Coco's example—he was at the local grocery store for their fortnightly supplies to re-kit the household. In the process, he literally bumped heads with someone. He had been pushing his old squeaky and rusty buggy down the wide wooden-floored aisles with well-stocked shelves well over head-height on both sides. He filled his cart with the collection of items they used on a regular basis until it was nearly overflowing. At the checkout stand, with the ample girth of Mrs. Leonard behind the cash register while the equally hefty Mr. Leonard worked meticulously at his fine meats in the back of the space nearly reminiscent of a small airplane hangar, Eddie was chasing a potato that had leapt from the basket. He should have engaged his peripheral agate-hunting vision but was concentrating on stopping the runaway spud before it got under the counter. Head down, he moved almost like a football lineman at the snap of the ball, ready to scoop up his prey, but instead banging his head into an equally sound item—someone else's head.

As it turned out, the lady behind him in the checkout line, with infinitely fewer items in her charge, had dropped a coin and was in the process of picking it up when she was nearly tackled by Eddie. As each straightened up, rubbing their heads, they exchanged some sort of mumbled embarrassed witticism and resumed their grocery business.

However, they met again in front of the store as Eddie was trying to cajole his uncooperative buggy over the stony pathway to his car—his victim parked right next to the Bronco.

Eddie felt he really needed to apologize for the blow to the lady's noggin. For the first time he really looked at the person upon whom he had inflicted such indignity—at least he felt he had abused her with his boorish behavior. She was roughly his age and height—with an amber complexion and long black hair.

Eddie excused himself, saying he was sorry to have been so myopic—hoping he had not caused any continuing discomfort.

The lady was most polite, assuring him she understood and that there were no lingering effects.

Nonetheless, Eddie asked if, to make up for his transgression, could he buy her a cup of coffee across the street at the bus station, to express his regrets. She agreed.

They sat in a cramped booth in the bus station waiting room and drank weak coffee from chipped stoneware mugs. At Eddie's prodding, his bumpee introduced herself as Louisa, Lisa to her friends she added. She lived in the port city where Earl had worked, was on her way home, stopping at the grocery store for some munchies.

Eddie was not going to let her get off that easily. With experience hewn from encounters in much more challenging environments, he smoothly spurred Lisa to impart more details as the waitress warmed their mugs. Seemingly with some reluctance, she was brought into a more detailed discussion that illuminated the fact that she was a true local—a member of the Siuslaw Tribe. She was, in fact, the chief counsel to the Confederated Tribes, at that very moment, coming from the county seat where she had been initiating a court case regarding encroachment on tribal lands.

As the coffee cooled, she seemed to warm at least to her subject if not to the surroundings. She informed Eddie, sure that he was unaware, that where they sat had once been part of the Coast Reservation, established in 1855 by President Pierce, covering a 120-mile band of seaboard from Cape Lookout to the Siltcoos River. The government had forcefully relocated tribes from all along the shoreline to this reservation in order to confiscate traditional tribal lands considered as having higher value. Then, realizing this reservation too was of considerable worth, in 1887 the government awarded 160 acres to each tribal household, selling all that was remaining to non-natives. Here, on these very shores, there had been another Trail of Tears as indigenous people were herded like cattle, moved to the reservation on foot and unrobed along the inhospitable strand, many falling by the wayside, never to see another spring. Those who had not been killed by the white man's diseases or avarice had managed to move through time as the marginalized and the forgotten.

Lisa concluded her monologue as though she were addressing the magistrate, adding great emotion and ending with her hopes the tribe could one day, if offered just a level playing field, reestablish itself as an important contributor to the local economy and society.

Eddie was impressed. Not so much impressed with the passion Lisa showed, although this was indeed impressive, but more with the great block of things of which he had no prior knowledge. Eddie was in truth now aware that he had been unaware—at least, heretofore he had not connected the dots.

Although he had had a close friendship with Willy and a cursory fifth-grade-introduction into indigenous people of his village, and while he had roamed the Crow lands and other Native American territories, he had not really grasped, until absorbing Lisa's descant, the full complexity and injustice of affairs.

Despite having been born and raised in the center of what had been the Coast Reservation, Eddie had, before now, never even heard the name mentioned. He had never considered the displacement and depravation of ancient cultures that once occupied this same space. He had seen the shell mounds, there was one very near his home. He knew the natives had made these with the heaps of byproducts when feasting on mussels, clams, and oysters. But he had never thought any further. He had never wondered where those shellfish-eaters had gone. Why they had gone? He simply saw a bunch of shellfish shells as a bunch of shellfish shells.

This was a new prism with which to look back. This was nearly an epiphany. Was this due to Lisa's eloquence? Was this, in fact, due more to Samantha's tireless efforts to sensitize him to the struggles of others? Was this due to seeing the plight of refugees in Spain and tea workers in Malawi? It was probably, Eddie thought, a result of the combined experiences of his life, heavily influenced by Samantha's ethos.

His revelry was burst like a carnival balloon popping—pierced not by a pin, but by the sharp jingling of a spoon in Lisa's empty coffee mug—his new acquaintance irritatingly swirling the unfilled Stoneware across the Formica as she waited for her companion to return from wherever he had gone.

With a sheepish smile, Eddie asked if she'd like a refill and a piece of pie—the bus stop rumored to have an excellent recipe for strawberry-rhubarb.

Even though she looked perplexed, Lisa accepted the offer. The pie met their expectations, offsetting the drab coffee, and offering a chance for Eddie to restore some sort of link with Lisa.

He chose the present over the past, asking her about the case she was preparing. She described a scenario where a large investment firm was asserting that a swath of tribal timber belonged to them. Instantly, Eddie had a flashback to the work he had done in Malawi. When Lisa finished outlining the situation, Eddie noted how ironic it was that he had previously dealt with just such a case.

For the first time, her green eyes seemed to twinkle as, in lawyerly fashion, she quizzed Eddie about his earlier work.

It seemed as though there had been a breakthrough of sorts. What had started as an accidental slamming of heads had transformed into putting two heads together to assess a common issue. An issue Eddie now wanted to pick up and to which he planned to devote his time and energy, having ample supplies of both.

The parallels between Eddie's previous work and the case in point were clear: some big outside financial entity wanted to encroach on the lands of an established group. It was nothing special. It was just that the clashing of crowns leading to Eddie's common-sense approach made Lisa feel as though she now had a clearer picture of a way forward.

By the time the pie was just crumbs and the coffee a cold slurry in the bottom of their mugs, Lisa and Eddie had formed some sort of still-to-be-defined bond. For her, it was an immediate action to compensate for the uncertainty of any legal intervention. For him, it was a dusting off of his old skills and a project to occupy his all-too-idle time. As the southbound Greyhound pulled in with a plume of exhaust, Lisa and Eddie left their narrow booth, stretching like old dogs warming themselves in the sun, and they promised to get back in touch soon.

※

It was nearly two weeks later, one of those bleak days that sort of compressed time and made Eddie wonder what he would do throughout the long night, when Lisa called. She invited him for a cup of coffee in Cushman in three days' time. At a point when even going to the dentist was a welcome distraction, Eddie jumped at the offer—trying to keep all excitement out of his voice as he replied in a forced monotone.

He knew Cushman, it was on a secondary road that branched east from the main coastal highway, following the river to the top of the Coast Range and then descending into the valley on the eastern slopes. On the appointed day, he and Coco headed south, crossing Cape Verde, driving alongside the wide sandy beaches and dunes that preceded the Siuslaw River, and then at the port town, heading inland along the river's north shore.

Just east of town, near Skunk Hollow, nestled under a cloud of steam and enveloped in a bubble of commotion was the sawmill where his father had spent most of his adult life. The site announced itself to the whole world on a slab cut out of the butt of a massive spruce, now carved with a logo depicting an old cross-cut saw and the name "Dodson Industries." From the road, he could easily see the mill's hurly-burly, almost hearing the sharp howl of the emery wheels as they precisely sharpened the great head-rig saws under his father's watchful eye.

Pushing thoughts of the past out to make room for today, he continued east, following the river. Both shores were lined with raft upon raft of logs secured to dauphins—a trio of pilings lashed together to ensure whatever they held stayed put, regardless of how it was pulled by tides and currents. Surrounded by boom-sticks, their fresh-out-of-the-woods color a golden brown, the fodder awaiting the mill's saws looked like loaves of French bread fresh out of the oven. Between these tawny pontoons, as the tide was rising, fishing boats headed downriver to the port and then the sea. Most were mid-sized salmon trawlers, their owners living upriver where they probably worked in the woods during offseason. There was, however, the occasional crabber and purse seiner. There were also the small bucking-bronco boats that laboriously hauled the logs to the mill—struggling with scores of trunks, each seemingly wanting to go its own way. Men sometimes jumped from these powerful river workhorses and ran across the flotilla, their calked boots keeping them upright on the rolling and slippery surface as they used their long pike poles to unjam logs and get the whole mass moving in concert. All told, the river was a busy place.

Another two miles down the road and he was at Cushman, a tiny hamlet including all the essentials: a small marina for sport boats, a campground for seasonal salmon sport fishermen, a trailer park for more long-term residents, and a gas station-*cum*-general store. He found Lisa at a small table in the rear of the store, seated in front of a picture window with a wonderful view of the river, drinking, as he was to find out, bland coffee that rivaled that of the bus station for lack of taste.

Once he was seated, she went headlong into her subject. They were sitting between the north and south forks of the river, an area surrounded by national forest, but an area that was traditional tribal land. Even after the carving up of native people's lands and the ultimate subdivision in 1887, the tribe had retained significant acreage of old-growth timber in this stretch between the two rivers. A belt with exceptionally large stands of cedar and even some spruce made it very valuable land indeed. The price of cedar shakes and shingles alone made these forests a goldmine.

Just two miles up the road from the gas station was Wedson Canyon, a small island of public land in a space occupied by tribal and non-native landowners. Simpson Investments, a highly diversified and somewhat nebulous Denver-based company, claimed large areas adjacent to the canyon as their land based on a century-old title they claim to have uncovered. She had initiated an injunction against Simpson pending a thorough examination of the deeds to the lands in question. Following their exchanges at the bus station, Lisa felt Eddie had the right tools to help her in her efforts—was he interested?

Yes.

---

This was what Eddie needed—and now he even realized himself that he needed this. Not just making it day to day, but something to really get him motivated—maybe even obsessed. Living, not surviving. A new assignment in which to dive and attack full bore. A strong magnet to pull his attention away from everywhere else and focus it on the work at hand.

His mother was getting better and needed him even less. Therefore, he decided to leave all the memories and emotions of home and rent a small place closer to the shores of the Siuslaw. He wanted to be near enough to the port town to have easy access to the amenities, but far enough away where he had his own space and maybe lower rent. He decided to look on the other side of the harbor, away from the city center. Finally, he expanded his search further south and found a cabin on Woahink Lake just five miles from the town's main shopping center.

The cabin looked like it had been built out of Lincoln Logs with a great green beard as the roof was supporting a record crop of moss and lichen. There were two rooms, one for sleeping and the other for everything else. It was located down a rutted track that often required four-wheel drive, on an isolated arm of the lake—it was perfect for his immediate needs. And it was cheap.

He and Coco had little to move other than the duffel bag that had remained in the corner of his bedroom, unopened, since he returned from Vanduzer. The cabin was furnished including rudimentary kitchen items so there was no lag time before he immersed himself in his new task.

He followed much the same strategy as he had in Thyolo. However, somewhat to his surprise, he found the historical data less readily available. This was likely due, at least in part, to the fact that the ownership issues in Malawi relied on documents that were only decades old while the present situation referred to papers that dated back a century or more—to a time when the local government, such as it was, was not noted for leaving a sizable paper trail.

He initially circumscribed a target that was a twenty-mile radius from the canyon. From the county, state, and private suppliers, he secured topo maps of this area. He was able to access aerial photos—something he had not had in Malawi—from the Forest Service to overlay the maps and then transcribe all visible signs of human activity. He then went to the county assessor's office and ferreted out all the available data on his target—again overlaying this with his baseline maps. Finally, he went to the state library and the county historical museum to read all he could about the area and its people.

Written records went back to 1846 when the first white settlers arrived. These expanded five years later when, named after the territory's first governor, the county was formally established. However, the forests between the forks of the Siuslaw were remote even today, historical information very sketchy at best. The biggest single block of background records came from 1887 when the 160-acre holdings were distributed and duly noted.

After nearly six weeks, Eddie figured he had accumulated about all that was readily accessible—more buried information only worth going after on a case-by-case basis. He then spent a fortnight in his Bronco with Coco, ground-truthing all that he had managed to synthesize into a working cartographer's model of the target.

At the beginning he would meet Lisa in a small coffeeshop on the bayfront every ten days or so for an update. His cabin had no phone so at each meeting, they would set the date for the next. At first, these were perfunctory, business-like appraisals of the status of Eddie's (volunteer, as he stressed) work. They migrated rather quickly, though, into more amicable chats that covered all the major points of the work at hand, but that also began cracking open the door into each's private lives. Quite simply, they enjoyed each other's company.

About two months in, Lisa invited Eddie to the celebration of Sovereignty Restoration Day, a prominent tribal festivity. This, Eddie found, was a lively event. He was introduced to and shook hands with far more people than he would ever be able to remember. But he did enjoy himself. He happily noted that, like the people he had encountered in foreign lands, the Siuslaw were welcoming and friendly. He contrasted this with his time in Vanduzer where he scarcely knew anyone well and could count no real friendships at the time of his departure. As he thought about the different scenes, he had to honestly admit that Lisa's presence undoubtedly made the current occasion more sociable in many ways.

Over the coming months, Lisa and Eddie attended numerous tribal affairs including a clam dig, a bazar of products produced by tribal weavers, and an exposition of beading work done by tribal members. At each stage, he felt he was slightly more accepted and that he understood slightly better the cultural context within which he was working. At each step, he felt a little closer to Lisa.

It was probably inevitable, but as he built a database for the lands surrounding Wedson Canyon, Eddie also, practically unconsciously at first, built a relationship with Lisa. Most of the people who saw them having coffee, walking near the boat basin, driving in the woods, or attending tribal events already assumed they were sleeping together, and eventually they did.

After discussing progress on Eddie's assignment one afternoon, Lisa proposed they go to the Rhododendron Festival, scheduled the following weekend, right next to the port. Having heard there would be abundant samples of local food and drink, Eddie was a ready and willing participant. After a pleasant afternoon listening to a local jazz band and munching on fried clams, all adorned with the ever-present rhododendron blooms, Lisa asked Eddie if he could drop her off as her car was in the garage.

Eddie knew Lisa lived north of town but had never known exactly where. He was pleasantly surprised when she guided him to Heceta Beach and a neat slate gray shake-sided two-story home at the corner of Third Street and Joshua Lane. Her house was just on the margins of the dunes and the wide sandy beach and, ironically, right next to the border of the Siuslaw National Forest.

Whether part of a plan or not, he never knew, but he gladly accepted when Lisa invited him in. He also gladly accepted the large portion of an excellent dry red wine as they sat on the couch and watched the waves run across the long sandy expanses not far from the house's big plate-glass windows. With the second glass, Lisa offered a tour of the domicile, leading him upstairs to a large master bedroom with a deck overlooking the beach. They watched the setting sun turn the wave crests fuchsia just briefly before finding themselves entwined on Lisa's sleigh bed.

At the onset, Eddie felt lost, guilty, insecure. He had not been close to a woman since Samantha's death. He felt clumsy. He felt ashamed. He felt he was violating the love he had for Samantha.

Yet, Lisa's patient tenderness and his own hormones overcame both concerns of ineptitude and propriety and soon he was overtaken by the moment—lifted on waves of desire that seemed stronger than the breakers he could hear in the distance. A page was turned.

Naturally, he imagined, after that Saturday evening of the Rododendron Festival, his relationship with Lisa evolved dramatically—an evolution for which he was deeply grateful.

They still maintained their same professional arrangements. Still meeting at the coffeehouse. Still carefully and thoroughly addressing the job at hand. However, at least twice a week they would dine together, either in one of their homes or in a local restaurant. They would then spend the evening together enthralled in passion, discovering each other's bodies—each other's sensitivities.

Eddie felt whole for the first time since leaving Zambia.

Lisa was also very satisfied, not only emotionally and physically, but nearly spiritually as she had been without a soulmate for months. Her last relationship had ended in misery and feelings of dejection when she discovered the law professor whom she felt she loved was married and had no intent of leaving his wife—his tryst with his former student only an amusing sideline to a rocketing professional career. Lisa really liked Eddie. She liked him as a person. She liked him as a friend. She liked him as a lover. And she liked the fact that he was generating ample material for her to prepare the legal framework she needed to combat Simpson Investments.

Her misgivings, which she always seemed to fabricate even if not originally present, were how to separate the private and the professional. She truly wanted an emotional attachment, a partner. But she was concerned the professional and private were so intermixed that each dimension could be adversely affected. She was concerned, and she was concerned that she was concerned. What was the problem? Was this simply an aversion to commitment? Was she scarred, the scar tissue preventing her from seeing the positive, accentuating the negative?

Despite all the questioning, she convinced herself to take things a day at a time. This could be a great flame that burned out quickly. This could also be something more permanent. This could be for keeps. But her training had shown her not to be preemptive. The jury was not even out—the presentations were still being made.

Lisa and Eddie entered into a period with new norms—or maybe with no norms. They were a team. They were working together on a common problem. They were, in fact, working together on two problems simultaneously: how to prevent Simpson Investments from stealing tribal lands and how to interact as team members.

They were very different. They were different races. And they were mixed in more than race. Eddie was spontaneous and pragmatic. Lisa was pensive and methodical. Eddie was an extrovert. Lisa was an introvert. Eddie liked strawberry. Lisa liked chocolate. From ice cream to mannerisms, they were different. Did this matter?

---

Regardless of time spent in contemplation, the work advanced. After four months Eddie had joined many pieces of the puzzle. He had produced a first draft of a multitiered dossier including detailed maps of the target along with a historical description of each structure. Although there was still some outstanding work and more detail required, the current set of documents unquestionably bolstered the tribe's case. Eddie was unable to identify any legal rights relating to Simpson Investments.

With this information, Lisa was able to be proactive, initiating a case against Simpson Investments, not only attesting they fraudulently claimed tribal lands, but demanding damages. While Lisa had been thinking about the impact of her emotional flame, she had equally lit a legal flame when she launched the case.

The reaction from Simpson Investments was rapid and sharp. They accused Lisa of libel and the tribe of unlawful expropriation of private lands. Concurrently with the legal filing, Simpson Investments applied to the state forestry department for a permit to haul timber from their lands—harvesting to begin within the next nine months.

Lisa was able to revise the existing injunction to cover any short-term removal of timber, thereby temporarily stopping Simpson Investments. As expected, her adversary demanded an expedited court hearing. The game was on.

Eddie had documented in the target area a number of large tracts that were still deeded to the tribe in spite of the 1887 move to subdivide tribal lands. Eleven tribal heads of household had been allocated 160 acres each. Of the total surface that Eddie had calculated as being 2,750 acres, therefore, 1,760 acres had been allotted to individual families, 890 acres was still under tribal management and one 100-acre plot had been assigned to a non-native owner in 1889. Nowhere on his map of the original situation did Simpson Investments even appear.

Any lack of clarity in terms of ownership, accordingly, did not come from the initial partition of the forested lands. Things became somewhat complicated as one examined the plots over the nearly hundred years that followed. Among the eleven families, only three remained with the same parcels they had received in 1887. Of the other eight, death and emigration led to lands being sold. In nearly all cases the parcels sold were purchased by members of the original eleven families—the lands staying within the community. One of the founding families bought the 640 acres from four relocated or departed members, while another purchased 320 acres from a pair of now absent owners. The thing was, Eddie could still not track down the current status of the remaining two families that had slipped away. To make things more curious, if not worrisome, the two missing families had been apportioned lands near Wedson Canyon.

Eddie knew the names of the two original families receiving the allotments: Bowden and Macnab. He also knew the exact boundaries of these two allocations. Unfortunately, the crumbling homesteads were now abandoned. No one seemed to know if the plots had been sold. So far, Eddie could find no registration of sales. No one knew what had happened to the Bowden's and the Macnab's. Times changed and some things simply were forgotten.

It was pretty much the same story for the one non-native land owner. There were Bureau of Indian Affairs documents recording the sale of one hundred acres to Emil Höltz with an address in the port. The transaction was well reported including the references for the survey markers. This homestead, like the Bowden's and the Macnab's, was located along Bernhardt Creek, the stream running through the Wedson Canyon site. Furthermore, like the other two locales, this homestead was apparently abandoned.

There were still critical holes in the picture—holes that Lisa highlighted at each of their business meetings. She had her fair share of anxiety over the case in hand. It was never easy going up against big business—especially big business, or what she assumed to be big business, that was so cloaked in the shadows.

The challenges of the assignment aside, Eddie and Lisa, each with their own (quite divergent) worries about developing a strong romantic bond with a colleague, attempted to draw some sort of a line between work and play. When the sun set, and they were together, they closed their files and concentrated on each other. They talked about current affairs. They appreciated good food and good wine. They watched the sea. They made love. They did not talk about Simpson Investments, Wedson Canyon, or even tribal or ethnic matters.

Simpson Investments succeeded in getting an early date for a pretrial hearing. Lisa was ill at ease. She had a lot, but she did not think she had enough. Eddie sensed the nervous tension rising.

After a particularly passionate interlude, before they dropped off to sleep in each other's arms, Eddie assured her he would find out about the Bowden's and the Macnab's—Emil Höltz too.

※

Eddie hoped he could keep his promise. Once again, for the umpteenth time, he and Coco were driving upriver to try and dig deeper, explore more, discover more about the three perplexing places.

As they had done so many times before, they turned north off the Siuslaw River Road and followed Bernhardt Creek. They cut the western corner of the Wedson Canyon public lands, continuing to follow the creek to the northwest. Leaving the commons, they crossed over a cattle guard traversing a small nearly dry tributary of the creek. For the first time, Eddie noticed a rusty sheet of metal that had partially fallen between the guard's rails. He stopped the Bronco, let Coco have a run, and pulled the legal-pad-size sheet from the goo under the guard. Through the maroon patina, the words were plainly visible, "No Trespassing! Arrow Head Timber and Cattle Company."

Beyond the cattle guard, the road continued on to part of the tribal lands and to the three baffling homesteads—all effectively neighbors. Each of the trio of problematic plots had had a house and some outbuildings. These were now derelict and unusable as, over the years, they had been overtaken by brambles and bracken—some even sporting small saplings.

Eddie and Coco walked around all these dilapidated structures looking for any clue, finding nothing. The debris looked like so many ownerless places scattered around the Coast Range. Buildings in shambles, no livestock in the dell, no gardens, no managed woodlots, no nothing. To most, simply a decaying sign of times gone by.

Eddie returned home as frustrated as ever.

Their next meeting at the coffeeshop took place after the pretrial hearing. Lisa and Eddie compared notes. Simpson Investments had had to stipulate specifically to which lands they were claiming ownership. Although they maintained they would only be able to present the full documentation at a later date, it came as no surprise that the objects of their endeavor were the Bowden, Macnab, and Höltz homesteads.

Lisa said the judge had ruled, based on some still-to-be-validated historical records Simpson Investments claimed to be bills of sale, there was a *prima facia* case and a trial date had been set for six months. The next week depositions would begin, and Lisa hoped she would be able to examine closely the papers presented by the opposition—items that had so far not been shared.

Eddie mentioned in passing the Arrow Head Timber and Cattle Company sign. While he had seen this just as a curious piece of forest flotsam, Lisa found it to be quite possibly much more. She proposed a division of tasks. After the first depositions, she was going to go to Denver to see what she could find out about Simpson Investments. If she was able to make headway, she would likely continue to D.C. to try and delve more deeply into the company, its history, and its associates. She suggested Eddie start at the state capital and then continue to the Historical Society and try to discover more about Arrow Head Timber and Cattle Company.

While the strategy made sense, Eddie was a trifle taken aback. Lisa had not mentioned any plans for travel, for separation. Had these truly just popped up or was this emblematic of her need for complete separation of public and private lives? Was not this the type of subject couples discussed?

Eddie realized this was not the time nor place to open such potentially emotional discourse. He just filed things away, hoping never to think of them again.

---

While Lisa flew to Denver International, Eddie left Coco with his mother and drove to the capital to probe as completely as possible the archives dealing with the lands of the Confederated Tribes bordering the Siuslaw, the distribution of lands between 1887 and 1892, and the story of Arrow Head Timber and Cattle Company. His search took him to a variety of agencies including state lands, forestry, tribal affairs, agriculture as well as branches of the Attorney General's office. He had copies of the first grants to all three obscure titleholders—he now needed to use these as springboards to leap through almost a hundred years during which these lands had been farmed, the timber harvested, families raised, and then the estates apparently cast aside.

As with all his duties, he took it a step at a time. Year by year, he began to pore over all the material he could muster. It was tedious and tiring work, the one big plus was that people were generally helpful, guiding him patiently through the halls of bureaucracy—not unlike when he first started hunting for facts and figures in Spain.

He would work two or three hours, then take a long walk and come back for round two—some days he would manage three rounds. He had a hotel room near the city center, thankfully paid by the Confederation, so he was never too far from a cozy bed when he became overloaded.

When he reached 1930, he began to see signs that he might be on the right path. In that year, soundly in the Great Depression, housing starts had fallen by nearly two-thirds, the lumber industry was in shambles, coastal communities were seeing unemployment increase by a third, and folks were moving out of town. It seemed at this time, although there were some records of timber sales in the early years of the twentieth century, by 1925 there was no further sign of any economic activity at the Bowden, Macnab, or Höltz homesteads. Then in 1931 he found the first reference to Arrow Head Timber and Cattle Company. Following this lead, he was finally able to determine that this enterprise had been established that year by Wilson

Bernard, one of the original eleven recipients of the lands in question. Apparently, it was a formal legal name Bernard had given to his primary 160-acre allowance.

From what Eddie could glean, Bernard had been advised that the Depression would force governments to help those suffering—this starting in 1929 with the establishment of the American Association of Public Welfare Officials. Bernard's tip seemingly indicated that the upcoming welfare programs would, to stimulate additional needed economic growth, be purchasing raw materials, together with lumber and beef, from smallholders in some of the worst-affected areas—the Pacific Coast included. This came right on the heels of the 1923 reduction in size of the county, whereby the new local government had considerably fewer public resources and was attempting to build partnerships with private operators. Bernard was doing all he could to set the stage for becoming a profitable entrepreneur at a time of extreme financial crisis.

Eddie was eventually able to follow this thread far enough to discover that it was Bernard who had procured the lands of Bowden, Macnab, and Höltz, when these families had left looking for greater opportunities than those offered by a reliance on a crashing lumber market and no other jobs to be had. Bernard had hoped to become a hub, supplying whatever materials he could to well-funded government programs ostensibly helping those in need of help. He was not too far off the mark. The Works Projects Administration, WPA, did invest lots of money to try and mitigate the terrible effects of the Great Depression. However, the WPA did not start until 1935 and, at least along the Pacific Coast, it had no need of beef or timber. It built bridges and highways that could not be supplied by Arrow Head Timber and Cattle Company. In fact, Arrow Head Timber and Cattle Company never did any business of any kind—a reason it was so hard to trace.

Wilson Bernard died in 1942, six months after his spouse. They had one surviving son, Jacob, living in Chicago. Jacob had inherited the 580 acres that had been Arrow Head Timber and Cattle Company but had not set foot west of the Rockies since his father's funeral.

It had taken nearly two weeks, hours and hours of concentrated effort, but Eddie now had a much more complete picture of at least part of the puzzle. Lisa would now need to fill in some pieces.

※

Lisa arrived at Denver International as the airport was under major renovations. Everything was a jumble including her own commission. She had to learn a whole lot about Simpson Investments without setting off any alarms and while garnering information that was reliable enough to use in court. In every way, she was far away from her comfort zone and felt the disconnect as almost a physical ache in her back.

She had reached out to a classmate who was now working in a local firm that specialized in environmental law. Alan indicated he was happy to help but was honestly not sure how much help he could be—he was pretty specialized and did not get out much.

Regardless of these doubts, Alan had already been most helpful. He had booked a room for her for a week, made some key appointments, and agreed to meet her at the airport. She spied him in the gaggle of welcomers as she left baggage claim—the whole airport feeling as tousled as her hair. Disheveled or not, she gave him a big hug and clung tightly to his arm as he shepherded her to the parking lot.

Within forty-eight hours, hair still tousled, but nerves now well-tuned like the strings of a fine violin, she was burrowing into a pile of dossiers. Some had been arranged by Alan and others she had secured based on her first meetings with possible parties of interest. At one point, Alan asked her why she had bothered to contact him because she did nothing but stay cloistered in her room going over files unless she was attending a meeting that produced even more files.

This really was the case. She looked into the Chamber of Commerce, the Better Business Bureau, the Business Development Center Network, the Secretary of State's office, the headquarters of major Colorado banks, Colorado Bankers and Lenders Association, Government Finance Association, and even ACLU. It was like moving a camera to different vantage points to take multiple pictures of the same subject, moving around until you had made a full circle and at which time you had a pretty good image of what the subject looked like from every angle.

There was only so much to see, but what she now saw looked totally different from what she had seen when sitting across from Simpson Investments in the courtroom. What might have appeared as a couple of hapless guys who innocently found something on a scavenger hunt, on closer inspection proved to be a finely-honed group of ambulance chasers who made their fortune by securing real estate where there were questions as to the ownership—real estate where there were holes in the papertrail such that someone could raise enough doubt and offer sufficient alternative hypotheses whereby they themselves could claim ownership. This was generally the pettifogger's tactic in the case of inheritance, sudden death, missing persons, or administrative negligence where the required details to emphatically declare the title were not apparent. In these cases of fray or fog, Simpson Investments could miraculously appear with some strange tale that made them a candidate and, if successful, the future owner. And it did often work. The number of properties officially owned by Simpson Investments was impressive. Additionally, there were a number of Lisa's contacts who surmised that for each property listed on their public register, there were three behind the veil.

The conclusion was obvious. Simpson Investments had not simply stumbled across the Siuslaw properties. They had painstakingly studied the terrain in many states looking for situations where deeds were prepared years ago and the owners effectively vanished from the picture. Simpson Investments then showed up with some papers, true or false, that indicated by some bizarre and twisted channel, the original owner had sold the real estate to them. They took hard-to-prove (or disprove) stories to court to try and legally divert ownership—ownership of not just anywhere, but high-value lands. Lisa noted that from the available census of Simpson Investments' holdings, roughly forty percent were choice industrial or residential real estate while sixty percent were undeveloped lands with significant mineral, forest, or water resources.

Lisa thought of how Eddie had explained to her about being an agate hunter. Well, while he was collecting a pocket full of stones, Simpson Investments was collecting a basket full of prized lands.

At the end of the week, she had a fairly good portrayal of Simpson Investments—of who they were, what they did, and how they did it. But that was qualified. She knew who they were in Denver and how the Denver crew worked when they went after real estate. She did not know who was really behind Simpson Investments. All enquiries in Colorado seemed to lead to the safe, and she felt unjustified, conclusion that Simpson Investments was a Denver company that was involved in land transactions across the West—full stop.

Lisa had a feeling, and at this point it was nothing more reliable than a feeling, that Simpson Investments was only one head of a Medusa. She felt quite sure there were mirror-image crews in other parts of the country doing the same thing. Her inner feelings went even further, somehow convinced this was only part of a wider web of profiteers. To try and peel back the layers to see the bigger picture, as she had thought from the onset, she would need to go to Washington, D.C.

Planning on this eventuality, and again relying on old classmates to help prepare the ground, she had contacted Sandra who had a mid-level position at the Antitrust Division in the Department of Justice. At the very least, Sandy was well-situated to be able to provide some very useful deep background on Simpson Investments.

She flew into National and, as had happened with Alan, Sandy met her upon arrival, whisked her away to a downtown hotel, chaperoned her to an initial block of meetings, and then remained on standby if needed. Lisa, buoyed by her momentum from Denver, focused initially on the Antitrust Division where Sandy was an excellent conduit, while examining other branches of the DOJ, and making appointments at a wide range of other agencies and institutions from the Bureau of Indian Affairs and other Department of Interior offices to the Departments of Commerce and Agriculture.

Here the question was no longer: How does Simpson Investments operate? It was: Who runs Simpson Investments—who really is the boss?

It was relatively easy if not quick to run down the key management of Simpson Investments as cited in the collection of documents she had amassed in Denver. Without exception, all these high-level executives appeared in decision and oversight positions within other important corporate structures. Simpson Investments was definitely not an island. However, the interrelationships within these commercial labyrinths, that, according to Sandy, had some of the trappings of cartels, were hard to tease out. These were people who took great pains to hide their actions—pulling back the curtain was not an easy nor rapid task. And, Lisa concluded, at this stage of the case, it was not necessary to reveal all the higher echelons. She had more than enough to work on herself. She had also piqued the interest of Sandy who would at least continue some level of investigation over the coming months to see how far she could look into the enigmatic world of Simpson Investments.

After a week, Lisa felt she had spent her time well, but that her efforts would now be best spent back on the West Coast. However, before flying off and following the sun, she had a final dinner with Sandy to lay plans they hoped would entrap the bad guys. Following Sandy's suggestion as to the best spots, Lisa treated at the Occidental Grill and Seafood on Pennsylvania Avenue—a treat for which she was really ill-prepared, at least financially, and was glad she had an expense account.

Probably understandably so, any restaurant that had welcomed Churchill, Patton, FDR, JFK, MacArthur, Teddy Roosevelt, JD Rockefeller, and even John Philip Sousa could not be cheap. Any restaurant that, since being built in 1906, sat less than 2,500 feet (as a bird flies) away from the White House was not just for anyone. If Sandy and she were to feel the ambiance of the center of power, this would seem to be the place; and it would not be cheap. But it would be a good place to plan and to say goodbye.

By the time Lisa opened her door at the corner of Third Street and Joshua Lane, she was bone tired. Nonetheless, the first thing she had to do was get in touch with Eddie. Since he had no phone, the best she could do would be to take a quick nap and then drive to his cabin at dinner time hoping he was eating in.

He was. But their reunion was a little anxious at first. There had been a separation. Was there a cooling of ardor? Was there a reassessment of emotional ties?

Here the answers appeared to be no. As soon as the initial brief awkward moment passed, they were entangled around each other in Eddie's wobbly bed—hoping the aging pallet would not collapse under their amorous dynamism.

It was not until breakfast that the two compared notes in terms of their recent investigations. While they did the dishes, she washed, and he wiped, they complimented themselves on jobs well done. Like a work of jurisprudence (which for her it was), Lisa encapsulated their recent progress. They now knew Simpson Investments' actions here were part of a wider game plan. They also knew all the land in question had legally been folded into the long-dormant Arrow Head Timber and Cattle Company. All this could be proven in court. It was beginning to look like Simpson Investments had no case.

The one loose end was Jacob Bernard. Eddie had what he thought was a current address in Chicago, but he had waited until discussing with Lisa before engaging the heir to the ossified Arrow Head Timber and Cattle Company. While she began working on transposing their disclosures into documents acceptable to the court, he would reach out to Jacob—traveling to Chicago if need be.

After a sudsy shower together, Lisa went to her offices at the Confederation to consult with staff as to how best to package the material they would need to prepare for court. She gave her key to Eddie who went to Heceta Beach and set up shop next to her telephone, his notes scattered about the dining table. He was prepared for a long stint and a sore ear in order to make contact with Jacob. He was totally unprepared to reach him on his first try.

Jacob was reticent at first, unsure what sort of scam Eddie was perpetrating. However, Eddie was able to fill in enough personal details about his father, about their homestead near the Siuslaw, and about Arrow Head Timber and Cattle Company that Jacob accepted Eddie's enquiries on face value and, still with some reluctance, provided more background.

He had left the family home in the forest in 1939 at the end of the Great Depression. It was clear that in spite of all the promises, in spite of all the bravado, his father's plans to make it rich (in a time of poverty) were futile. They were, and they would always be poor Native American folk living in the woods. He was twenty-three and he wanted more. He took the train to Chicago and was able to get a job as a shoe salesman at Sears, Roebuck, & Company at their store on Lawrence Avenue. He worked hard, went to night school, and was able to move up in the company that was at that time becoming one of the major retailers in the country. He became a regional manager and, in 1973, with the opening of Sears Tower, he moved into the skyscraper as a senior member of a core marketing team. But he had now been retired for several years. His wife of thirty years had died a decade earlier of cancer, their son was at a military base in Georgia and their daughter was doing something or other in California. He then added as almost an afterthought, he was an avid Bulls fan and a volunteer at his local YMCA. He kept busy, and he never thought of returning to the woods.

Eddie felt he had an adequate understanding of the owner of Arrow Head Timber and Cattle Company—an attribute he never sought and apparently never wanted. But it was what it was, and he needed to secure Jacob's position in relation to the case at hand.

Eddie did his best to summarize the situation, emphasizing that some out-of-state crooks were trying to steal Jacob's land. This of course impacted the tribe and the tribe was taking the necessary action, but they needed Jacob's help. Eddie hoped they could send Jacob an affidavit that he would sign stating he was the owner of the 580 acres that had been Arrow Head Timber and Cattle Company. Furthermore, they hoped that if they needed Jacob to testify, he would come to the West Coast—they would pay his expenses.

Jacob insisted he wanted to help. Even if he had turned a page, or so he felt, he could not deny, would not want to deny, his roots. When all was said and done, he loved his parents—they had done all they could for him and he did truly want to reciprocate. However, he was worried. He was not concerned at all about contradicting the thieves who were plotting to take his land. He was concerned about back taxes. It had been nearly half a century. What exposure did he have?

Eddie assured Jacob he understood. These plots were, after all, part of tribal lands. He did not anticipate any problems, but he would pursue this specific issue and make sure that the tribal officials addressed it when they wrote him to send the affidavit.

Jacob still seemed shaky on his commitment to dig up the past and open doors he had kept shut for so long. Nonetheless, he offered his personal guarantee to Eddie that he would do whatever was necessary. This was all that could be expected for the moment.

That evening, sipping margaritas, huddled on Lisa's deck against the cool wind, Lisa and Eddie recapped. The documents would go off to Jacob the next day, the full packet of material should be compiled, double-checked, and ready for trial within a month.

Lisa was ill-at-ease in regard to doing any forecasting. In principle, it was open-and-shut. The area in question could all be traced to Jacob, they had copies of all the deeds and related documents. At the highest level of analysis, Simpson Investments did not even enter into the discussion—they were quite simply wrong. Whether intentionally or erroneously, Simpson Investments had been giving incorrect information to the court. The lands along Bernhardt Creek belonged to the tribe and its members.

If Simpson Investments refused to accept reality, she would describe to the court what kind of business they really were, how their main business was cheating people, and how they had no credibility. Sandy was still probing and by the time of trial she should have even more facts incriminating Simpson Investments, albeit they themselves were not on trial and hence could not be found culpable.

All this fine strategizing notwithstanding, Lisa wanted Eddie to stay on the job. Once the court case had begun, once she had received all her opponent's material, she needed Eddie to root out the background to any records Simpson Investments were using to show any claim to ownership. Who was maintaining they had sold tribal lands to these outsiders? Just as Lisa and Eddie now knew, Simpson Industries likely knew their claims were patently untrue. Nonetheless, someone was pushing the case forward—doubling down on the falsehoods. Eddie needed to try and determine who this was and then verify that the parcels in question were exactly those of the Bowden, Macnab and Höltz homesteads.

※

Things unfolded pretty much as Lisa had foreseen. Although they had what she considered an air-tight case with Jacob's affidavit and all the supporting historical paperwork. Simpson Investments insisted they had the true title and that all that was being offered by the tribe was make-believe—the tribe, in truth (according to Simpson Investments), acting out of ethnic hegemony—opposed to Simpson Investments purely because they were not Native Americans.

As Eddie had predicted after boring into the opponent's documentation, Simpson Investments twisted the truth, taking the position that it had been Emil Höltz who had purchased the Bowden and Macnab properties. They further maintained that, before his death in 1938, he had sold the full 580 acres to Fir Products, a sawmill eighteen miles upriver that intended to harvest the timber from the Bernhardt Creek plots. Fir Products never managed to harvest the timber before it closed three years ago. Simpson Investments had then purchased the land from the defunct sawmill's creditors. Finally, and unfortunately, they submitted, Mr. Höltz was dead as were those from Fir Products who had been involved in the transaction. Simpson Investments could call no witnesses but could offer as defense exhibits clear, if rather old and well-worn, documentation attesting to their claims.

After lots of homework, Eddie had been able to provide Lisa with enough iron-clad information to perforate the Simpson Investments story. Over an eighteen-month period covering 1931 and 1932, Wilson Bernard purchased the Bowden, Macnab, and Höltz properties as verified by the deeds and bills of sale on record. In August 1932, Emil Höltz purchased a gas station in Weed, California. He passed away in Weed in 1937. He could not have sold land to Simpson Investments in 1938. Moreover, there was no record at county or state levels of any purchases by Fir Products in the area in question—such a corporate transaction certainly being noted in public records if it ever occurred.

Lisa provided the final blow when, using documents provided by Sandy, she was able to show that Simpson Investments had attempted exactly the same tactics twice in the past three years: once in Idaho and once in New Mexico. Both of these cases had been thrown out of court.

There was no real choice; Simpson Investments lost.

※

Lisa was happy with the outcome. Yet, to Eddie's surprise, she was not ecstatic. She saw the judicial victory as a sign of foreboding—a symptom of weaknesses heretofore unappreciated.

Simpson Investments were ruthless modern-day rustlers raiding unsuspecting landowners. But they were not alone. There was a growing number of individuals and companies wanting to pilfer other's riches—doing so in the full light of day, in an open courtroom. Lisa realized the best protection against such unscrupulous persons was truth.

The tribe needed to bolster its defenses. They needed to ensure all the yellowed and dog-eared documentation upon which they based their lifestyles and livelihoods was, indeed, factual and up-to-date. They needed current and verifiable records of their assets. To the extent these were lacking, they needed to be provided.

She convinced Eddie he had a part to play—validating and documenting all the tribal lands. It was no small undertaking. It would be costly in terms of time and finances. While the tribe could cover much of the cost, as part of the payment he extracted, he moved into the house at the corner of Third Street and Joshua Lane.

*Book Seven*

# Full Circle

Eddie spent a total of five more years working for the Confederated Tribes. During this period, he and Lisa maintained their bimodal existence—keeping some sort of curtain between their professional and private lives since they effectively worked for the same employer.

This blind, more show than substance, probably did little to affect their work and it certainly did not hamper their lives away from work. Their personal lives bloomed. They established a deep and loving relationship—Lisa knowing she could not replace Samantha and not trying to—Eddie finally realizing there was enough love to go around—keeping that that he had for Samantha, while still having enough to share with Lisa.

Irene and Lisa became good friends—the three of them spending a weekend together every other month. There was a normalcy he had missed. He felt as though his own roots were struggling to penetrate parched and hardened ground.

Then, seemingly as always, the unknown became the known. Lisa had continued her relationship with Sandy, still pursuing the shadowy figures behind Simpson Investments—expanding the scope to study a wider panoply of antitrust issues that affected the tribe in particular and native people in general.

Eddie used to kid Lisa that it was always the tribe first. She did not disagree. She would always add something about the greater good, but ultimately, as she knew he knew, native people had been marginalized for so long there was really no honest way to reset the equation.

Now, this commitment to a higher goal had been recognized. Partially with Sandy's prodding, DOJ offered Lisa a special post linked to the Bureau Indian Affairs but housed in the Antitrust Division. It was a rare opportunity. It was a chance that could not be overlooked. Lisa postponed accepting until she had spoken with Eddie, but she knew immediately that she could not let this one go.

Eddie was stoic. It was the prevailing fatalism that had infected his view of his life; uncertainty was to be his benchmark. He understood Lisa's position. Intellectually, he even agreed that she should not forego such an extraordinary moment. However, just as clearly as he saw this as part of Lisa's trajectory, he understood he would not survive D.C.

Lisa too, when she scraped off the emotion and should'a been's, recognized this as that fateful fork in the path in the woods. She and Eddie would have to take different directions.

They tried to plaster over the probable shock that would likely end their relationship by agreeing to meet every three months to keep the flame burning. Both knew the chances were slim. But they wanted to do all they could.

Eddie moved home and Lisa moved east.

※

Coco was getting along in years, but she still loved to run on the beach. She and Eddie spent hours among her favorite haunts as they readapted to a home that was not a cabin on the lakeshore nor a modern residence at Heceta Beach—rather an old-fashioned and just plain old house that was Eddie's birthplace—carrying all the baggage of the fountainhead.

Irene too was getting along in years. She was brave. She was strong. But she was old. Nevertheless, she was completely mended and basically of good health and sound mind. She filled her days with her faith and by puttering around the house that had become her realm. She dusted, she cleaned, she rearranged. Although she had fewer commissions with Father Chris (who was still around), she was always busy.

Elsie had died suddenly the previous year and Eddie found he could now be of some more practical assistance to his mother—running errands, buying groceries, taking care of the outside of the house and the garden. Yet, by and large, Irene was still the chief and she knew exactly how she wanted things done.

This time, however, Eddie was not awash in waves of doubt and blame. He had established himself through his work with the Confederated Tribes, receiving a nearly continuous series of requests from which he could pick and choose jobs that seemed more interesting or were simply the right place at the right time.

Eddie was soon to be a quinquagenarian. While he did feel as though he had accumulated a half century's worth of knowledge or wisdom, he definitely felt as though he had accumulated fifty years' worth of knocks and bruises. He was still in denial, but he was growing old.

If he felt he continued to lack wisdom, he had, nonetheless, developed a keen sense of *savior faire*. He could carefully peruse the requests for his time, selecting just enough to keep him busy and adequately financed so as not to have to worry (his bank account, if not overflowing, still more than generous). He made sure he had time every day for his two girls: Irene and Coco.

He also kept time for his third girl, Lisa—although this was not on a daily basis. They did talk on the phone several times a week and were making all efforts to meet every few months (this, at times, binging painful remembrances of rendezvous with Samantha all those years ago). This hit-or-miss schedule was not easy for either of them, but it was most rewarding, both emotionally and romantically.

They would try to find a location that was affordable and accessible; places like Kansas City, Tulsa, or Albuquerque. Each for their own reasons chose to not include Denver in their list of reunion locales.

These were hot and passionate meetings. They often stayed in the hotel room for forty-eight hours straight—and, could not describe the room later. These were impassioned, really lascivious, reunions. There was no discussion about families, tribes, or even the weather. There was only steamy flesh and salacious acts.

But it seemed to be working.

Somehow their long-distance relationship was still holding together—although they both were too worried about its durability to examine it too closely. They happily applied the old adage, "if it ain't broke, don't fix it."

Eddie successfully orchestrated this juggling act for three years—evidently all parties accommodated and content with the status quo. Then, once again, as Eddie was accustomed, the unthought-of became reality.

Eddie had been splitting some alder for the fireplace when a large sliver, more of a sharpened chunk really, flew off the piece on the chopping block and, in the most unlikely of happenstances, like a spear shaft, it hit Irene who was coming back in the house after putting a rug on the clothesline to air. Although Irene insisted Eddie just pull it out as though it were a tiny sliver in her finger, her son was more than a little reluctant to try and fish a three-inch shard from her thigh. He finally convinced her, or more truthfully, forced her, to go with him to the emergency room.

This was both a good and a bad decision. The wood was close enough to an artery that it required an hour in the operating room under local anesthetic to get it out. Given the tissue damage and the possibility of future bleeding, Irene was admitted for observations—in theory only overnight.

To everyone's great surprise, as opposed to her lively self, Irene was lackadaisical when Eddie came to take her home the next morning. The doctor extended the observation period by another day and the next day Irene was worse. Over the next twenty-four hours her health declined while the doctors and nurses did what they could to find the cause. They diagnosed drug-resistant pneumococcal pneumonia. They assured Eddie they could treat it with Penicillin G—his mother would be fine in a few weeks. She was old, but she was tough, and she would be fine.

Irene died two days later.

Eddie blamed himself for insisting on going to the hospital. To add to the burden, even with his grief, even with his shock, a hospital administrator pulled him aside and told him, because he needed to know, that he should have no thoughts about suing the hospital. He waved a sheaf of papers under Eddie's nose, saying that, on admission, Irene had agreed not to hold the hospital responsible for any illness or health issues contracted while on its premises. The administrator wrapped up saying he was sorry for Eddie's loss, but was sure he would not see him again.

Eddie had obviously known his mother was truly getting along in years. He had thought about her passing but had always pushed these thoughts to the dark recesses of his mind. She was there and she had always been there. But now she was no longer there and he blamed himself.

He wanted to run away.

The only place he could go was to Lisa.

He boarded Coco and flew to D.C. She met him at National and took him to her apartment. This time there was no steamy flesh or salacious acts—there were only tears.

Three days later he was back on a westbound plane. Lisa had managed to lessen his self-blame, if not his grief. While he still harbored some guilt—not only for the hospitalization but for the wood chopping itself—maybe he had done something wrong—he realized that the elderly routinely go into the hospital. If it had not been this, it likely would have been something else. Drug-resistant infections were becoming notorious in hospitals. This was just bad luck. But the bad luck should definitely be tempered with the good luck that Irene had led a long and loved life.

There was a lot to do. Eddie needed to go home.

Lisa promised to look into the legal ramifications if Eddie ever decided to pursue the issue; she also promised to come to see him within a month.

When Eddie had picked up Coco and was pulling into the driveway, he found Hal sitting on the backdoor stoop.

There was a lot to do, and Hal was a big help. A week after Irene was once again resting next to her beloved Earl, they had attended to most of the big items. He was the sole offspring—things were generally straightforward.

Eddie and Hal were sitting in the living room of what was now his house, sipping beers and marveling at the crash of the waves. Eddie was getting used to this, the latest page of his book of life. He realized he knew virtually nothing about the man seated across from him. Nothing.

Eddie thought, *If not now, when?* The direct path seemed best. He simply asked Hal what he did.

Hal took a deep swallow of beer and stared at the open beam ceiling. Slowly his eyes met Eddie's and parried with his own question, recalling Eddie's probable surprise and inquisitiveness when Hal had flagged the little-known fact that Diversified Western Forest Products was a part of Delpro.

Eddie nodded his affirmation but remained silent.

Hal apparently felt he owed his nephew a fuller explanation. He confirmed that what he had told Eddie when they were in South Luangwa was true, but just the wrapping paper—the real story was complex and much of it confidential. He then spent the next twenty minutes going into great detail about his work. Eddie was enthralled.

Hal, unbeknownst even to his sister, had been a CIA agent and was still affiliated with the agency. As an active agent, he had been assigned to stations across southern Asia, Latin America, and Europe. He had been involved in combating human trafficking, smuggling, and piracy. He painted vivid verbal pictures that made Eddie think of chasing the buccaneers across the Caribbean in the seventeenth century.

After a long stint with the agency, during which he worked in more than a dozen world capitals, his effectiveness and drive came to the attention of several experts on international criminality who were trying to identify the role of US businesses in illicit global markets. They wanted him to agree to a secondment to a clandestine interagency task force operating out of the Division of Enforcement of the Security and Exchange Commission. He agreed.

He was still doing task force work. In fact, when he had come to visit Eddie in Zambia, he had been on the job. In Jo'burg he had told his sister he was going to take VARIG to Rio, but after they separated, he took South African Airlines back to Lilongwe. It was not an accident that he knew that Diversified Western Forest Products was a part of Delpro. Delpro had been one of the prime targets of the task force for years.

Hal's voice then softened to almost a whisper as he told Eddie there was more. This was not simply about bad business practices. These people were criminals. They were dangerous. He was really sorry to open old wounds, but he felt Delpro was involved in Samantha's death. It was not an accident. He could not prove it—not yet. But he was sure there was a connection. Somehow Samantha posed a threat and they had dealt with her as they dealt with all threats—quickly and without pity.

Delpro, Hal emphasized softly but sternly, needed to be dealt with.

Hal wrapped up his story with a childhood remembrance. He recounted to Eddie that when he, Hal, had been young, really young, his mother (Eddie's grandmother) had put him in the bathtub with all his toys while she filled the basin with hot water to scrub off the day's accumulation of grime. While Hal played with his tugboat and yellow duck, while the hot water filled the tub, his mother left to answer the doorbell. The water started to get really hot. Hal's chest started to burn. Hal knew he had to stop the heat. He began by throwing his toys at the incoming flow—hoping somehow this would ease his growing discomfort. Fortunately, his mother returned, turned off the faucet, and set about her scrubbing, never knowing her boy had just passed through a period of fear and near panic. She never knew, Hal never forgot.

The possibly obtuse moral Hal was trying to impart on his young nephew was that, to get the job done, you needed the right tools. Throwing a rubber tugboat at a spigot will not do it. Simply turning the handle will. He and Eddie needed to have the patience to do things in the right way that would yield the needed results.

The rapture with which Hal's story held Eddie ruptured like an overripe tomato with the mention of Samantha and her death. Eddie was ill-prepared to re-open a door he had closed so tightly. This was not at all what he had intended. This was not where the discussion should go. This was desecrating hallowed ground.

※

Hal let things sink in. He did not want to add to Eddie's load as he adjusted to losing his mother and now to new issues surrounding Samantha's death. He stayed another week on the beach, as the affairs of funerals and estates abated, he and his nephew spent more time walking along the rocky shores—Eddie, as always, looking for agates.

When Hal left, he knew he would be back, just not when.

Eddie nearly fell back into the hole where he had played hide-and-seek with reality. He began looking at his life as wasted. He would have been better simply following his father through the gates of Dodson Industries. At least then, having spent his lifetime in his familial territory, he would be part of a wider community and not, as now, just a loner who had lost the last living person who loved him—intentionally keeping Lisa out of the equation. In his musings, he did not include Hal. He really did not think of Hal. Perhaps he had pushed him back into the same box—the same mental mothball-filled trunk—where he had encased all his misery and madness when Samantha died. Perhaps he honestly did not feel he knew Hal well enough to even be angry with him.

Again, and he felt he had done this far too often, Eddie adjusted to a new set of surroundings. He did less work and spent more time with the surf ringing in his ears to stifle the other ringing that was, he imagined, the tolling of the bell of time.

He spent two years in some sort of self-induced mental bondage. He would periodically meet Lisa. These encounters were both physically and emotionally soothing. Lisa tried. She tried very hard. But he often seemed lost in the fog.

Then, Coco died. This all but pushed him over the edge. The void was closing in.

There was Lisa, but she was too far away. There were no longer any hooks on which to hold, hooks to keep from falling into depression and despair.

Six weeks later, a bleak evening when Eddie had shifted from beer to whiskey, there was a knock at the door. To his complete consternation it was Lisa.

Lisa gave him a big hug, but said nothing, only handing him a rather heavy basket. He opened it right there on the porch. It was a puppy: Coco II.

Lisa spent a week while all three of them bonded.

Over the coming months, Coco II grew and grew totally attached to Eddie. They spent all their time together. Eddie took pains to do more, to introduce her to more. He even took on more jobs—ostensibly so his pup could see more of the country.

Soon thereafter, one day Hal was back sitting on the stoop when Eddie returned from a job on the northern coast.

Hal was not checking up on his nephew. He had come with a proposition. If Eddie had had time to think it over, and if Eddie wanted to do something about Samantha's death, then Hal had a plan.

Consciously, Eddie felt he had relegated any thoughts of Samantha— her death or her life—to the tightly locked compartment in a hidden alcove of his mind. However, he now realized that subconsciously he had been pondering the possibilities that Samantha's death had not been an accident. He had to admit; it was certainly possible. But why?

The realization of this uncertainty, the offer from Hal of taking some sort of action, these lobbied his brain to accept his uncle's proposal. Logic and common sense told him to get Hal a beer and then politely decline his suggestion. Logic and common sense did not win out.

✳

Hal's proposal was more a pre-proposal. He invited Eddie to meet with him in D.C. in two months' time.

As it turned out, Hal had an assignment on the West Coast and thought it opportune to see if Eddie was up to a new and very different challenge. Now, with Hal's coaching, Eddie could prepare for a lengthy absence from the shores he knew so well—preparing to enter into a totally new reality.

It all sounded overly theatrical to Eddie. But he was ready for something new and he followed his uncle's advice. He arranged for neighbors to look after the house. He put his Bronco on blocks. He prepaid his utilities. And, he arranged with Lisa to take care of Coco II—the puppy accompanying Eddie to Washington, D.C.

This seemed to Eddie like one of those rare defining moments that you vaguely see coming, but that are mostly visible in the rearview mirror. Not unlike the proverbial fork in the path in the woods he had recently experienced with Lisa, this had all the trappings of a pivotal moment.

Looking into that rearview mirror, Eddie realized there had been a number of these junctures. If that terribly failed date in eighth grade with the infatuating Barbara Ward had not been such a crash-and-burn failure, their relationship might have flowered to the point where they had settled in the shadow of Cape Verde, he working at Dodson Industries to this day to pay for his three kids' studies. Then, of course, if he had not left college, he might be living in some west coast megalopolis with his equally career-orientated spouse, commuting to a fancy white-collar job, and taking equally fancy vacations skiing in the Alps or bronzing on the Riviera Maya in Yucatán. Obviously, if that horrific day had not happened near Lusaka Airport, he and Samantha would likely still be living somewhere with refugees—certainly not here.

There could have been many permutations. There were many could'a been's.

But now, as he and Coco II exited National Airport and took a taxi to Lisa's, there was only the present—a present largely unknown and even frightening. Yet, one that could not be ignored.

When Lisa and Eddie had rekindled their flame, and reinforced their joint rapport with Coco II, they sat down, with a glass of good wine, to review the here and now.

Lisa, as hostess, went first. She highlighted work she was doing jointly with DOJ's Antitrust Division and the Bureau of Indian Affairs. It all boiled down to trying to identify and define illicit business activities that entwined major American corporations and Native American groups and their investments. There was a tangle of pathways to follow, but Lisa was looking most at possible use of casinos in laundering large sums of offshore monies coming from prostitution, the drug trade, pirating pharmaceuticals, human trafficking, and a variety of other criminal acts.

This all set the backdrop perfectly for Eddie's explanation, or better put, further explanation of why he was sitting in her living room. Lisa had met Hal, but never had any real contact with him. Eddie, therefore, tried to fill in the blanks for his enigmatic Uncle Hal.

Not wanting to breech any confidences, Eddie provided an attenuated sketch, basically recounting how Hal worked with a clandestine group through the SEC to examine very much the same topics Lisa was pursuing. The overlap seemed uncanny—raising questions as to why there was not more collaborative effort.

Not wanting to get ahead of himself, all too aware he knew far less than perhaps he should—or than Hal wanted—Eddie dodged the majority of the subject, suggesting Hal, Lisa, and he have dinner to discuss things more thoroughly.

Given the possible delicacy of their planned discussions, Lisa proposed they dine in her functional but not too luxurious apartment. She added; these arrangements would keep Coco II company.

After spending another day with Lisa, Eddie called Hal to let him know he was now lodged in their nation's capital, inviting him for dinner at Lisa's at his earliest convenience.

Hal's busy schedule gratefully provided Eddie with three unencumbered (and uninhibited) days to spend with Lisa before their dinner date. Despite Eddie's visit, Lisa still had a job to do. Her apartment was on Second Place NW, near Fort Solcum Park (for which Coco II was most thankful), while her office was at Two Constitution Square on N Street—about a half-hour commute one-way including a bus trip and almost a mile on foot. She often left early and got home late—making time to celebrate their reunion limited—these limitations extending to little time to have any meaningful exchanges with Hal.

With these constraints in mind, with Lisa's blessing, for the dinner with Hal, Eddie arranged for take-away from a nearby well-reputed Korean restaurant—thinking the piquant kimchee could spice up the discourse—cutting out externalities to get right to the core of the issue.

Eddie's wishes were granted. It seemed as though Hal came primed to have frank and serious discussions. They sat in a relaxed tension scattered around Lisa's living room as though to establish a personal territory, a sort of home turf, that would somehow insulate them from the gravity of the discussions upon which they were embarking. Each in his or her own corner, they sipped highballs that seemed never to empty, presenting tales that in any other setting would appear as pure fiction.

Hal started. Delpro had been the object of his work for years. In fact, Delpro was so big (Mr. Smith's words came back to Eddie; Delpro was, "very, very big and very, very diversified. They were everywhere.") there was an entire team engaged in the investigation—Hal only covering the agricultural part of the large and varied Delpro portfolio. His portion of the case encompassed farming, forestry, and fishing. He was still building his case, but he had solid information that Delpro was involved in human trafficking and smuggling agricultural products—chiefly from Africa to Europe. He also had strong evidence that Delpro was actively embroiled in misappropriating land for agricultural use—citing, to Lisa and Eddie's surprise, the recently uncovered intelligence that Simpson Investments was part of Delpro. As if there were not already enough serious concerns, Hal added that his probe, partially undertaken when he was with Eddie in southern Africa, had unearthed explicit proof that Delpro clandestinely grew crops like cassava, maize, and yams on unrecorded farms across Africa—drying and pulverizing the harvests into a sort of unrecognizable organic powder. The powder was then exported in large quantities to Spain where they had equally clandestine factories that converted these powders into totally worthless pharmaceuticals that were then shipped back to Africa as well as to Latin America and Asia where regulations were weak and they could make immense profits from selling useless, even dangerous medications.

Hal wound up by confirming why he had invited Eddie to come east, so they could go over his files to try and ascertain if Samantha's death had been a result of Delpro's nefarious workings in Zambia, Malawi, or Mozambique—countries where the Chipata AMORE office had activities. Up to now, he had no idea if anything he was doing was related to Lisa other than the now closed case with Simpson Investments.

Right on cue, Lisa picked up the discussion without a pause. However, her intervention was much crisper and concise. Albeit she was completely surprised at the hidden links to Delpro regarding the attempt to defraud the Confederated Tribes of their land and timber along the Siuslaw, she was certainly aware of mega international corporations that made millions through a multiplicity of illegitimate acts—her own work linked to DOJ also looking into these malefactors, but these efforts still really only in the start-up phase. Thus, Hal, with a significantly longer track record, could be a real resource for her own efforts. Affirming her willingness to get involved in any way, she conceded she was uncertain as to the best next steps.

Hal was ready for the question. He restated his long-time association with this subject and, regardless of all the months and years invested, the fact was that this remained a work in progress—nevertheless, a high priority for US law enforcement. Big conglomerates were obscure entities that could disappear and reappear in a different form on very short order. They were multi-tiered with iron-clad firewalls between different levels and compartments. Lower echelons could be picked off as their misdeeds surfaced, but the senior coordination remained cloaked in layers of stealth and crews of highly paid lawyers. While all knew, to be really effective, the head had to be severed, pragmatically, removing low hanging fruit was seen as success.

For better or worse, this was the approach. There were no clear pathways to the top. At the ground level, there were scores of flags identifying wrongful corporate-sponsored activities covering a wide range of crimes. Yet, no ties to the higher-ups.

Hal hoped, with Eddie's help, he could burrow deeper—climb higher. But this was still to be seen. Until he had some real meaningful and incontrovertible evidence leading to management levels, he did not feel there were any tangible things DOJ, and by default Lisa, could do. Most of their present focus was offshore and outside the realms of US justice. If they could excavate deeply buried threads leading back to these shores, there would be a lot of work for DOJ. Until then, in Hal's view, this was a time for preparation, but not concerted joint action.

That seemed a suitable note upon which to pivot and change the subject to more pedestrian topics that would go better with dinner.

Hal left after dessert, having made a rendezvous with Eddie at a downtown café in two days' time. Lisa and Eddie then carried their wine glasses to the bedroom for more after-dinner sweets.

Eddie and Hal met as arranged. Hal started off with a cautioning: if Eddie chose to go ahead, it would require considerable effort, time, and sacrifice—possibly even danger. Hal would cover all the expenses, but Eddie's role would be totally unofficial—if things took a turn for the worse, Hal might have to disavow any contact with Eddie other than that of uncle and nephew.

Eddie, thinking all the histrionics might have been more appropriate for a youngster of half his nearly three score of decades, repeated to Hal that he was all in. If there was any chance at all that Samantha's death was anything but a gruesome accident, Eddie wanted to know. And, he wanted justice.

So it was, they went ahead.

Hal first set up a calendar whereby he and Eddie would meet three times a week. To start with, Eddie would provide Hal with all the documents he had at his disposal from his work for Delpro in Spain, Malawi, or Zambia. Hal would cross-reference these with his archives and then get a full set of documents back to Eddie for his review. They would spend the next six to eight weeks analyzing what they could. Then they would retrace Eddie's steps, going back to his old job sites.

The deskwork only reinforced what they already knew: Delpro did a lot of things in a lot of places and took a lot of advantage of (most would say, abused) its partners, collaborators, and employees. Moreover, there were a lot of holes in the data. There were a lot of questions. Many facts were buried beneath layers and layers of incongruous reporting.

One of the surprising features that surfaced was that Delpro had no real history. Unlike most present-day big businesses that have followed an often-lengthy trajectory, Delpro seemed to just appear out of nothingness: one day it was not there and the next it was. There had not been slow and steady growth. There had not been incrementally increasing investment and expansion. Delpro seemed to have shot up overnight around the world. The company's officially cited holdings had not changed appreciably over the past thirty years. It had started big and it had stayed big.

Hal indicated this type of corporate growth curve was indicative of massive mergers and buyouts done covertly over a long period. The "new" company would sprout as though fresh growth in the spring, when it was, in fact, a large number of repurposed old businesses. He had staff trying to dig out these old building blocks in the hopes Delpro's present areas of interest reflected the specializations of those past enterprises that had been folded into the new conglomerate. This could show how far the tentacles had reached. But it was a long and uncertain process.

It was also a frustrating process—especially for Eddie. He wanted action.

Hal and his team went meticulously through all of Eddie's work in Spain and Africa. They made copies, they took notes, they asked Eddie questions, they referred to the latest detailed satellite maps. They needed to distill everything down to a few key points upon which Eddie and Hal could focus when they traveled.

Finally, after hours and hours of tedium, the first drops began to come from the still. His trail with Delpro had left some valuable crumbs. And, in many cases, his gut feelings had been spot on, regardless of how these sentiments had had to be packaged to be acceptable to Delpro itself.

Early results from Eddie's precise work in Spain, when he visited what he had called his "Phase One" farms with Alberto, while Maria Helena and David dug into the archives of these operations, had concluded things were fuzzy and elusive. Adding new information and putting all into today's context, Eddie and his team had glimpsed what had been and still were lies hidden in plain sight. Hal's crew had accumulated good evidence, strengthened by Eddie's work, that the disparity between the recorded size and scope and what Eddie had found on the ground was not an accidental error from one side or the other—it was the desired situation. Delpro paid big bucks to keep this make-believe error on the books. These farms were more than farms. The proffered miscalculations were intentional, creating the smokescreen Delpro wanted to envelop its activities.

The same applied to the Delpro farm in Zambia near the Msandile River, and probably other farms across that country—soy and maize were not the only products. With Delpro, there was always the overt and the covert.

Eddie's examinations, ironically at Delpro's behest, had exposed an unintentional window—one they now undoubtedly wanted closed, but one that Hal hoped to use to his advantage.

While these dual visible and invisible functions did not seem to apply to Eddie's work in Malawi, he did not only have contacts within Delpro in that country, but he had perhaps inadvertently cracked open a long-protected door on human trafficking.

Hal's associates had followed up on Samantha's efforts to find the children of the Thyolo lady. They had pursued the reports from the AMORE office in Granada, they had been able to ferret out more clues about the teenagers. Additionally, they had connected a number of dots and reached a yet-to-be-confirmed conclusion that Delpro was recruiting people, chiefly in the vicinities of the Mlolo and Chilengo border posts. In truth, they were nearly kidnapping refugees from the Mozambican war—snaring them with lies and then literally shipping them to Spain with false promises of finding Eden.

With strong emphasis on a disclaimer that this was still conjecture, Hal told Eddie he felt Samantha's pursuit of the Thyolo children and her growing interactions with refugees from Mozambique was seen as a threat by Delpro. With her growing concerns and Eddie's (from Delpro's perspective) closeness to veiled Delpro activities, it did not seem like too much of a leap of faith to imagine that Delpro management wanted these two nuisances, Samantha and Eddie, out of the picture. Believing rightly that Eddie was there because of Samantha—remove one and both are gone.

Most of this was still a working hypothesis. But it was more than enough to begin building a case. It was time to go to the next level.

※

It was hard. Hal explained to Eddie that the retracing of his steps was not expected to be an effort to reopen the doors through which he had already walked. This was not to be a revisitation of the past, but a snapshot of the present. The intent was simply to update, possibly expand the situation. Visit the Spanish sites to verify if they still had the same status. If possible, chat informally with Maria Helena, David, or Alberto to glean any morsels that may have not already been included in the existing documentation. Then, moving on to Zambia and Malawi, doing very much the same thing—trying to fill in any possible blanks that would help them move forward with their case against Delpro. With Eddie as the sounding board, their task was to refresh their significant body of information.

Eddie wanted action. Hal understood. However, this was not the time for the type of action Eddie wanted. This was working on the soft side.

Once they had renewed their data—revised their case—they would focus on individual Delpro actions. Hal's team would then get their own people inside questionable farms in Spain. They would follow specific shipments from Beira to Rabat—the routing Hal's associates thought Delpro used for trafficking people and pharmaceutical products into Spain. They would delve deeply into specific legal authorizations and approvals issued for specific investments. In short, they would try and turn the places Eddie had worked inside out. But, as always, it was a slow and methodical process.

Eddie was not happy. Eddie was shocked. Eddie was bewildered.

Eddie was ready to rush into the nearest Delpro office and wreak vengeance for Samantha. Eddie was ready to scream at the moon.

Hal could not console him.

With great patience, and no small dose of hard love, Lisa was able to refocus Eddie's now hyperactive thoughts. In spite of himself, he was finally able to see that there were no quick fixes. This was insidious. This was a major threat. They had not even begun looking into the questions of culpability at other times when Eddie's life had, unknowingly, met Delpro—times at Vanduzer or Wedson Canyon. And still, even with the tiny slice of the massive Delpro pie that was in their sights, they had been able to validate vast corruption, colossal wrongdoing. Eddie subconsciously knew, but consciously resisted, that he had to be resigned to enduring painful, even lethargic, processes to reach the end he knew he had to achieve.

Beyond this stellar effort of building, with Lisa's help, a bridge from the past to the future, Eddie tried to spend some relaxing—even romantic time with his now long-time partner. The two of them, with Coco II, walked about the enclaves of the capital, seeing things never seen before and appreciating anew long-cherished sights.

They had quiet moments when the world seemed welcoming and no larger than the four walls of Lisa's bedroom. But, inevitably, the uglier side of human behavior would reappear—they, somehow, trying to float above the waters draining into the sewer of greed and abuse.

As the discoveries by Hal's team evolved, more evidence surfaced of the truly mammoth scale of misconduct.

Lisa was, officially, so far just a spectator. None of Hal's speculations were sufficient at this stage to formally engage the DOJ. Nonetheless, both she and Hal were sure that as the investigation progressed, there would definitely be a role for DOJ once justice was sought. For the moment, it was necessary to keep their heads below the parapet. Their results had to be incontrovertible. They were, however, creeping to the the point of public confrontation with Delpro.

※

Hal and Eddie flew to Granada via Madrid. Eddie was unsure how he would handle this trip back to his past. Following Lisa's advice, he tried to internally frame this as a journey to places he had never been before. After all, it had been quite some time. Things had changed. He should focus on the newness.

This enforced naiveté was facilitated by the structure Hal had imposed on their mission: Eddie was solely the conduit. He was to verify the farm sites—nothing more. He was to introduce Hal or his on-the-ground colleagues to his old co-workers and mates—nothing more. Eddie was the hood ornament, the whole car behind doing the work.

This meant Eddie's time was needed for a few days early on at each stopover—then Hal took over. Again, with Lisa's help, Eddie had devised a tactic to prevent him from spending most of each stay despondent and alone in his hotel room. At the Duty Free, while in transit at the Madrid-Barajas Airport, he bought a top-of-the-line SLR camera. With Lisa's guidance before leaving D.C., they had selected worthy places Eddie had not visited in his other life. This time, he would visit these spots and prepare a spray of photos for each site. Perhaps just busy work—but it would keep him busy.

Hal had pre-planned a series of convoluted tactics for each visit, requiring the least amount of direct personal intervention (always preferring the shadows to the spotlight), relying mostly on the skills of his Spanish crew to actually unearth the morsels they were seeking. The strategy was assembled one piece at a time.

Eddie had no good contacts for his former team members but was able to trace Maria Helena through a cousin to whom she had introduced him and who ran a restaurant not far from their old apartment. Eddie presented Hal as his uncle, using the story that Hal was a university economics professor and the lady accompanying him (actually one of Hal's top researchers) was one of his graduate students. The lady was doing her dissertation on rural economies in Spain and, knowing her prof's nephew had spent time in this area, had asked him to arrange a meeting with Maria Helena who, according to the nephew, was most knowledgeable on this subject.

With that entrée, the cousin restauranteur was most amenable. He quickly arranged for all the parties to gather at his establishment for a tasty meal prepared under his own watchful eye.

Maria Helena was happy to see Eddie—embracing him with a strength that reflected real affection. But she was also saddened by the memories—both difficult and pleasant—this reacquaintance rekindled. Pushing back these thoughts, she assured her new guests of her willingness to help a young student with her studies. Arrangements were made. Eddie was then able to bow out, as was Hal.

Next, they went by Delpro's office, which appeared unchanged—at least on the outside. Without entering, Eddie briefed Hal on Mr. Smith. One of Hal's colleagues would visit the offices later to see if the good gentleman was still there and if he would be willing to talk to a journalist about the company's farming program. Hal's researcher this time posed as a reporter for a well-known northern European newspaper for which she had documents (excellent facsimiles) to prove her bona fides.

Hal and Eddie, in Hal's rental car, then spent the next several days visiting all the farms that had been involved in Eddie's study. Eddie pointed out all the anomalies for each operation, but they made no contact. Later, Hal would send his people to each estate with different cover stories ranging from agricultural inspectors to fertilizer salesmen. They would target the irregularities flagged by Eddie as well as assess the overall functioning of each unit—preparing thorough reports thereafter that Eddie would review.

With the groundwork set, Eddie now had at least a week to himself before he had to begin providing Hal feedback on the work of the various inquirers. He intentionally avoided all the old haunts he had frequented with Samantha. He grabbed his camera and visited some sites outside the city center that he had not yet seen, including the Sacromonte Abbey and the Basílica de Nuestra Señora de Las Angustias. After a day of photographing rare Baroque architecture, relics from hidden caves, and panoramas of the city from Mount Valparaiso, he felt he needed to leave the past to find the present.

He rented a car and drove to the coast, to Torrenueva, about sixty miles from the city. Here it was not to appreciate the differentness, but to seek the commonness. It was not to admire the past, but to try and feel the present. To look to the sea. A very different ocean than the one next to which he had been born, but still endowed with the reassurances of Neptune and Poseidon. The salt in the air, the cry of shore birds, the tang to the breeze—it grounded him. He remembered a quotation Samantha had loved to recite at the seashore, a quotation from Henry Wadsworth Longfellow:

*My soul is full of longing for the secret of the sea,*
*and the heart of the great ocean*
*sends a thrilling pulse through me.*

※

When Eddie met Hal back at his hotel, he felt rested and somehow enthusiastic. His efforts not to look back notwithstanding, he uncontrollably thought back to the small auberge where AMORE had reserved a room for them when they first arrived in the city. The opulence of the Hotel Alhambra Palace, Hal's present choice of accommodation, perhaps due to his ample expense account, was a blatant comparison to the frugality of their lodgings those years ago. The Palace, built in 1910 by the Duke of San Pedro de

Galatino and inaugurated by King Alfonso XIII, had provided accommodation for none less than Charles De Gaulle, the Dalai Lama, Cole Porter, and Henry Fonda. It should certainly be suitable for an aging civil servant and his no-longer-young nephew.

Hal had a prime room overlooking the city. Upon Eddie's return from the coast, as when they first had arrived, Hal had booked a slightly less palatial room for his nephew—overlooking the forest of the Alhambra as opposed to the urban lights. But the view was the least of Eddie's concerns. In his absence, his uncle had also prepared a pile of reports for his nephew's review. Roughly half of the agents had already submitted some documentation. This now needed to be contrasted with Eddie's unofficial findings. They needed to have a current description of Delpro's overall activities, highlighting any major changes since Eddie had first examined these facilities. Thereafter, they would select up to four of the most curious operations where they would try to infiltrate inspectors to look in depth into all the goings on. These would be those enterprises with verifiable, major anomalies between the official description of their operations and those activities Hal's team felt were likely ongoing.

Previously unbeknownst to Eddie, Hal had also had colleagues contact AMORE to follow up on the Malawian teenagers about whom Samantha had enquired as well as any similar cases. He had also had agents in Morocco check on Delpro shipments from Beira to Rabat and subsequent transshipments to Spanish ports along with possible transshipment overland.

There were a lot of reports to examine.

Eddie spent the next three days cloistered in his room, only going down to the main restaurant early in the morning for a lavish breakfast and then having dinner in his room as he dug through the pages and pages of reporting. Just when he thought the end was in sight, Hal brought another pile for his perusal. It took five days to go through all the material. Hal had then reserved a discrete and almost intimate meeting room in a little-used corner of the hotel where he and Eddie, after spreading all the documents on the burnished conference table of Spanish Chestnut, interviewed various agents as the team plowed ahead.

After another three days, they had, to Hal's satisfaction, updated their files on the broad Delpro program in Spain. They had identified the farms where they would try to insert people to collect specific incriminating information. They had boiled unanswered questions down to a list of ten critical outstanding matters—most of these relating to human trafficking and pirating pharmaceuticals—these more carefully guarded activities that would be at the core of any major judiciary case. These were acts that were enshrouded in complex and effective levels of secrecy.

While the underscored ten matters were the core, their answers would not just pop up because Hal needed them. The answers had to be dug out like getting a splinter out of your finger. It was hard work. Hal knew this. It was a slow, iterative course of action. Results could take a long time.

Hal organized his Spanish crew. He gave each an assignment, each with monitoring mechanisms and reporting procedures. Then it was up to them—those dedicated agents spending the coming months, or even years probing the secrets of Iberia.

Hal and Eddie moved south. While Hal, as he explained to Eddie on the flight to Jo'burg, expected to use much the same methodology in Zambia and Malawi, these were paths less frequently traveled. In Granada they blended in, their fact-finding unlikely to attract attention. This was not the case in southern Africa. They were more visible. They would attract attention. For this reason, he had decided to rent a car in Pretoria and drive north. There were lots of South Africans on the road and perhaps in this way they could be less conspicuous. They would drive across Zimbabwe to Zambia. They would go straight east, spending only a minimum of time in Chipata, basing most of their work out of the Makkokolo Retreat—a high-end tourist resort on Lake Malawi where, again, they would be part of a larger expatriate crowd—hopefully an invisible part.

The roads were relatively good and, once they left Harare, offered only light traffic. As they progressed north, Hal felt viscerally the anguish Eddie was suffering as they neared the Lusaka airport junction. His nephew closed his eyes well before they got to the intersection, only reopening when they were well clear.

Hal understood all too well Eddie's apprehension about revisiting Chipata—concerns about reviving demons that had only partially been put to rest. Their stay needed to be as brief as possible.

There was a job to get done. They needed to get there and get it done quickly.

Eddie's main inputs would be needed regarding the Delpro farm near the Msandile River. Fortunately, Hal's local team had already visited the site. There was a rise about a mile from the farm that offered an excellent vantage point to review the now fully functioning operation without creating any concerns about a too close for comfort examination by a couple of foreigners.

Hal hoped he had arranged a schedule that would minimize his nephew's discomfort. They would leave the InterContinental Hotel (having avoided the memory-bound Pamodzi) in Lusaka well before sunrise to begin their run east to the Malawi border. With such an early start, they would arrive at the Msandile River well before noon.

Back on familiar ground, from his preselected lookout, Eddie took his time to examine the entire farm headquarters site through powerful binoculars. He then sketched what he saw on sturdy A1 sheets provided by his uncle. Although the farm covered almost 150,000 acres, it was improbable major infrastructure had been built outside the headquarters hub. Any meaningful new construction at a second site would require building roads, bringing in utilities, and, most importantly, getting clearances from an ever-watchful government. Given the tensions that had accompanied the initial lease, even with the substantial sums that had passed under the table, prudence on the company's part was required. There was considerable anti-Delpro sentiment among the local communities, to the point that central government felt it must oversee the site attentively.

A sheaf of Eddie's notes carefully stowed in Hal's suitcase; it was just about midday when they pulled back onto the T-4 to continue east.

Out of respect for Eddie's already taut nerves, they did not even stop in Chipata. They headed straight on to the border and from there directly to their hotel in Lilongwe. Hal did not think there was anything to be gained at this time from trying to get fragments of new information from the AMORE office that Samantha had headed. If, at a later date, something was needed, he would be able to send someone to follow up.

They left Lilongwe after barely twelve hours in the country's capital, driving down the escarpment to lake level and the Makkokolo Retreat. Right on the shores of Lake Malawi, the resort was classed as among the elite spots for the astute tourist—if not due to its fine amenities, then due to its very pricey room rate.

Eddie and Hal had adjoining lakeview rooms that were sufficiently large to allow them to spread out their work and get right to the task at hand. Eddie's main inputs were again needed for the field sites: Thyolo and Tedzani. As they had done in Granada, they would verify that the Delpro office was still in Blantyre. They would check the status of Delpro activities in the Southern Region and then across the country. But they would make no face-to-face contacts. They themselves would do no ground-truthing. Hal's local staff would do all the foot work.

Eddie had no idea how Hal had all these contacts virtually anywhere they went. It was uncanny the team he had been able to mobilize nearly overnight in Spain. Here again, in even a more isolated piece of real estate, Hal seemed to have absolutely no worries about having all the staff he might need to do whatever needed to be done. Eddie really did not understand. Nevertheless, it was what it was.

After they had reviewed all the available reports prepared by Eddie and others, they made day trips from their lakeshore base. They went south to Blantyre, Thyolo, and Tedzani and then west to Lilongwe. Eddie used his camera to document the present situation at sites he knew. But they were able to glean very little in terms of actual reconnaissance—having to leave this to the agents who would follow.

Hal would leave Eddie at the hotel to update documents while he went foraging on his own. Hal would then fill Eddie in as they had dinner together on the terrace that overlooked the massive lake before getting ready to sleep at an early hour to be prepared for another busy day to come.

Thinking Eddie might still be recognized, Hal alone had pursued two channels in Lilongwe—making headway in each. A number of NGOs and UN agencies based in the capital had been working with Mozambican refugees. They had lists of people reported as missing by their families as well as names of unaccounted persons who had entered resettlement schemes but disappeared in the process. Hal had also been able to forge some special friendships with a few high-up customs officers. These officers were responsible for the freight that was trucked south into Mozambique to the port of Beira—Malawi's major access to sea-lanes. Hal's connections had been revitalized by his generosity—results pending.

With the right stimuli, Hal knew there could be payoffs. Even under relatively difficult circumstances, these benefits could come rather promptly.

After two weeks, both Hal and Eddie felt they had amassed a worthy amount of information and were beginning to operate under diminishing returns. There was little else to do at this time.

In what seemed like a blink of an eye, Eddie found himself back in Lisa's apartment, patting Coco II, sipping a beer, staring vacuously at Lisa, wondering if what he thought had just happened had really happened.

---

The easiest next step, and maybe the best next step, was to let things carry on at their own speed. Eddie had provided critical assistance, filled in key pieces, provided important contacts and context. Hal was now trying to push the string uphill.

However, Eddie did not want to slack off just yet. He owed Samantha all he could give, and he felt he could give more.

He and Lisa discussed over a midnight snack accentuated by an excellent Beaujolais after an early evening of ardent lovemaking. She was happy to have her lover closer to her. Eddie adamantly and amorously maintained he too was more than content to be close to his dear Lisa. But Lisa knew he missed his home. He was, at least for the moment, only amenable to stay in D.C. if he could pursue the case. They both realized he needed to take a new tack. But not wanting in any way to jeopardize the intricate actions Hal had already set in motion they were not sure what the best course of action would be.

Lisa suggested looking for others who had been used and abused by Delpro. Given the scope of their operations, she reasoned, there had to be some who had managed to escape and somehow make it to the US as part of the bands of refugees that, legally or not, came to our shores.

This seemed a natural next step and Eddie was energized. Late the next morning, as Eddie's uplifted energies were now not limited to pursuing known malefactors, Eddie walked to the nearby Lamond-Riggs Neighborhood Library to begin his research for new names, new people of interest. After a few days here, he shifted to the better-endowed Georgetown Library; this required a Metro trip, but also opened an opportunity for him to have lunch with Lisa on library days as their job sites were not that far apart.

※

When Eddie was not digging in a library, he was often walking with Coco II. They both felt lucky to be so close to Fort Slocum National Park. This Civil War fort, while not huge, offered grass fields and woods including some of the original wartime earthworks used when the Second Rhode Island Infantry successfully defended the city against the advancing forces of Confederate General Jubal in 1864.

While Coco II and Eddie nosed around the long-abandoned emplacements of Fort Slocum's twenty-four-pounder howitzers and Coehorn mortars, Lisa thought of Eddie as she gazed out of her office windows through the vapor rising from her ever-present coffee mug. They were so different and still so similar.

Lisa was eight years Eddie's junior, but at their age, what difference did this make? They came from similar places. They had both grown up feeling the throb of the great Pacific Ocean; Eddie had been not even a stone's throw from its crashing magnificence, while she, as the bird flies, had been thirty miles inland in a small community along one of the coastal rivers where her great grandfather had settled in the mid 1860s after being released from an internment center. Her forbearer had managed to sustain his family doing a little bit of everything—hunting, fishing, and odd jobs. His eldest daughter was of such rare beauty the well-to-do local Norwegian store owner had asked for her hand when she was still a teenager. Disregarding her father's strenuous objections, the teenager had agreed. Beyond all odds of success, the mixed marriage proved to be solid and loving. They had two children, a boy and a girl. The girl was Lisa's mother. While she had much of her own mother's elegance, there was strong sentiment in the minds of many locals against what they labeled as half-breeds. This was a period of racial reactiveness. There was a backlash from the forced relocation of Japanese Americans during the war that went all the way to the Supreme Court. There was an even more galvanized effort to combat segregation and repeal Jim Crow. During these changing times, communities seemed to either engage the fight, sometimes literally, or to bury their heads in the sand. Much of the Pacific Northwest considered itself outside, or perhaps above the fray. They reacted as though in the great new West there was no racism—conveniently completely ignoring all the injustice and discrimination that continued up to that time to be levied against Native Americans.

These stances of denial had many implications on policy as well as on private lives. One of these was an overt and malicious debasement of Lily, Lisa's mother, because of her mixed blood. Whether through choice or pressure, Lisa never knew, Lily left the multicultural, comfortable environment in which she had been raised, returning wholeheartedly to the community of her grandfather. When she was just sixteen, she met Bobby, three years her senior, at the annual powwow for the coastal tribes. A flame was lit that day that continued to burn brightly up to the present as they were still completely devoted to each other as they entered their eighties.

Bobby had worked in the woods. Lily, who was an accomplished chef due to the influence of her paternal grandmother, did custom baking for marriages, other celebrations, or local gatherings. They had three children, Lisa the eldest. Their other two children, both sons, followed in their father's footsteps and worked in the woods. Lisa's younger brother, Nathan, was killed in his early twenties when a log rolled off a deck and crushed him. The middle brother, Ralph, had lost his long-time slot in the woods in the eighties when mills were closing left and right, but managed to get along with his new job at a small roofing business.

Lisa, regardless of her deep love of her family and clan, always felt there was something special waiting for her over the next hill. She had been top of her class in high school and got a scholarship to a state university. Over school breaks she worked in a marine supply store in the nearby port city. The summer of her sophomore year, while in the store, she was accosted by three drunk fishermen calling her a "heathen," a "squaw," and a "timber nigger." They yelled, "Where are your braids, Redskin?" They took a filleting knife and prepared to slash her hair. She snatched a boat hook and hit one along the head, smashed the other in the solar plexus, and cracked the third in the groin. They left howling only to return with a sheriff's deputy.

They demanded he arrest the godless forest dweller as she had ruthlessly and without cause attacked them.

Fortunately, the deputy had a sense of humor. Stifling a laugh, he chased the three fishermen away with a warning not to come back. Then he apologized to Lisa for the comportment of his "brothers." While Lisa was glad things had not got even more out of hand, she was troubled by the deputy's humorous dismissal of a potentially violent act. She would forever wonder if the fact that the deputy considered the fishermen his brothers meant he did not consider her his sister. Were they not all God's children?

This event was the pebble in her shoe that continued to bother her for the remainder of her studies. It was not that she was so grievously attacked. Sadly, this could happen to anyone anywhere. It was not that she had been so maliciously insulted. These people were ignorant. They were idiots. There were idiots everywhere. It was really the question of whether or not the deputy considered her his sister if he felt the fishermen were his brothers. Lisa was not big on seeing acquaintances as siblings, but she was big on equity. She fervently believed in equity.

As she approached graduation, she realized this was in fact the theme she wanted to adopt for her life—her beacon. In this pursuit, she had gone on to law school, sat for the bar, and become an attorney. She had taken successive positions in several large prestigious firms—demonstrating keen skills in each. She was on a trajectory to a partnership and a very profitable law career. But this was not what she wanted. She finally found her special something over the hill when she accepted the post of chief counsel to the Confederated Tribes. She was now where she needed to be. The pebble in her shoe now was Eddie. If she was where she needed to be, was there a place for Eddie?

※

Unaware of Lisa's pondering, Eddie finally had the results he needed to take his next step. He had drawn up a list including such organizations and groups as the UN High Commission on Refugees, the Immigrant and Refugee Program, the New Refugee Council, the International Rescue Committee, the United African Immigrants' Organization, and the African Immigrant Alliance. He had addresses, he had names of contacts, he even had a list of D.C. restaurants and bars reportedly frequented by southern African immigrants. He now needed to go out and test the waters. However, before he got too far down this path, he wanted to check in with Hal.

The two met at a small café in Silver Spring. Eddie was sipping an espresso when Hal walked in. He thought of Hal like a much-loved old pair of blue jeans. Hal was slowly changing color—slightly fading—becoming softer. But there was still great strength in his gate, as he slowly approached Eddie's table, he thoroughly yet stealthily checked out the premises while he advanced.

After some casual chat, Eddie explained his plan to Hal. Hal played with his latté as he mentally examined Eddie's suggestion. Gradually he smiled, and Eddie knew he had his uncle's blessing to go ahead.

Eddie dove full force into the African diaspora.

Very quickly he was inundated with names of, or sometimes vague references to missing southern Africans. He had to impose some filters. He assumed Delpro's aim in ingraining itself into the lives of others was for its corporate benefit—simply put, they needed labor, even if effectively slave labor. In this vein, males between fifteen and thirty-five could well be the prime target. However, Eddie was looking for those who got away—those who had endured the deception and the abuse but had managed to breakout. This meant his window was for slightly older men, maybe those from twenty to forty-five.

Distilling responses in this way, he had a lot fewer names—but still hundreds. He then reasoned, his desire to follow up on the children of the lady in Malawi who had begged him to help aside, Mozambicans would be a prize target for Delpro. With the war raging, people were afloat everywhere—no deep roots and close community ties to monitor the movements of a young man. Better still, lusophone Mozambicans would have a better level of communication with the overseers of the Spanish operations than Malawians or Zambians—Portuguese sufficiently close linguistically to Spanish to facilitate basic exchanges from master to vassal.

Applying further criteria, Eddie was able to reduce his candidates to a workable list of twenty-three Mozambicans who had been reported as being missing specifically in the areas of the Mlolo or Chilengo border crossings in Zambia or the Dedza crossing in Malawi. These were the most accessible exits from Tete Province which was the closest war zone to Delpro's activities.

For the twenty-three, he was able to get fifteen discolored photographs—chiefly from international refugee groups. Taking these pale representations along with a one-paragraph synopsis of the individual and whatever background was available, Eddie began a tour of the coffee houses, diners, and bars tagged as being frequented by Portuguese speakers from Mozambique, Angola, Guinea Bissau, Cape Verde, or São Tomé and Príncipe.

As he had experienced in his other life, when he entered a locale where he was the interloper, there was an immediate raising of the defenses. Eddie the intruder was automatically met with distrust and even outright aggression. However, if he was able to identify one of the crowd with more curiosity than apprehension, he was most often able to make inroads.

After several weeks, he had been totally unsuccessful in getting any leads on his list of fifteen. He was beginning to think he needed to change track when one afternoon, while enjoying a bowl of *caldo verde* with crusty *alentejo* bread at a small café he had recently begun visiting, an unremarkable man approached his table. He was in his mid-forties and wore sneakers, jeans, and a T-shirt. He introduced himself as Alfonso. He said Agnes, the waitress with whom Eddie had been trying to curry favor over the weeks, had told him Eddie was trying to locate some Mozambicans who were lost to their families.

Eddie offered Alfonso a seat and a coffee before explaining in a truncated way his work in southern Africa, how he had been asked by families to help (a bit of a twist of the truth here), and how he had, with the help of international agencies (another twist) established a list of people who could be in the D.C. area but whose families had no idea they were still roaming this Earth.

As this initial explanation did not seem troubling to Alfonso, he embellished it a bit more, saying he knew that during the Civil War, Mozambicans were continuously separated from their families, hence these issues of missing persons seemed to be exceptionally prevalent among the Mozambican Community.

Again, Alfonse seemed unfazed. He sipped his coffee, saying nothing—as if waiting for Eddie to say more.

Finally, Eddie felt Afonso had something to say, but was waiting for him to somehow open the door. He took a gamble. He asked if Alfonso had ever heard of Delpro.

This seemed to prompt a stirring in Alfonso, but he remained silent.

Eddie then went all in figuring he had nothing to lose. He explained he had worked for Delpro in Europe and Africa. His work had led him to believe that the company was involved in human trafficking—quite possibly engaged in slavery to run its operations on the Iberian Peninsula.

This appeared to be the card Alfonso was waiting to fall. His dark eyes focused on the man across the table as he told Eddie he was in fact in the US as a refugee from the Mozambican war. However, he had not been unfortunate enough to have encountered Delpro. Nonetheless, his cousin Jordao, who had also fled the war, had not been so lucky. As he was trying to get into Zambia at the Mlolo crossing, someone from some big European company offered him free passage all the way to Spain if he would only agree to work for the company for one year. The company told him after that time he would be free to do whatever he wanted, and they would even help him arrange all the official paper work necessary to stay and work in Europe. Jordao had jumped at the opportunity.

His new saviors shepherded him across Zambia and then across Lake Kariba in a large canoe filled with others fleeing war or other unpleasantries. They then were transported in a large enclosed truck to the Mutare border crossing where they crossed on foot back into Mozambique—this time into Manica Province. They took a mini bus from the border town of Villa Manica to the provincial capital of Chimoio where they were kept in a sort of barn-like structure until a large truck arrived with a long container on its trailer. According to Jordao, the eighteen Europe-bound, soon-to-be farm workers followed the truck to the port city of Beira in two vans. They followed the truck all the way into the container loading and unloading area where their guides explained to them there were a total of four containers bound for Europe. Three were full of produce, the fourth was to be their home for the rest of the journey. Although shocked and frightened, the travelers had come too far to turn back now. They then spent a hideous twenty days thrown about in the horrors of a sealed container with minimal food and water, only seeing sunlight again, to their great surprise, in Rabat. Here they were split among a variety of vehicles for the last leg to Spain and to different farms scattered around the country.

Jordao had spent over four years working at a facility in Andalusia. Despite his expectations, despite the promises made, he did not spend this time working as a farm hand. He spent this time working in a factory that was housed in an enormous multipurpose shed on a farm with expansive olive, lemon, and fig orchards they saw when they first entered the estate.

The part of the factory line where Jordao worked was involved in bottling pharmaceuticals—according to other workers, these products were prepared in another cubicle of this spacious enclosure, apparently using materials similar to those that had come with them on the freighter.

The workers were in effect prisoners. The expansive building had but one set of large reinforced, electronically controlled doors for the entry and exit of both people and materials. This passage was guarded twenty-four seven by guards as well as monitored by closed circuit TV. The workers themselves were accommodated in another cubicle where there was a dormitory and cafeteria—the prepared food coming in from the outside.

As he concluded his cousin's tale, Alfonso added that if Jordao had not had the good luck and foresight to hide in a truck that had just dropped off a load of agricultural powders, he would probably still be there today. His escape had only been possible because a small fire had broken out in the truck's engine compartment (Alfonso had no idea if his cousin was involved in setting the fire), and the truck was rushed out of the structure without the normal security check. Jordao had secretly clutched the chassis as the truck left the building. His cousin had made it to Lisbon and from there had contacted his family in the US. The family was able to send some money to their heretofore lost member to get him as far away from trouble as possible. Alfonso himself had met Jordao in Montreal and smuggled him across the border into the US. In other words, his cousin was an illegal alien.

Jordao's legal status notwithstanding, Eddie was able to confirm through Alfonso that his cousin saw Delpro and similar profiteers as hideous threats to innocent people—especially people of Africa. He was willing to help, but obviously he needed to protect his status at the same time. He was now married with a three-month-old baby girl.

Eddie and Alfonso exchanged contacts and Eddie hurried off to brief Hal and later that evening he shared his excitement with Lisa.

※

Hal maintained his typical stoic posture while Eddie effusively told him about this fortuitous find: Jordao. When his nephew had finished retelling the story, Hal simply said he would include Jordao in the investigation.

Eddie was not satisfied. This was a goldmine. This was the proof they needed. They could rush ahead and take Delpro to court. Jordao would be the nail in the company's coffin.

Hal saw his nephew needed better perspective. He quickly summarized all the pieces of the puzzle he and Eddie had already identified during their recent trip. Jordao was another piece. And, there were many other pieces. Hal had an entire team of agents, specialists, researchers, and consultants looking into a spectrum of issues. Each group had to follow its leads, secure its pieces of the puzzle. As he had said all along, this was a slow and methodical process. There would not be a court case today, none tomorrow, and not even one this year. This was an assignment that required great sensitivity, tact, and foolproof data. Eddie could not get in a rush. He had to have patience. It would take time—a long time.

Hal also reassured Eddie that he was not saying this to discourage him. They had made and were making good progress. Things were going even better than Hal had hoped. On this note, he wanted to sit down again with Lisa.

That evening Eddie filled Lisa in on all the news—thankful she was much more optimistic and reassured. Before rushing off to the bedroom to celebrate, she indicated she would call Hal the next day to arrange for a meeting for the three of them.

It was four days later when they met in a café in Reston. As was beginning to be the pattern, Lisa and Eddie arrived on time, ordered coffees and brioche, already ready for a refill before Hal appeared. He first seemed to head for the restroom, but then changed course and came to their table with a nonchalant but attentive demeanor.

After warm greetings and cool chitchat, Hal went quickly to the subject at hand: Delpro. He felt, as he had told Eddie a few days earlier, they were moving ahead at a good pace. He and his team, however, would only be undertaking the investigation and collecting the data. They did not have the mandate, nor did they want the visibility, to lodge charges against the company. He looked to Lisa for this.

His proposal was simple. He and Lisa would meet every two weeks to review progress. Once the pieces had fallen into place, Lisa would take over. In the meantime, she needed to do her homework, so she knew how best to handle the case and what actions to undertake once they had concluded the inquest. Hal was fully confident it was not a question of if, but of when. They would ultimately be able to take Delpro to court for a variety of very serious charges.

Throughout, Eddie listened carefully. He welcomed the positive assessment. But he was unclear as to his role, asking Hal for details.

With an unaccustomed smile, Hal simply told his nephew, "Go home."

This was the last thing Eddie wanted to hear.

Nevertheless, as Hal once again recapped the situation, with Lisa's full assent, Eddie realized this was the only logical course of action. He had done what he could for the moment and, as long as Hal promised to call him when he needed him, in truth he would be happy to get back to his home turf.

※

Eddie spent another ten days in D.C.—not because of Delpro but because of Lisa. They had been able to spend an extended period together and now this separation was particularly painful. They made plans to meet periodically as they had before, but they were both saddened to see the end come to this phase of their conjugal lives. It seemed so unfair they had to pull themselves apart just when they were getting used to living as a well-tuned twosome. At the same time, they knew and understood it was what it was.

Eddie and Coco II were glad to get back to where, when they would awake each day, they could taste the sea breeze and relish the chorus of the gulls.

With amazing speed, they fell into their old routine—the routine they had haphazardly followed before their sleuthing and globetrotting.

Eddie was able to get word out that he was back. A few jobs came his way—his skills were kind of like those of a cobbler, only sought when needed. He and Coco II spent hours on the beach, his collection of agates growing one stone at a time.

The old habits reappeared. The old became the new.

Every three to four months he and Lisa would find a way to arrange a rendezvous—most often in D.C., since Lisa's workload was swelling. As their relationship matured, these meetings were less about romantic release and more about emotional attachment—not to say they lacked amorousness. Each took great pains to reinforce the commitment of the other—acknowledging the challenges of living on opposite edges of the continent, redoubling their pledge to do all they could to make their cherished alliance work.

And it did work.

During these liaisons, Eddie took care not to mention the Delpro investigation nor Lisa's preparation for a possible court case. He had complete confidence in Hal that his uncle would let him know if he needed any help, while making sure to keep his nephew abreast of any breaking news. In this case no news was not good news. It was just vindication that the process was slowly ticking onward.

Gloomily, Eddie speculated when back at home, "slowly ticking" was exactly what was happening. In truth, it felt like nothing was happening. He should probably forget the whole matter.

Just when he was about to become completely dejected about bringing Samantha's killers (he had by now fully accepted that she had been murdered) to justice, Hal called and asked to meet in New Orleans—the Hotel Montleone nonetheless, once accommodating Ernest Hemingway, Tennessee Williams, and William Faulkner; as Eddie was to learn.

Eddie had no idea if there was any significance to New Orleans or the Hotel Montleone, but he immediately accepted. In a week's time was sitting across a French Provincial coffee table from Hal in his imposing hotel suite, tasting chicory-laced coffee, and trying to absorb the impressive stack of papers Hal had heaped on the hopefully sturdy table.

As before, Hal had booked the adjacent room for his nephew. He suggested Eddie move the papers into his room and spend the rest of the day looking them over. They would then meet in the evening to recap.

The papers were astonishing. Most were executive summaries, linked to full reports with annotated bibliographies—these latter not among the documents provided to Eddie. Yet, even without the full text, it was clear that Hal's team had been very busy. Agents had infiltrated five operations in Spain, they were working with AMORE and other groups to get comprehensive data on people missing in the area of Tete Province as well as digging into the legal status of Delpro operations in Iberia, southern Africa, and elsewhere around the world including the US. They had interviewed and continued to keep in touch with Jordao, with his help, identifying three more people who had successfully fled the terrors of Delpro. They had clandestine operators enter Delpro offices in Granada, Lusaka, Blantyre, and a score of other cities to furtively audit their figures in the dark of night and there was even more. Hal's crew had cast an impressively wide net—now they were beginning to pull it in.

When Hal and Eddie discussed later, it was clear to the uncle that the nephew finally understood much better the breadth of the investigation, the need for a slow and steady pace, and the present real opportunity to be able to take definitive action—but not immediately—still more patience was required.

In the meantime, as Hal and Lisa were meeting regularly in D.C., Hal suggested Eddie feel free to discuss each and every detail with her as her role was becoming increasingly critical.

It had been a worthy meeting—perhaps, more emotionally than professionally. But, of course, Hal and Eddie had both an emotional and a professional relationship.

Maybe, just maybe, the truth of Samantha's death would surface—not vengeance, simply justice.

Progress was being made.

They celebrated by going out for some five-star Creole food at Restaurant R'evolution in the French Quarter. Hal always seemed to know the best hotels and the best restaurants.

After a superb meal, Eddie suggested they stop by the Penthouse Club. He had read a flyer in the hotel and it was billed as the ultimate club with VIP rooms available for hotel residents. Hal appeared to have an immediate allergic reaction, as though he had eaten a bad oyster. He put on his doting uncle cap and said that was no place for his impressionable nephew—guiding them instead to the Spotted Cat Music Club where they had some excellent drinks and listened to even more excellent jazz. It was a good choice.

While they were enjoying their Sazeracs, awash in an outstanding rendition of Basin Street Blues, a pair of very beautiful, very buxom ladies came over to their table asking if they would like some company. Eddie was just getting ready to politely decline when Hal had an even more noticeable reaction than he had had at the mention of the Penthouse Club, nearly driving the girls from their table. Embarrassed afterwards, he bought a series of drinks such that uncle and nephew were totally plastered when they wove their way back to their hotel rooms. The next day, they were most appreciative of the fact that, in their grossly inebriated condition, they had not been mugged before finding their beds.

Day two, nursing massive hangovers, was more subdued than day one. Now comfortable that Eddie understood well the bigger picture, Hal wanted to examine some issues more closely. He had some questions that had arisen from the various agents who were following up on his nephew's leads. He also, figuratively speaking, bared his chest and let Eddie ask any question he may have. Probably fortunately, Eddie felt so badly that the extra thought required to probe more into his uncle's investigation was simply too painful to conjure up.

They ate a much more modest meal that evening in the hotel, following it with just enough alcohol to ensure a sound sleep before their departure the next morning—one flying east the other west.

Hal's flight to D.C. was at sunrise, he and Eddie having said their goodbyes the night before.

Eddie's flight was not until mid-afternoon. Before checking out, he went to the hotel restaurant for one more sampling of Creole cooking. The waiter recommended Cajun fried rice with crawfish and green onion sausage—reportedly a recipe dating back to the family of Charles Louis Fonteneaux who had come from France in 1767. Whether or not it was Charles Louis' dish did not matter, Eddie found it to be splendidly spiced, providing enough sustenance for the rest of the day.

When Eddie later went to the reception to drop off his key, the clerk handed him a note on hotel stationary. It was from Hal:

> *My Dear Nephew,*
>
> *It is 0430. I am off to the airport. I hope you are sleeping soundly. I just wanted to let you know that I am sure your mother is very proud of you—of how smart you are, how hard you work, and how dedicated you are to doing the right thing. Your mother always tried to do the right thing. She raised you well.*
>
> *Take care,*
> *Uncle Hal*

*P.S.: I am sure your mom would also say she would not want you to drink too much, but that she is so happy you do not pick up hookers. H.*

※

Eddie was flying west, but not all the way. He was only going as far as Dallas on the first leg of his return to the Northwest. He and Lisa had decided he was already close enough to the Eastern Seaboard that they should get together. Admittedly, Dallas was far from the East Coast, but any excuse worked.

Eddie took the shuttle to the Crown Plaza downtown, finding Lisa had already checked in. After they had sated their abstinence, they enjoyed room service as, following Hal's recommendation, they briefed each other on the subject that occupied much of their time: Delpro.

They spent four days in the Big D; alternatively, they enjoyed romantic intervals (sometimes surprisingly frisky), dove as deeply as possible into Delpro, and visited the World Aquarium, Arboretum, and zoo. Then, as always, the clock ran out and they went to their respective corners.

Lisa went back to D.C. to the full slate that dominated her work. She was becoming more and more occupied with the minutiae of possible legal action against Delpro. It was demanding. It was more than a job—it was a cause.

Eddie went home to Coco II, the beach, and the random (now increasingly rare) small jobs.

Life cycled as though carefully planned. There were sporadic passionate rendezvous—the passion both emotionally ardent and professionally stimulating. There were increasingly frequent telephone calls—especially as Lisa began to get wrapped-up in the work and had numerous questions for Eddie. He still took long hikes on the beach—with a growing collection of new agates.

Weeks ran into months, soon another three years had passed. Eddie began to think it had all been a dream. Samantha was now almost a mystical character from a novel describing someone else's life. Far off places seemed better placed in National Geographic than in his own memory. Delpro seemed like of group of characters out of the latest popular thriller.

The sea, the waves, the rain—this was the limit of reality. All else was imagination.

*Book Eight*

# Shiny Scraps

H<small>AL</small> was dead.

It was totally unexpected, but one day he just was not there any longer.

Eddie received word via Rodney, one of Hal's colleagues. Eddie had been named in Hal's personnel file as his family contact—his next of kin. Rodney was direct; Hal had been found dead that morning. No further details were available. Apparently final arrangements were to be made in D.C., was Eddie coming or did he want to stay on the West Coast and liaise with others who would take care of the details?

Eddie said he would be there in three days' time. He was able to get a booking on an eastbound flight, expedited on companionate grounds. He boarded Coco II, called Lisa, packed his bag, and was off.

He went straight to Lisa's; she was shocked nearly as deeply as Eddie by Hal's untimely departure. The usual passion of their first meeting was replaced by remorse, sorrow, and nostalgia. The next morning, Eddie took a taxi across the district to the address he had been given, a nondescript office building among a row of 1950's brick apartments along Blue Plains Drive, not far from the Potomac Job Corps Center.

The stodgy exterior belied a modern and bustling interior that was somehow reminiscent of his first visit to Delpro's office in Granada. There was a swanky reception with an equally fashionable elderly lady behind the high oak table. When Eddie asked to see Rodney, with no preliminaries, she immediately accompanied him to a spacious corner office—his host seated in one of a trio of leather-covered club chairs, as if he knew his visitor was coming.

When Eddie entered, Rodney stood to shake his hand. He was above average height, lanky, but somehow sinewy. With few formalities, Rodney told Eddie he needed to tell him about his uncle.

Eddie obviously knew Hal as his uncle, his mother's younger brother. But what else did he know?

Eddie, preempting Rodney in the storytelling, had to admit he really knew very little about this man. He had only first chatted with Hal when his uncle had accompanied Eddie's parents on their visit to Zambia. Then, when his mother had died, he had had a better chance to get some more details about his long-lost uncle—these limited snapshots of his uncle's background and life had been expanded upon when the two had recently worked together on the Delpro case. Yet, in the face of all, he knew he still had a very narrow view of this quiet and complex man.

Eddie's family had always been rather reserved—even closed. In regard to his overall family's life history, he often felt there was more he did not know than he did. With respect to his uncle Hal, this knowledge gap was much larger.

He knew his mother had spent her life in one place—being born not far from where she died. She was the second child, born to a smallholder dairy operator who had probably never seen a 100-dollar bill in is life. Her older brother, four years her senior, Wilfred, had initially done odd jobs around the family's home range. He had been responsible for introducing Eddie to agate hunting. But he had drifted away. According to his mother, given his upbringing, he migrated to Wisconsin to work in dairies—something he did up to his death in 1987 when he had been the victim of an automobile accident during a particularly severe winter storm.

The way Irene later had told it, after Eddie had seen his uncle that Fourth of July at the river, Hal had been an "oops baby"—fifteen years her junior and an unplanned and in some ways unwelcome addition to the struggling family. His middle-aged parents had no time to wrench away from their cows to coddle a youngster. Hal had pretty much been left to his own volition—almost a non-entity. In fact, as Eddie disclosed to Rodney, for a long time he was unaware he even had an uncle Hal.

Irene had explained they were not hiding Hal, not keeping him a secret. It was just that his life had somehow become clouded—the clouds growing thicker as Hal grew older. Irene herself knew so little about what he did, where he lived, or even what he liked and disliked. There was really almost nothing she could say about her younger brother. He had had a difficult time growing up and when he turned seventeen, he had left, never coming home again.

Rodney jumped in before Eddie could continue to wax wistfully, assuring his guest that he could fill in a lot of the blanks.

As Rodney recalled, Hal had indeed left home in 1960. He had joined the Army. He was not satisfied with just the mundane—he never was. He pushed himself and, with the Kennedy Presidency, by the end of 1961 he was in Special Forces. In December of that year he had been among a small group of Special Forces to go to Buon Enao, Vietnam. This was an area where the US, assisting President Diem, was trying a new holistic model to counteract insurgency; not just dealing with arms, but also trying to promote social and economic improvements.

The CIA was working closely with the Special Forces. They took notice of Hal, his motivation and drive. They recruited him on the spot and sent him back to the States for additional training. In February 1962, the US established the Military Assistance Command under General Harkins. In July of that year, Hal was back in Vietnam, in the Central Highlands, working with the Montagnards for the CIA. By the end of 1963, the war effort was putting down roots with 16,000 US troops. Over the next three years, as troop numbers ballooned to almost 200,000, Hal stayed in the Highlands. Then, in 1967, as part of the Studies and Observation Group, he moved into Cambodia where he stayed until bombing started in 1970. By this time, Hal was an experienced, most would say talented, senior operative. He began taking shorter-term assignments all across the globe.He had led an unhampered vagabond life until he was asked to set up a team in D.C. under the Division of Enforcement of the Security and Exchange Commission.

This building where they sat, Rodney concluded, was the team's offices. The officers Eddie saw around him were the nucleus of the investigation of Delpro. While Eddie did not know them, they knew him. They had followed all his work with Hal in Spain and southern Africa and were most grateful for Eddie's services.

Eddie thought Rodney had finished his review—his eulogy. But after a big gulp of air, Rodney said there was one more thing Eddie should know. This was completely off the record, but Rodney felt it was his duty to make sure Eddie knew—at the same time asking for his discretion. Hal had been gay.

Not only was Hal gay, but Rodney was his partner. They had broken two sacrosanct rules: one against homosexuality and the other against fraternizing with colleagues. Eddie needed to know, but for all their sakes, he also needed to keep this knowledge to himself.

Eddie returned to Lisa's in a daze. By the time she got home from work, he had drunk three beers and did not know if he was in better or worse shape to tell her about Hal. Regardless of the condition of the teller, Lisa was enthralled by Hal's story—impressed by the events of Southeast Asia, sympathetic to the love of a workmate (regardless the situation) and amazed she and Hal had worked so long together and she had known so little. The story proved Hal was an exceptional human being in many different ways. She cried for Eddie's loss. She cried for her loss.

The next morning, just as Lisa was ready to go out the door for her trek to the office, Rodney called. There was a meeting that afternoon in the offices of Stanley Cooper Esquire, Hal's lawyer, on the corner of nineteenth and Q, near Dupont Circle. The meeting was at 3:00 p.m. If possible, Rodney would like to meet Eddie at a coffee shop right across from the circle and then the two could go to Cooper's office together. Eddie agreed to meet him at two. He then arranged with Lisa to meet in town for drinks at seven. The day was already buttoned up.

Over coffee, Rodney reiterated to Eddie the urgency in not talking about his uncle's private life. He was the next of kin and the sole survivor, so any estate matters should be able to be settled very promptly. He, Rodney, would update Mr. Cooper about the status of Hal's death vis-à-vis the agency. Mr. Cooper should take care of the reading of the will, with any footnotes necessary. Then they would be done.

Things almost went as Rodney had described, at least in terms of following the prescribed outline. However, the particulars under each heading were quite unexpected.

Rodney informed Mr. Cooper that, as a senior employee of the agency, there was a mandatory postmortem. The autopsy, moreover, would be performed by an agency coroner and, as needed, a team of forensic pathologists.

Both Mr. Copper and Eddie enquired if this implied some questions surrounding Hal's death. Rodney replied that this was completely routine and there were no worries at this time about Hal's demise. As he had been in his seventies, it was fully anticipated the cause of death was natural causes.

Feeling somewhat reassured, Mr. Cooper then read Hal's testament. It was simple and straightforward, if somewhat unforeseen. Hal had lived a very simple life, at least materially. He did not own a home nor a car. He had few earthly possessions—none worthy of any special notice. But, through the years, with skillful investment, he had accumulated a considerable portfolio. At the time of his death, this was worth $7.8 million. As his only heir, this was passed to Eddie. Even after taxes and other costs including attorney fees and a few specific gifts stipulated by Hal, this was still a handsome bequest.

Mr. Cooper estimated, due to the relative simplicity of Hal's estate, probate would take six to nine months. If things did not change demonstrably, no major problems should arise and within a year's time Eddie would be a much wealthier man.

Potential wealth notwithstanding, there was, according to Hal's instruction in his will, the matter of attending to his final wishes. Hal had managed one final time to catch Eddie off balance—after cremation, he wanted his ashes spread over the Pacific Ocean. This was Eddie's task.

The meeting wound down as technicalities were discussed and contacts exchanged. Rodney promised to keep the others informed about any worries from his side, Mr. Cooper affirmed the same, and each went his own way.

Eddie and Lisa had agreed to meet at the Off the Record, the bar in the Hay-Adams Hotel. The hotel on sixteenth Street, dating back to the 1920s, was about as close as someone could get to the White House without an invitation. The bar, hailed by Forbes as one of the world's best, was rumored to be the heart of the city's informal information mill. The hushed atmosphere was the perfect place for Eddie to bring Lisa up to speed about Hal's status—more correctly put, update their status in a post-Hal world.

Lisa was overwhelmed by the fortune Hal had been able to amass.

Eddie felt uncomfortable even talking about the estate. It seemed clear that, although he was officially the only heir, Rodney was the person who had truly shared Hal's life and to whom the assets of this life should pass. The prevailing, but perhaps unjust realities made this difficult.

Lisa, so often seeing tough subjects through a clear lens, suggested Eddie not get too tied-up about this now. He did not need the money—there was no urgency from his side. Furthermore, with probate, everything would be blocked for some time to come. There was plenty of time and a lot of flexibility to see how best to arrange matters. After all, she took a loving jab at her paramour, he, Eddie, was almost sixty-five—retirement age, what would he need money for—he was too old to enjoy it!

Eddie laughed, but the age remark had some bite in it—totally unintended by Lisa, he knew. Still, he would not look back, so, looking forward, Lisa's perspective seemed to make sense. He ordered a round of fresh drinks.

Over the next several days, Lisa and Eddie simply seemed to soak in the new reality.

Then Rodney called. He suggested they meet at a Cajun coffee house off Clarendon Boulevard in Arlington. Eddie accepted, the Cajun reference stinging a bit, and the constantly changing venues also reminding him of his uncle's habits. Maybe it was standard operating procedure for the agency?

As they enjoyed the bitter taste of the chicory coffee, Rodney began with a solemn face. This was the first time Eddie took real note of Rodney the person as opposed to Rodney the messenger. Eddie had originally thought he was in his forties, but on close inspection he was considerably older (Eddie would later learn he was fifty-nine). He had short-cropped hair and a tawny complexion that could have been due to the sun or genes or both. He moved in a relaxed way that should make the observer think he lived a stress-free, even mundane life. To belie this, he demonstrated a sharp mind and an eloquent tongue. He was physically and mentally a force with which to be reckoned.

Rodney's first news was that Hal's autopsy had not been as straightforward as they had hoped. There were no signs of force or attack, the odds continued to greatly favor natural causes. However, some of the initial biochemical analyses had provided confusing results and another battery of tests was being run. These were very complicated, involving a number of labs around the country. It could take up to six weeks to get the new results.

The next point was more tangible. Rodney had taken over the Delpro investigation from where Hal had left it. The same large crew was still working on the same basket of issues, places, and problems. Very recently, yesterday in fact, there had been what could turn out to be a breakthrough. After literally years of trying, they may have pierced some of the walls protecting the very highest echelon of Delpro management. Rodney wanted Eddie to take a little road trip with him when they left the coffee shop.

Eddie agreed.

They left the greater metro area via I-95, going south to Fredericksburg where they took Highway 17 to Tappohannock, crossing the Rappahannock River on the Highway 360 bridge. This road turned into the Northumberland Highway which they followed almost to Burgess, turning north to Edwardsville and then moving onto County Road 706 which took them to the confluence of the Potomac River and Chesapeake Bay, at Candy Point, on the Virginia-Maryland border.

They came to what appeared to be a large residence shielded from the outside by a nine-foot-high brick wall only broken by a twelve-foot-high wrought-iron gate monitored by numerous cameras. From the road, the impression was that the property ran all the way to the shoreline—the wall blocking line of sight to confirm this supposition. Rodney pointed out the holdings, then turned around and retraced their steps for about five miles to Blue Heron Lodge on Hull Creek. At this rather isolated retreat, they easily found a secluded table given there were few clients at this time of day. Eddie ordered coffee while Rodney removed several files from his briefcase.

Among the papers bulging from the khaki folders, Rodney first presented some aerial photos of a very impressive mansion, clarifying this was what was behind the brick wall they had just visited—a home of truly royal opulence. He then showed Eddie a grainy color eight by ten of a man with a remarkable mane of alabaster hair that offset a pink complexion. Despite the poor picture quality, Eddie immediately recognized the man he had seen in Granada and Blantyre.

Rodney opened a file, pushing it to Eddie, stipulating these were Hal's notes about Eddie's previous sightings of this man. They now knew his name was Robin McCandless. The big house on the shores of the estuary was among his many residences. They believed McCandless was the top of the vast Delpro pyramid—he ultimately called the shots.

Rodney emphasized this was all speculation. There was, as of now, no hard and fast proof of McCandless' involvement with Delpro. But Rodney's team was getting closer. Eddie's testimony about seeing McCandless with known Delpro operatives could be critical—crucially, his observation that in Granada Mr. Smith gave McCandless his report.

Outside the scope of the present investigation, McCandless was a highly respected, if largely invisible, philanthropist and conservative benefactor of a variety of charitable causes. Even with the resources of the agency, there was very little known about McCandless' youth. He seemed to have fallen out of the sky when he married Maribel Dubois.

At the end of the nineteenth century, when the Rockefellers were making a fortune in oil, the Carnegies in steel, and the Vanderbilts in railroads, the Dubois' were reaping their own riches from industrial chemicals—everything from fertilizers to fabric dyes. The Dubois' wealth rivaled that of any of the richest families in America.

However, what had started as a family enterprise changed into a global conglomerate run by professionals in a score of different disciplines—the family relegated to figurehead positions on the board. Concurrently, Lady Luck began to abandon the family. Several of the second-generation male heirs were lost to ghastly accidents. By the fourth generation the atrophy was nearly complete. Only one sibling remained of what had been a clan. Maribel, daughter of an aging and ailing Wilson Dubois, took her seat at the board when her father was no longer able to attend. Within a year her father had passed, and she had married McCandless. Within five years she too had passed, and McCandless assumed her seat.

Maribel's death had been shrouded in mystery. She and her long-time school mate from Wellesley had gone to a celebrity tennis tournament followed by a $5,000-a-plate dinner for a local charity—her husband reportedly out of the country on business. The ladies had declined their chauffeur, saying they wanted to have the evening to themselves to relive their old college highlights. It was unclear how much reliving happened, but it was noted the two ladies consumed large quantities of intoxicating beverages as they enjoyed being the center of the rich and famous. Returning home in the early hours of the morning, they apparently took a corner too fast as they approached a bridge, plummeting into the river below—both old friends succumbing to the accident. There was a closed-casket service, Maribel promptly cremated, her husband devastated at the loss of his much-loved wife and the family they now would never have.

After a week of mourning and regret, demonstrated across the full spectrum of Dubois interests, McCandless made a tearful eulogy for his beloved spouse as he commemorated a new wing at a local hospital in her honor. He concluded with, "life goes on," and promptly took his seat on the board.

Two weeks later, it was rumored a reporter was prepared to break a story that the official version of Maribel's death was patently untrue. Close colleagues had attested to the fact that Maribel did not drink. She could not have been drunk. The reporter was apparently able, through unknown means, to access Maribel's medical records and confirm she had clinical alcohol intolerance. The story was a sham.

Rodney underlined the agency had been able to track down this story after a great deal of dredging into newsroom archives. The story never went public. The reporter disappeared—acquaintances saying he took a job in Europe. Officially or unofficially, no one ever openly questioned Maribel's death. Nevertheless, to insiders it remained an unresolved case—most suspecting some sort of treachery. For these insiders, McCandless was feared, not liked.

Rodney stopped. They knew a lot. There was a lot more to know.

As had become their new routine, Lisa and Eddie discussed the day's occurrences over dinner. Some subjects related directly to her own work, others were more abstract. Of course, there was no crystal ball. They could only guess and try to plan or react accordingly.

Eddie spent two more weeks in D.C., wanting to make sure Rodney and Mr. Cooper had all they needed from him. Final results regarding Hal's death were still outstanding, but Rodney seemed to be moving ahead on sure footing. No other new considerations had surfaced relating to Hal's estate. Mr. Cooper assured Eddie (as everyone these days seemed to be doing) that he just needed to sit back and let things take their course.

The eve of his departure, Eddie invited Lisa and Rodney to dinner at a Spanish Bistro in Bethesda—it seemed somehow appropriate for their work while being somewhat out-of-the-way as Rodney appeared to like. He wanted to thank them for all they did for him—all they did for Hal. He also wanted to talk in complete candor and confidence about Hal's estate. This was, he knew, premature. The estate was still in probate. But he wanted each of them to think about the very sizable sum that would in all likelihood soon be liberated by the court. It should really be their money, not his—they, the three of them, were all more than vested. Eddie was not sure exactly how each of the trio could benefit—how much each of them really could use given their ages and lifestyles. It appeared the total amount was more than enough for all. Thus, in view of their needs and priorities, he wanted Lisa and Rodney to devote some serious thought as to how they could best use these assets. What could they do to make a difference? What goods or services could they consider? What shiny scraps could they envision to leave in their wake to let the world know they had passed, and they had cared?

This seemed nearly so ponderous a topic as to distract from the redolence of the paella they were sharing—taking Rodney and Lisa somewhat aback. Eddie quickly deflected any dour spirits, reiterating he was only broaching the subject for their future thoughts. This seemed a chance to have a legacy that was more than how much income tax they had paid or how many houses they had owned.

They all took gulps of sangria, complimented Eddie on his insightfulness, and dug into the brimming plate before them.

Later that night, as Eddie and Lisa hugged, steeped in the fog of their afterglow, Eddie whispered in Lisa's ear that he was very serious about how to spend Hal's monies in a meaningful way. Lisa sighed, "Of course you are."

The next day Eddie flew back to a joyful reunion with Coco II.

It stunned Eddie how seamlessly he was able to reenter the routine he had had before Hal's death as though nothing had happened. As though nothing had happened, but in truth, a lot had happened—more than a lot, a great deal!

Eddie was back in his old ways—the same but different. Strangely, it became apparent only now that many of his customary practices had been overtaken by his old nemesis: time. These changes had been oozing slowly forward, almost imperceptibly. Somehow Hal's death made that that had been unseen for years, now visible—that that had been transforming and unnoticed, now eye-catching. What he had seen as his comfort zone, he now realized was a facade for a remodeled world.

For years his ancestral hamlet had been self-contained, at least as regarded the basics. There had been, he recalled, a primary school (his primary school), grocery store (actually, two—but the Leonards' was the best), a gas station, a hardware store, a post office, a bus stop (his genesis with Lisa), a bar, along with an assortment of restaurants and motels. This was how he had grown up. No one needed look beyond the village for their needs.

A changing economy and a brave new society, without regard to the past, had totally changed the present. While the restaurants and motels had multiplied over recent decades, much of the rest was gone. There was no school, no post office, no bus stop, no hardware store. Commercial life had magnetically been pulled to the two port sites to the north and south, leaving the community to focus on accommodating transient tourists. At the same time, mills had closed, fish stocks had depleted, the traditional means of supporting a family had vanished. Most year-round residents were now pensioners originally from out of state.

Eddie did not know if this was development or back-slipping. He knew it was different. He knew he did not like it much. Yet, he also knew it was what it was. The human flotsam they all were had only modest (if any) control over the currents that pushed and pulled one's cruise through life.

These realizations, all the same, did not make Eddie pine morosely for days gone by. They did not make him strike out at an unsympathetic modern world. They did not make him angry nor sad. They quite emphatically reinforced his determination to address his legacy. He wanted to do something that would leave a positive sign of his passing even with the impersonality and perhaps uncaring of today.

As Eddie was getting back into the rhythm of his old routine, much like the cadence with which the tides rose and fell, he was contacted by Rodney. The results of the additional tests on Hal had come back. Rodney did not want to sound an alarm just yet, but there were reasons to question further the causes of death. There were unusually high and imbalanced levels of liver enzymes alanine transaminase and aspartate transaminase consistent with some foreign substance in the body—a substance no tests done so far were able to reveal. This was troubling.

They would continue their exploring, searching ever deeper into what had been happening in Hal's body at the time of his death. At the present stage of this examination, Rodney was not willing to make any definitive statement as to the cause of death. The case was still open.

This did not, however, require Hal's presence (so to speak). The agency coroner had an ample supply of samples, so they could go ahead with Hal's final wishes. With Eddie's consent, Rodney would arrange for the cremation in D.C. At a later date, when they, including Lisa, could make the preparations, they could deal with spreading the ashes at sea as Hal had wished.

This was all fine with Eddie.

The next week Eddie got a call from Mr. Cooper. The attorney expected the estate to be settled shortly. As they had envisioned, there had been no surprises. Everything went smoothly. He, Mr. Cooper, would prepare letters and checks for the gifts Hal had specified. Then, once the fees and any miscellaneous charges were settled, the balance would be available to Eddie.

Eddie, having already anticipated this inevitability, informed the lawyer that he would consult with Lisa and Rodney. They would identify an investment firm in the D.C. area where they would temporarily park the funds. Once the trio had identified the best choice, Eddie would officially inform Mr. Cooper and the assets could be transferred.

Mr. Cooper indicated this would be fine. As part of his work, he would be preparing a series of letters and other documents for Eddie. He would include these financial arrangements once formally informed. In the interim, he wanted to describe a little bit more about the gifts Hal had requested. He assured Eddie that, although generous, these would not have a major impact on his inheritance.

Hal had designated $100,000 to each of three NGOs: the Hebrew Immigrant Aid Society, the Red Cross, and Mercy Corps. This was easy. Mr. Cooper would prepare checks and letters for Eddie's signature as executor.

There was a fourth recipient. This was somehow different. Hal had provided $200,000 to General Industrial and Chemical Products. So far Mr. Cooper had no idea who this was. Hal had provided no details whatsoever.

Eddie said he would discuss this with Rodney who probably had access to vastly more resources than they to get what they needed regarding the company.

Mr. Cooper hung up after assuring Eddie that even after all the payments, he would still be very rich by any standards.

---

Part of the renewed routine that was reestablished was the regular rendezvous with Lisa. Eddie intuitively avoided discussing what he now thought about as the "legacy thing," their meetings more about them and, to some extent, about Lisa's work.

During one reunion in St. Louis, Eddie brazenly raised the taboo topic: what of them? He had to shield his incredulity when Lisa reacted much differently than previously. Heretofore, she had taken all efforts to shun the topic—prudently pushing it off the agenda as an item to examine tomorrow, when the dust had settled. It looked as though she felt that this time the dust had apparently finally settled, as she fervently embraced the matter.

Maybe it was age. Maybe it was D.C. burnout. Maybe it was homesickness for the Pacific Northwest. Maybe it was the increasing difficulty with which she met each separation with Eddie. Maybe it was all the things. For whatever reasons, Lisa announced emphatically they needed to have a plan—a real plan they would follow—not just some cosmetic disposable thing that would change next week.

She revealed she had nearly completed the task upon which Hal had set her. This remained somewhat of a moving target given all the unknowns inherent in any case against Delpro—including the unknown of whether or not there would even be a case against Delpro. She had, nevertheless, done extensive research and prepared an in-depth outline of all the steps that would need to be taken to initiate a legal case—offering a lattice-work of different scenarios and different legal options.

She did not feel she, she did not feel Eddie, she did not feel they, should tie their lives to Delpro. Hal had done all he could. Rodney was doing all he could. Something might happen. Something might not. Delpro had ruined the lives of many. As Eddie knew all too well, Delpro had killed and corrupted. They should not let Delpro further ruin their lives by waiting and waiting and not doing what they wanted to do but waiting to do what they felt they should do. She did not want them to die waiting. It was time to move on.

✳

What Lisa and Eddie intuitively understood was that the first step in moving on was to mentally prepare to move on. They took the first step.

While his new friends were trying to find simple ways to undertake a complex refocusing, Rodney continued his overall investigation. Then Eddie asked if they could talk about "their dilemma." Eddie called not only for an update about the definitive cause of Hal's death, but also to brief Rodney about the details of Hal's endowments as explained by Mr. Cooper, so they could think more about moving forward on defining those shiny scraps they wanted to survive their own passing. Although the latest tests regarding Hal's death were still outstanding, Rodney was very curious, as obviously was Eddie, about why Hal had included such a generous bequeathment to an apparently unknown company.

Rodney selected a particularly savvy member of his crew and began a new research avenue: who and what were General Industrial and Chemical Products?

They started with Hal's unusual donation. This turned out to be a rather uncomplicated knot to untie—at least superficially. The company had a foundation that provided scholarships to students in developing countries to study chemistry, mechanical engineering, food science, or related fields. Though the foundation officers with whom they spoke could not recall a specific promise of support from Hal, in fact, they could not even recall Hal, they assured Rodney that such silent donations happened all the time. Two or three times a year they had a program on public television describing their work while highlighting specific students from poor countries who were excelling thanks to the opportunity they had been given by General Industrial and Chemical Products. Frequently, immediately after these televised programs they had an influx of funds, many anonymous.

Getting the real specifics from foundation staff was not, however, a pushover. They showed a serious reluctance to stray beyond the normal public relations line memorized by all for general public consumption. It was only when Rodney recalled Hal's planned exceptional generosity (charity that needed some more information for validation) to those who were so dependent upon the foundation's fine works, that the officers showed any willingness to discuss outside the prescribed lines.

Once the hatch was opened, however, Rodney quickly asked if they had an annual report that gave more specifics as to the students granted the scholarships and the work they did after graduation. The foundation's director proudly confirmed this information could be found in their periodic reports, volunteering to send these promptly to Rodney.

Leaving this as a subset of the General Industrial and Chemical Products research—what Rodney now referred to in shorthand as the "General Problem," they moved to the more entangled matter of who General Industrial and Chemical Products really was. This took great effort. It was like trying to follow a single leaf in an autumn wind storm. After looking through heaps of domestic and international data, they could only conclude General Industrial and Chemical Products was a shell corporation. There seemed to be a mesh of subsidiary enterprises scattered around the globe. Many, at first glance, looked like relatively small companies targeting localized markets. There were, however, some large and, in their own right, perplexing operations. Two that stood out were Ace Foods and Farm Services. Simple names for multimillion-dollar undertakings with on-the-ground presences on at least three continents.

Ace Foods was highly diversified but seemed to concentrate on fruit and vegetable products grown on large farms in Africa, Asia, and Latin America to supply European and North American markets. Perhaps logically, Farm Services addressed the other end of, in many cases, the same value chain—providing fertilizers, agrochemicals, and machinery to some of the same farms as well as a broader swath of clientele.

Among others, Rodney noted Ace Foods had farms in Ghana, Mozambique, Tanzania, and Sénégal. What really caught his eye was that produce from farms in these countries was processed in Spain for sale in the European Union. It was surely no coincidence that one of the principal agriculture supply vendors in these countries was Farm Services. This batch of interrelated activities seemed a good place to concentrate effort.

This decision was confirmed when Rodney obtained the General Industrial and Chemical Products Foundation's documentation. When he perused the annexes where there were lists of all the individuals who had profited from foundation assistance, breaking these down by country, a full two-thirds of the African recipients came from Ghana, Mozambique, Tanzania, or Sénégal.

A real breakthrough came when they went back to Evergreen Ocean Transport. This was the company that had owned the containers that had carried Jordao and the powdered agricultural products from Beira to Rabat. This was also the company that transported Ace Food's fruit and vegetables from Ghana, Mozambique, Tanzania, and Sénégal to Spain. Scouring the records, it was finally revealed, moreover, that Evergreen was owned by Delpro. This was the first Ace Foods-Delpro link.

It took weeks. It required five more highly-trained staff. But ultimately an intricate three-dimensional pyramid took form with Delpro at the apex. Delpro was indeed networked with Ace Foods and Farm Services as well as their parent General Industrial and Chemical Products. By far the majority of General Industrial and Chemical Products Foundation graduates now worked in positions linked to Delpro. Delpro's tentacles went from kidnapped refugees to highly trained scientists.

On this basis, Rodney expanded his team and his geographic area of interest. He sent agents to work on Ace Foods' farms, Farm Services' depots, and ports using Evergreen containers. It took months, but in the end, they had some new dependable reconnaissance. They had had to narrow their efforts considerably to be able to bore to the core but bore to the core they did. In Ghana they found Ace's major investment to be in pineapples. Ostensibly, they sent boxes of pineapples to a wholesaler in Granada for onward shipment to retailers across Europe.

This was indeed what happened. However, there was more. Through Evergreen and Farm Services, the Ace operations in Ghana had connections with businessmen in Guinea Bissau. Officially, for reasons no one could explain, fertilizer for the pineapple plantations was imported from Bissau. Upon careful covert examination, it was discovered it was not fertilizer that was being shipped from Bissau but cocaine. The cocaine was then carefully wrapped and inserted into hollowed-out pineapples for delivery to Spain.

This became a very big piece in the Delpro puzzle. Rodney concluded his dear Hal, whom he missed terribly, had concocted the bequest intentionally—providing bread crumbs for the very investigation that had taken place.

Rodney thought of Hal continuously. While he and his colleagues had been overloaded with Ace Foods and Farm Services, he had received the final test results. The agency coroner did not believe Hal had died from natural causes. He believed he had been poisoned. Sadly, there was no proof. This deplorable act had been committed with the greatest of skill—greatest of forethought. The products used were unknown to the agency. Without a full confession from the culprits, there was no way to know more.

Once more, connecting the dots was more based on his insight into the individuals than on the hard facts, Rodney concluded, at least to his personal satisfaction, Hal had uncovered far more than he had shared with the team. Understanding well Hal's ways, Rodney appreciated Hal did not want his conjectures to get ahead of the truths they were able to document and verify—this was not about innuendo but about law. Although he was always five moves ahead, he did not share his deductions—he wanted the team to follow the facts.

Somehow Delpro had obviously known Hal was well on his way to exposing their labyrinthine affairs. He had to be removed much as Samantha had had to be removed as she began to unearth the reality concerning many of the lost souls she was trying to help.

---

Rodney was in frequent contact with Lisa and Eddie. When he had the final word about Hal's death, he liaised with the other two to meet on the coast where they would be able to rent a small airplane, fly out to sea, and spread Hal's ashes as he had wished.

When their assignment had been accomplished, they had agreed to spend the next day together to drink to Hal and to pick apart the results of their joint efforts to date. Rodney filled his co-conspirators in on all the things that had happened when they followed up on General Industrial and Chemical Products due to Hal's inexplicable and sizable bequest. Rodney reiterated that the donation was surely done intentionally to set others on the right path in the event he should be gone. Lisa and Eddie were impressed albeit it not astonished—having already realized that Delpro was probably larger than the Church of Jesus Christ of the Latter-Day Saints.

After they had gone full circle (again) on all that was Delpro, the verdict was still the same: they were not there yet. They had a large and diverse quantity of evidence. Rodney hoped this would soon be considered by those making the decision as adequate to launch an official case—to go before a Grand Jury and begin legal proceedings. But as of now, it was still a game of wait and see.

Lisa and Eddie echoed their earlier conviction that they could not wait and see forever. They were adjusting their plans to carry on in an admittedly uncertain new world but without an anchor of Delpro—without closure. They were trying to acclimatize to a new normal. So far, it was uncertain if they would succeed.

All these incidences notwithstanding, Eddie wanted to bring up yet again the ever-burning (to him) question of legacy—the shiny scraps they could leave as affirmation they had been. Mr. Cooper had wrapped everything up, including his own bill. There was over $6 million remaining from Hal's estate. Eddie wanted to divide this into four pots—one for each of them and then a fourth for the "legacy litany" as Rodney began calling

Eddie's now very persistent refrain—this moniker replacing the previously favored "legacy thing".

Lisa and Rodney were still uncomfortable in discussing what they felt was almost unseemly, as though, in their minds, they were serving a Thanksgiving turkey and discussing who wanted what morsel. Hal was not a turkey.

Eddie was well attuned to their discomfort. Nonetheless, as the eldest among them, by quite a few years if anyone was counting, he was feeling the pinch of time. They needed to move ahead on this too—Delpro was not everything.

To Eddie's credit and satisfaction, they did not just kick the newly baptised "legacy litany" can unopened down the road. They agreed with Eddie's overall suggestion; each confirmed that he or she would objectively assess how they felt the assets should be divided. At least they had agreed to agree.

---

A month later, Eddie received a large manila envelope with the return address of Mr. Cooper's office. Inside was a second manila envelope and a cover letter from Mr. Cooper's legal assistant. She informed Eddie that after Mr. Cooper had collated and finalized all the estate documents—sending these earlier to Eddie—they had discovered the enclosed unopened envelope from Hal. Apparently, it had got mixed in with a pile of other unrelated papers, only now surfacing. She apologized for the inconvenience and wished Eddie well.

Eddie opened the second envelope to find a third, smaller envelope addressed to Rodney and a seven-page handwritten letter from Hal—the precise and tidy script reminiscent of the thoroughness with which Hal dealt with everything. Stifling a gulp, Eddie read, then reread the pages from his uncle.

The letter was almost melodramatic. Hal stated, just like in the movies, that if Eddie was reading this, this meant he, Hal, was dead. Therefore, he trusted that his written words would be taken to heart by his nephew whom he dearly loved and honestly respected.

His uncle then proceeded to tick-off the key points one by one.

He was completely devastated by Samantha's death. He was convinced it was foul play although he recognized this would be very difficult to prove legally. Samantha had been a very special person. It was, in fact, due to her influence that he had donated modest amounts to various NGOs working with refugees. He was most grateful to her for the way she opened his eyes with kindness and generosity.

Speaking of his will, as Eddie had undoubtedly discerned by now, the bequeathment to General Industrial and Chemical Products was Hal's play at a hunch—a follow-up to a gut feeling that heretofore had not warranted the time of professional investigators. By throwing money down the rabbit hole, he hoped maybe the white hare would appear. It was a gamble, but one he was willing to take and one he knew Eddie, with Rodney's help, would be able to scout out.

There were a lot of bad folks out there. His nephew and Rodney needed to be extremely careful. But it was a job that needed doing.

Furthermore, Hal wanted to underscore what he had told his nephew so often—these things take time. Sometimes they work out, sometimes they do not. He could only refer his dear nephew to the Taman Shud Case in Australia, the Glico-Morinaga Case in Japan, and the more recent Gardner Museum Case in Massachusetts. These were just a few of the myriad of cases that do not get solved, the most scurrilous often never even reaching the public's eye.

Hal was sure Eddie would recall how his mother suffered after his father's death. One of the coping mechanisms she adopted was to turn to religion—to believe. In addition to her close ties to local clergy, she found solace in the words of Joyce Meyer. There was one quote from this Christian author she particularly cherished—so much so, in fact, she had sent it to her little brother. Her favorite was, "*Patience is not simply the ability to wait—it's how we behave while we're waiting.*"

Eddie should remember and be guided by this.

Hal wanted to stress that Eddie should not be put off by the size of his uncle's estate. He should never consider this as ill-gotten gains. Hal had been very lucky in his investments and had led a low-maintenance life. There had been no shenanigans. It was what it was, but it was Eddie's free and clear. He knew his nephew would know best how to use these assets and that he would use them well. He should not fret too much about his new-found wealth. He should, rather, think of it as the gods smiling on him. He deserved their good will.

Finally, Hal was sure by now Eddie had met Rodney. His uncle had enclosed a letter for Rodney, he hoped Eddie would make sure Rodney got it. Hal categorically stated what Eddie had observed, he loved Rodney and Rodney was an exceptional person. Hal was not sure if Eddie would understand. He hoped he would. In the event he could not understand, he hoped his nephew had a big enough heart (as he knew he did) to accept.

As always, Hal could not just close, full stop—there was always a footnote. In this final appendix to his final communication, he started with an apology—he did not really mean to meddle in Eddie's private life—although, as his uncle, he felt he had every right to do so. So it was, he wanted to remind his nephew that, as he had said at the onset, Samantha was a terrific person. Yet, totally independently of this fact, Lisa too was a wonderful person. She and Eddie were good for each other. In his ending admonition, he wanted to lovingly advise his young, in spirit if no longer in body, explorer nephew to not let Lisa get away.

Eddie put the letter down, feeling a tightness in his chest and a lump in his throat. He missed Hal and knew he would soon miss him even more.

※

Eddie forwarded the letter to Rodney, then called Lisa. They agreed to meet the next weekend in Seattle.

They stayed at the Edgewater, with a dockside room overlooking the Sound. It was not exactly Eddie's domain, big city and all, but they were lulled by gusts from the Pacific and the calls of the seagulls.

Eddie shared Hal's letter with Lisa.

She read attentively. Her face, which Eddie watched studiously, changed like shadows from clouds moving across the sun; there were smiles, almost scowls, and there was deep sadness. When she had finished, there was a bittersweet moment when they simply stared at each other.

Eddie broke the spell. It was a delicate bubble and it popped with just two words, "And so?"

Lisa frowned, looked nonplussed, then grinned. She was equally curt, "OK."

They both understood. This was the end. Each had done all they realistically could. There were many players on the field, and it was time for them to take (hopefully cushy) seats in the bleachers.

Within three months, Lisa had moved back to her traditional lands, back to her beloved ocean, back with Eddie and Coco II. Before leaving D.C., she had compiled up-to-date and explicit documentation on how to proceed with the Delpro case, should it go to court.

With their resources, they could have lived anywhere. But they stayed where they were most comfortable, in Eddie's family home. Lisa put her home at the corner of Third Street and Joshua Lane up for rent until they decided what to do with the property. They did splurge on some renovations that Eddie felt were superfluous, but that Lisa found mandatory.

They then stared an uncertain future in the face.

※

Once they were totally settled, the first thing they did was to invite Rodney to come for a visit and a housewarming. It was almost six weeks before he could find time, but the trio did get together to, one more last time, make a toast to Hal and then, under Eddie's guidance, discuss the "legacy litany."

To Eddie's enjoyment, even if a bit unexpected, both Lisa and Rodney now had clear ideas of what to do. They agreed to set aside $1.5 million for their personal use—this to be divided equally among themselves. This would leave a balance of somewhere in excess of $4.25 million. They agreed this would be used to establish the SAMHAFRI—for Samantha and Hal's Friends Foundation. In the spirit of Samantha and Hal's priorities, the foundation would aim to help refugees and other vulnerable people get adequately settled in the complex and challenging ecosystem that was the United States.

They realized it would start as a modest effort. They would, in Hal's words, have to be a patient. They would all pitch in and also hire a part-time manager until they had a better idea of what services they could provide and how much money they could bring in. They would locate the new non-profit organization—NPO—in Portland; this was accessible enough to where they could go if need be, but far enough not to be a chain around their necks.

The agreement had been far easier than they had imagined. Now the hard work would start.

With this item now off their to-do list, at least for the moment, Rodney took advantage of their get together to update all on the Delpro case. Without going into specifics, the team was making exceptional progress. They felt that within three to six months they would have compiled all they needed to go before the Grand Jury.

While this was good news, the even better news was that, in Rodney's judgement, for now, they had all they needed from both Eddie and Lisa. The couple was now free to go clamming, hunt for agates, or climb trees for all Rodney cared—it was a job well done.

※

Lisa and Eddie were able to spend quite some time on the beach, although they did not climb any trees. They, along with Coco II, were all getting older. They also now had a big job in setting up their NPO. The initial phases were able to be done by phone and correspondence, but ultimately, they had to spend a lot of time in Portland building the foundation for their foundation.

They found, fortunately, a welcoming climate that facilitated the arrangements. They were also very lucky, they hoped, as they found a young lady, Valentina, who was well-suited to run the foundation and, more importantly, interested in doing so. Lisa and Valentina had an almost immediate connection. Lisa's skills were invaluable in getting the NPO off the ground. But Lisa was very much aware she did not want to build a dependence on her inputs—taking great efforts to build the needed capacity in Valentina.

---

Things were moving smoothly when one day, after a jaunt up the river, Lisa and Eddie returned home to find Rodney on the stoop—recalling almost painfully to Eddie how Hal would miraculously show up at the strangest of times.

When they were all settled in the living room, Rodney explained he had news that he felt better to deliver in person. As he had planned, they had made good progress on the Delpro case, actually going before the Grand Jury and getting an indictment of Robin McCandless as the key conspirator on a wide variety of federal charges—state charges still pending.

Rodney and his crew were confident their evidence was compelling. Apparently so was Robin McCandless. He had tried to flee the country by boat, leaving from Candy Point evidentially to meet a seaworthy craft somewhere in Chesapeake Bay. However, his speedboat had just left the dock and crossed the Virginia-Maryland state line when the boat exploded.

Rodney and his team had immediately seen this as a ploy to vanish. They were sure Robin McCandless could not have been on the demolished craft. However, when they reviewed the images from the surveillance cameras, they had surreptitiously placed all around the McCandless Estate, there was incontrovertible proof that Robin had indeed boarded the boat. Moreover, when the Coast Guard came in response to the explosion, they were able to recover three badly burned bodies. It was difficult, but the coroner had finally been able to identify Robin McCandless through dental records.

Rodney and his superiors as well as key staff from DOJ had painstakingly reviewed all the available information, declaring McCandless as dead (probably at the hands of his colleagues), but feeling they still had a case against Delpro, and deciding to continue, seeking indictments against Delpro management.

They were moving ahead. They had to retool some, but they expected the indictments against five top Delpro officers to be handed down in the coming weeks. There would then be a variety of legal gymnastics and they would be fortunate if they could get a trial date for next year. When the trail did start, there would be an initial period where the prosecution would have to build the case—tell the Delpro story. Depending on how well they were able to get the message across to the jury, early or late in the process they would need Eddie's testimony. He would need to be available for several days. Right now, regrettably, Rodney had no idea of when this could happen.

Rodney interrupted himself to go to his rental car and retrieve a package. Returning, he handed it to Eddie who opened it hurriedly, looking almost like a kid at Christmas. His anxious countenance, however, changed to incredulousness when he saw the contents. It was one of those modernistic cell phones. Eddie, no longer a champion of the latest fads or highest technologies, had done all he could to avoid just such a contraption.

Rodney explained. He did not want Eddie tied to his home phone, but he had to have rapid communications with one of his star witnesses. He apologized for the inconvenience, but he needed to ask Eddie to carry this so that the two of them could talk as needed.

Eddie reluctantly agreed.

※

Eddie did carry the cell phone. But it received very little use. He and Lisa were fully occupied with their routine. Delpro seemed like an old wives' tale. Washington, D.C. seemed like another planet.

Then again, like a will-o'-the-wisp, Rodney appeared at their door. As before, it was not as the bearer of revelations, but simply as a partner bringing the news. He felt Lisa and Eddie needed their information refreshed (Eddie thought Rodney was talking like one of those cutting-edge computers which he also disliked strenuously).

After a stout cocktail, Rodney settled in to provide the latest on Delpro. They had been able to get indictments on the five officers they had hoped to indict. However, Delpro had brought up a hoard of top-drawer lawyers who had done their best to create a smoke screen and have the charges dismissed. Although they had not succeeded, they had managed to muddy the waters sufficiently that there were now several additional steps necessary before they could actually get these guys in a courtroom.

These delays were unfortunate, but Rodney wanted to make sure Eddie was ready on a moment's notice as things could evolve very rapidly without much advance warning. To this end, he wanted to spend as much time as was necessary to make sure Eddie was prepared.

They devoted the next two days, with Lisa as the external arbitrator, going over the entire Delpro story from Granada to Chipata to Blantyre. They reviewed what to say in regard to Samantha's death as this was mostly speculation and they did not want to have it become a centerpiece that would ultimately backfire. They included Diversified Western Forest Products where Rodney had been able to uncover considerable background material that highlighted irregularities in accessing national timber sales. Lamentably, Eddie's testimony could not provide an entree directly into this malfeasance, but if he could manage to bring up his time in Vanduzer, this might open the door to this discussion later on with other witnesses. They analyzed the Wedson Canyon Case, seeing this as an example of how deeply and clandestinely Delpro could ingrain itself. They revisited Jordao and how his experiences were symptomatic of others—with some of whom Eddie had been in contact. They rethought how to bring up Robin McCandless. He was dead, but he had been one of the focal points—a focal point Eddie could place as he engaged in Delpro activities in Africa and Europe.

There was a lot of material to cover. Nevertheless, regardless of the high degree of Eddie's involvement, Rodney wanted to strongly emphasize that he was only a corroborating witness. In some ways Eddie was the human face of Delpro's accusers—but looking at the entire body of evidence, he was really second string. Their case did not hang on Eddie's testimony. They had years of investigative results providing conclusive information.

Rodney stressed further that Eddie's role was not simply a matter of semantics. He was not the dominant deponent. They, Rodney's team, needed to make this point clear to the defense. If Eddie was seen as the key to the case, there was no reason not to believe Delpro would do all it could to remove Eddie. As government had amassed a tremendous volume of objective facts sourced over years from a multitude of places, Eddie himself did not pose the primary threat to Delpro and there would be little reason to think they would try and eliminate him. Rodney hoped this would be a consolation to Eddie and Lisa.

Rodney felt they should be consoled. Yet, he did not want his words to be interpreted as minimizing what he was asking Eddie to do. This would change Eddie's life. It would undoubtedly change Lisa's life as well.

Given the importance of this case, the trial would be public. Eddie, by nature a private person, would find his image in all the newspapers and on television. As Rodney had said, Eddie would find himself as the face of the case against Delpro.

Samantha would be there too, next to him. If they brought up her death, and they needed to, she would be resuscitated by the press, and possibly not in the most flattering of ways.

Nothing was free. There were certainly costs for Eddie, and by default, Lisa, to continue along this path they had embarked upon so long ago. Eddie was, Rodney pointed out with great emotion, doing the right thing. Sadly, doing the right thing was frequently not easy.

There was one more crucial point Rodney felt he needed to once again accentuate: as Lisa could verify, this was a long process. Even if they got a conviction, it was guaranteed Delpro would appeal. Moreover, this was only a case involving five top managers. As Delpro had demonstrated time and again, if the visible head was cut off, another appeared to take its place—evidently these actions orchestrated by the invisible powers that controlled the empire. In the best-case scenario, this was a tiny step. If there was the political will and the judicial willingness, it could be a tiny step leading to a major shake-up. Or, and this was much more likely, it could be a flash in the pan with the sacrificial lambs offered and sacrificed—business as usual returning promptly.

In all candor, Rodney had no idea as to the higher-level outcome. If history was a guide, it did not bode well. Entities like Delpro were obviously a manifestation of political and financial power—a manifestation of an abuse of this power, well and good, but nonetheless, a presence reflecting man's greed and insatiability regardless of the consequences. This drama was of course as old as man himself. Would they really effectively curtail this through Delpro? Rodney thought the odds were against it.

This portrayal of the stark realities was nearly an epiphany for Eddie. Somehow, in the back of his mind, he always hoped for the best—always had a feeling that good would prevail. Rodney had given him a slap with reality. This did not mean he would not go ahead and do all he could to combat these evildoers. This did mean, or should mean, that he needed a better perspective. Even if not through his own eyes, in the eyes of others, he was an old man. Biologically he was an old man. He would give it his all—he owed this to himself, to Samantha, to Hal, to them all. But he needed to ground himself. Whatever fruit was born from the seeds he had sewn, he would unlikely be around to taste it. It would be another shiny scrap left in his backwash.

It was an unusually warm and calm day for October. Eddie was sitting on an outcropping about a half mile from home, enjoying the warmth from the setting sun as it began to cast long shadows—slowly arching to the horizon then seeming to fall the last few feet into a boiling sea. The cell phone rang in the breast pocket of his Filson. He answered. Rodney had a date—he would testify in five days.

He turned back to go home. A fresh gust of sea breeze hit his face. It felt right.